I0604622

Beatrix Bellafonte And The Castle In The Sea

by Kirk Thomas

The Bellafontes

The girl dreamed, her blanket pulled comfortably up around her chin, a look of utmost contentment on her face.

"Mmm", she moaned softly.

She was dreaming of a happy place. A fascinating place. A **magical** place.

She was in a castle, of sorts. At least it looked like a castle. She couldn't tell right away.

That was the annoying thing about dreams, they rarely began at the start.

There were stone archways everywhere. The floor was stone, everything was stone! There were torches in braziers on the walls, lots of twists and turns, and a high, curving ceiling.

But it didn't seem like just any castle.

She stopped and marvelled at a large window. It was high and arched, like the window of a church. It was a window of blue. And aquamarine and black and grey. It was a window to wonder. A window to whimsy. It was a window...to the sea! Was she beneath the sea?

She felt dizzy and put her hand against the wall to steady herself.

A blonde girl skipped past her then, hand in hand with another girl. She turned to look, and the blonde girl winked back at her over her shoulder. She blushed and felt a little better.

Suddenly, the hallway was chaos. There were lots of girls in checkered pinafores and black shoes. They all had the same ribbon in their hair, and the same badge on their pinafore, like they were wearing a uniform. Their shoes struck a symphony of tips and taps on the floor, and their happy voices washed over the girl like when you first sink into a warm bath.

She shrunk back against the wall, as the girls swept past her, books in hand, carefree looks on their faces.

Was she in a...school?

She put her hand to her chest as her heart started to flutter, and stayed pressed against the wall until the girls had gone. And then, as soon as it had begun, it was over, and the corridor was quiet again. She swallowed and detached herself from the wall.

She began to wander aimlessly, taking twists and turns as they came. Before long, she found herself in a long, narrow corridor.

At the end of it, was a door.

It wasn't like the other doors she had seen.

This one had a misty, ethereal quality to it, like it wasn't really there. It seemed to shift and twist like smoke, but it wasn't dark like smoke, it was lighter, like fog.

She walked toward the door, pulled by some eldritch quality, some unknown song that only she could hear.

The door called to her.

She desperately wanted to touch it.

To walk through it.

She knew something waited for her on the other side.

Something wonderful.

Something magical.

She was in front of the door now.

She reached out her hand.

She was so close.

Her fingers reached for the handle, heart beating like a drum in her chest.

Her stomach was in knots.

Her fingers were only inches away now...

She licked her lips, and prepared to grasp the handle, when suddenly, everything went black.

*

"BEATRIX, WAKE UP!"

The wall of her bedroom shook, as her mother thumped it with her first.

"Ughhh", Beatrix moaned. "Ohhh!"

She was ever so frustrated. She had been having the most wonderful dream.

She pulled the blanket right up over her head and buried herself beneath it, squirming agitatedly at the rude awakening.

"GET UP! The Mistress is coming!"

Her eyes shot open, wide with fear.

She kicked the blanket back and jumped out of bed. She daren't be late for The Mistress. She ran across to her mirror and began pulling her hair back into a tight knot.

3

The door to her room whipped open, and her mother stood there, rolling pin in one meaty hand, white puffs of flour all over her apron. "Are you up?"

"Yes", Beatrix replied irritatedly. She didn't know why her mother insisted on asking silly questions, she could already see that she was up.

"Don't yes me", her mother retorted. "Just get ready".

The door to her room closed, and the girl turned back to her mirror with a sigh.

The girl looking back at her was a strange one, or so she thought. She had round, brown, twinkly eyes, like a cat. They seemed to sparkle with promise, or perhaps mischief. And she had a little button nose that she hated.

She scrunched her nose up and stuck her tongue at her reflection.

The door to her room whipped open once more, and Beatrix's tongue retreated quickly. Her mother left, and she stuck her tongue back out at her through the closed door.

But really, she must get ready now. Wasting no more time, she picked out a plain grey dress from her little wardrobe.

She slipped it on quickly against the chill morning air, shivering as it touched her skin.

Her room was at the back of their little log cabin, away from the fire, so it got cold a lot. Sometimes she cuddled up in the bed with Felix, their cat, for warmth.

Felix liked cuddling with her. Or perhaps he just liked the warmth. She liked to think it was the former.

Felix was a black cat, in every sense of the word. He was dark, mysterious, and aloof. He came and went as he pleased, much to the chagrin of her mother.

Mother didn't like when Felix brought back mice to the house. He'd often sneak in through the crawlspace under the house, and pop up into the living room, with a mouse dangling devilishly from his mouth.

Mother would scream and shriek and shoo at him with her broom, and he'd run nimbly into Beatrix's room and hide under the bed.

Mother would chase him and try to whack him with her broom, but he'd hop out and jump out the window, which Beatrix often left open as an escape route for him.

Mother would shout at her to leave her window shut, so she would close it, but somehow it was always open when Felix needed it to be.

She shook her head, ponytail waggling and bouncing behind her. "Now is not the time to be daydreaming, Beatrix Bellafonte".

She straightened her dress and left the room.

*

They were all assembled in the town square, and there was absolute silence.

Mistress Madele was pacing slowly in front of them, hands clasped behind her back, ponytail rigidly trailing her neck.

Every now and then, she would slow, as if to turn and look at someone, then as if she thought better of it, she'd keep walking.

There was lots of nervous swallowing and gulping, and lots of nervous shifting of feet.

Beatrix's father licked his lips, and her mother gave him the most imperceptible of elbows in the side.

He pursed his lips and straightened himself like a soldier, looking resolutely ahead.

Their "town" was more of a village. And their "village" was not much of one at that. There were sixty-three people in Winterweld. Sixty-three.

The thought saddened her. No prince for her here. Half of the boys were her cousins, and the girls...

She didn't get on with the girls. They didn't like her and excluded her from their games and their frolics in the meadow and the barn.

She didn't know why. She'd only ever wanted to belong. To be part of their fun. But they didn't like her, and that was that.

She dreamed of running away to the city and working as a barmaid in one of the taverns. There were lots of interesting city boys, and lots of beautiful girls.

If she worked as a barmaid, she was bound to meet people, and bound to get into adventures.

It was probably easier when there more than sixty people, and half of them weren't your cousins.

She frowned as she looked at Dullen, her first cousin, who was picking his nose absentmindedly.

His ma, Hildy, pinched him hard, and he gasped. She was glaring at him with eyes like burning arrows, like she was trying to fry his brain in his head.

Dullen bit his lip and looked down at his feet.

Thankfully, The Mistress had missed the exchange. She was looking over their heads into the distance, head cocked to one side, as if thinking.

What was she thinking, Beatrix wondered...

You never knew with The Mistress. She was flighty, and volatile. Beatrix hoped it wasn't anything bad.

The Mistress sighed and looked at them as if they were a particularly disappointing bag of potatoes. "That will be all".

They breathed a sigh of relief, and began to disperse back to their houses, or shops, or bakeries.

Grizzly, the smith, gave The Mistress a scathing look, and stomped back to his forge.

The sound of his hammer soon rang out. Beatrix thought it sounded rather aggressive.

Grizzly frightened her. He was a big man with wild auburn hair down to his shoulders, and a beard just the same. He often had bits of food caught in it, which she thought was rather gross.

At the village dances he would always lift a keg of beer over his head in an attempt to down it, but it would inevitably end up sloshing everywhere and he'd look like a drowned rat by the time he thumped it back down.

Well, actually, a rat was rather wrong for Grizzly. A drowned bear, perhaps. He reminded her of a bear. Big and scary and covered in hair. And he sounded like a bear when he was angry. He'd shouted at her da once in the tavern, and her da had gone white as a sheet and raised his hands as if to say, "I don't want any part of you bear".

"Come on now, don't be dawdling". Her mother's impatient voice rang out beside her.

She sighed and followed her mother. It was time to do the laundry. She hated the laundry. But one of her chores was to wash the clothes with the other women, in the stream that ran behind the village. It was always so cold! And she hated the cold!

Sometimes the other girls would splash her when her ma wasn't looking. She hated that. Especially Fiona. She hated Fiona. She was so sneering and waspy and permanently looked like she'd smelt sour milk.

She smiled, as she remembered the time when Felix had followed her to the stream and pushed Fiona into the water. Fiona had been splashing her, and egging the other girls on, who of course, were obliging.

Felix had padded up behind her, stealthy as a jungle cat, and sprung at her, ninja quick. He landed on her back and Fiona had stumbled forward and lost her balance. She'd fallen right into the stream, face first!

Beatrix's laughter had peeled out wildly, and all the other women had looked to see Fiona spluttering and beating at herself feebly in the water.

"Oh, my dress, my new dress!" Fiona had wailed.

Fiona's mother, Muriel, had run over as if Fiona had been maimed by a horse. The look on her face! It was so angry and concerned. Beatrix couldn't believe it; it just was just a bit of water!

"Oh, look what you've done!" Muriel had cried, turning her eyes on Beatrix, and narrowing them like daggers.

Beatrix had been taken aback, and her laughter had fled. "I didn't do any-" she began to explain.

But Muriel had cut her off, waving her hand dismissively. "I don't want to hear it".

She never wanted to hear it. She only wanted to give it. Muriel was quick to open her mouth, but slow to open her ears. And her daughter took after her rightly enough. At least that's what Cath, Beatrix's mother, said. Cath didn't like Muriel. And Muriel didn't like Cath.

Muriel and some of Fiona's friends had pulled Fiona out of the stream like she was a newborn, or a frail old lady, fussing and fudding over her.

Beatrix had snorted, and they'd glared at her. She'd picked Felix up and given him a kiss on the head and walked away.

Cath, who'd been working further down the stream, pretended not to see.

There was always drama at the stream. Beatrix didn't like drama. She found it pathetic, to be honest. She just wanted to wash the clothes and go home.

Well, she didn't want to wash the clothes at all, to be honest. Why couldn't the men do it themselves? They were the ones who got the clothes stinky and dirty, not her.

They were always covered in food, or beer stains. Could they not feed themselves? Worse than babies some of them. Slopping and sloshing over themselves like pigs in a rush to empty the trough. Bleugh. She hated watching them in the tavern. But mother insisted. She must go and socialise; she must meet a man. How else was she to find a husband?

Maybe she didn't want a husband. Maybe she just wanted peace and quiet.

She turned then and stared at the sky.

Or maybe.

She wanted adventure.

The White Hair

Beatrix woke up and rolled out of bed.

Felix glared at her.

"What? I have to get up, I'm sorry", she said.

Felix wasn't impressed. He stretched, then rolled over, showing her his back.

She petted him, but he didn't turn back.

Felix didn't like it when they got up this early, but they were going to the city today, and she had to get up early and get ready. Mother insisted that she look her best and had laid out a hideous pink dress at the end of her bed. She hated it. She hated pink.

The door to her bedroom opened. Seeing that her daughter was already up getting ready, her mother simply nodded and left, closing the door behind her.

Beatrix sighed, and sat down, staring into her mirror. "Mirror, mirror, on the wall, who's the pinkest of them all?"

She looked back in disgust at the dress on the bed.

"I am, I'm the pinkest".

Felix was looking at the dress with interest.

"You like it? You can have it".

Felix waved his tail mischievously.

"No? Didn't think so".

She put the dress on and started pulling her hair into a bun.

"Leave your hair down", her mother called through the wall.

She scowled and began brushing her long black hair out. It was naturally curly, and she liked to leave it curly, but mother insisted she brush it straight.

"Brush the curls out, brush the curls out! A modest girl doesn't have curls. Curls suggest a mischievous nature. A modest girl wears her hair in a ponytail, or carefully brushes it, so that it runs down her back, not too short, not too long".

Her mother had read one too many fairy tales. Stories written by men to fill girls heads with nonsense and fancy.

She'd run away one day and wear her hair as curly as she bloody liked. The thought filled her with glee, and she smiled back at herself in the mirror.

When her hair was suitably modest, and she had her obnoxiously "look at me" dress on, she joined her mother and father in the kitchen.

Her mother smiled at her sweetly, and her eyes filled with tears. "Oh my". She gripped her husband's arm for support. "Doesn't she look beautiful?"

"My bootiful baby girl", her father said gruffly, biting back tears.

Beatrix shook her head and looked down at her dress. "I look like a courtesan".

Her mother blushed. "Beatrix Bellafonte! Mind your tongue, or I'll snatch it out!"

Beatrix scowled.

"Now stay here, I'm going to get Meggie, and she can have a look at you-" Her mother started,

"Ma, no!" Beatrix wailed.

"What do you mean no-" her mother replied.

"I look like a frickin strumpet!" Beatrix blurted.

"BEATRIX!" Her mother started to swell up like a balloon, her cheeks had gone red, like a lady who'd drunk too much sherry.

"Beatrix", her father repeated sternly, though it looked like he was struggling not to laugh. He had a little twinkle in his eye.

Cath turned a calculating eye on her husband, to make sure she had his support. "And what are you looking at, Mr Bellafonte?"

"N-nothing, dear", Mr Bellafonte stammered.

"Should ope not", Cath warned. She dropped her h's when she was angry. And some other letters sometimes, depending on how angry she was. When she was mad, she often ended up sounding like Banny, the barmaid.

Banny was tough as old boots, her father used to say. Don't mess with Banny, he'd warn. Beatrix rather thought her father liked Banny a little. He used to stare at her longingly out of the corner of his eye sometimes in the tavern, and when Cath caught him watching, she'd scowl and tell him to put his eyes back in his head.

Mr Bellafonte shifted on his feet awkwardly. "You musn't curse, girl. It ain't right".

"Not right", Cath corrected.

"Not right", Mr Bellafonte repeated.

A crack of sun shone through the bottom of the living room curtains then, casting a nice yellow glow on the wooden floor of the cabin.

"Will you look at that!" Mrs Bellafonte exclaimed. "Look at the time already. Meggie will have to wait; we really must get going!"

"Oh, no, what a shame", Beatrix said quietly, with a fair amount of cheekiness in her voice.

Cath narrowed her eyes menacingly at her daughter.

"There, there, love", Mr Bellafonte said soothingly, rubbing his wife's arm.

"Don't you love me, Graeme Bellafonte", Cath replied sharply.

Graeme winced. He was in for it now. He should have told Beatrix off a bit more enthusiastically when she spoke like a sailor.

Beatrix caught her father's eye and winked.

Graeme's mouth twitched, and Cath detached his hand from her arm.

"That's it!" Cath said. "We're going. Fat lot of good it will do, taking a bunch of degenerates like you two into the city! They'll send you home at the gates, and I wouldn't blame them one bit!"

Cath turned to her daughter. "Beatrix, get your coat".

"Ma", Beatrix moaned. It was bad enough she was in this stupid dress. Not the bloody coat too.

"I said get it! We're goin, now!" Cath barked.

*

They were scrunched comfortably into the back of the wagon, as it trundled down the dirt path toward the city. The path wasn't very good, it wasn't maintained all that well by the king's men, but it was alright, Beatrix supposed.

She'd ridden the path through Darkwood once when she was wee, and that was horrible. She had leaned out of the window to be sick twice on the way.

That path was horribly uneven and bumpy and there were big stones and lots of dips and rises. It hadn't helped that the driver had been a horrible creepy man that stunk of alcohol and had red eyes with bags under them.

Her mother had said that he was a vagrant, and she wasn't to speak to him. It felt kind of rude ignoring him when he addressed her, but she didn't want to rile her mother up, and her mother had glared at the driver when he tried. He quickly thought better of it and just focused on driving.

Well, this ride was better than the one through Darkwood, thankfully, and she only felt a little bit sick. The air was cool and refreshing and there was a nice breeze today, which made it better.

She leaned over the side of the wagon and gazed out across the meadows.

Brightcastle was surrounded by fields and hills and meadows. It was like somebody had rifled through a book of fairy tales, picked out the most cliche looking city they could find, then dropped it here.

She stared at the men and women working the fields. Their skin was brown and rough from long days under the sun, like leather. She didn't want to look like leather. She turned away, but curiosity soon got the better of her, and she turned back to look out the window at the sound of children playing.

They were close to the city now, and a group of children was chasing each other through a field alongside the wagon. They had worn shirts and pants that were probably once white, but had faded to a creamy yellow colour, like the sun kissed wheat they were running through.

One of the boys caught a girl and wrestled her to the floor where he began tickling her. The girl began giggling then kneed the boy in the stomach. He grunted and rolled off her. "Ow, Sar, too hard". The girl cackled then ran off into the field, pursued by two other boys. Another girl set off after them. "Wait Sar", she yelled. They were soon swallowed by the wheat and out of sight.

Beatrix grinned and turned her eyes to the front, where the city could be seen in the distance.

Brightcastle. The name alone filled her with excitement. The name came from the dark ages, before The Mistresses came, when the dark ones were prevalent.

It was said that the dark ones didn't like light, twisted things they were, so the king had a rolling watch of men man the walls with lanterns. The men patrolled the walls, lanterns burning bright, day and night, guarding the castle against the darkness.

The dark ones didn't trouble them anymore, but the tradition had stuck, and the lantern watch remained, even to this day.

They were called Torchbearers, the men who held the lanterns. Perhaps the king was scared they'd come back, the dark ones. Whatever the case, it was how the castle got its name. And the city had sprung up around the castle soon after, starting inside the walls, then expanding outside into little towns and hamlets, all feeding back into the city.

She shivered, as a chill breeze gave her goosebumps. It was an odd time of year. Not Summer, not yet Winter. Autumn, she supposed. But it didn't feel like Autumn. Felt like Summer one minute, Winter the next. Where was the consistency?

She closed her eyes as the sun fell on her and warmed her skin. It felt like she'd just sat down in front of the fire.

The wagon rumbled to a stop.

"Brightcastle", the driver grunted.

Her mother went in her purse, then leaned forward and gave the driver some bronze coins.

"Thankin you". The driver got out of the wagon and held his arm out for Cath.

"Why thank you", Cath said, surprised. She obviously didn't expect much in the way of manners from his man, though she could sometimes be quick to judge others on their appearance, and the driver didn't look like much.

"And for you, m'lady". The driver offered his hand to Beatrix, who grinned.

Cath frowned at this, and watched closely as the driver helped Beatrix hop down onto the path.

"Ta", Beatrix said.

"Thank you", her mother corrected, with a warning glare.

"Thank you", Beatrix repeated insolently, lowering herself into a curtsy.

The driver snorted, then got back into the wagon. He turned the wagon around then rumbled back the way they'd come.

Cath opened her mouth to tell Beatrix off some more, but Graeme placed a hand on her arm and shook his head gently.

"Right, this way then", Cath said, deciding to drop it. She clutched her purse primly under her arm and began picking her way toward the gate, which was open and manned by two sentries, sturdy men in plate armour. They looked like knights. Maybe there were.

"Hello", Cath said nervously, adjusting her purse and handing the nearest sentry a piece of parchment.

The sentry took it, then gave them all a piercing look, as if he was looking for any trouble. Cath reddened. Beatrix stared back at him.

"We're here to see the sister", Cath volunteered, a little uncertainly.

The sentry looked up, then back down at the parchment. He turned it over. There was a gold seal on the back. It looked like a woman in a shawl holding a baby.

The sentry nodded. "Through there, up the road a ways then turn right at the inn. Carry on up the hill and it's the big building at the top, can't miss it".

Cath nodded. "Thank you". She curtsied. It was an ungainly thing and Beatrix snorted. The sentry pretended not to notice, but Beatrix could have sworn his mouth twitched.

Graeme cleared his throat. "Thank you, ser". He pulled Beatrix by one arm, Cath by the other, and started guiding through the gates.

There were people coming in and out, and a wagon rolled past them into the city, giving Cath a fright.

She jumped and her hand leapt to her heart. "Goodness! They really should announce themselves; he was so close!"

"Ma, this is the city, ain't nobody gotta announce nothin", Beatrix said sassily.

Cath's mouth dropped open. "Who taught you to speak like that?"

"Ain't nobody taught me, I learned, all by myself" Beatrix retorted.

"She's jus rilin you up", Graeme muttered in his wife's ear.

Cath, seeing the smirk on her daughter's face, shook her head and swept off ahead of them.

"You've done it now, girl", Graeme mumbled to his daughter.

Beatrix grinned up at her father. He smiled at her fondly, then pushed her on ahead.

Beatrix was in her element, and her head was turning left and right on a swivel. There was a group of men playing dice in the corner by a seedy looking tavern, but Graeme steered her away. She'd been gravitating towards them, a look of excited glee on her face.

"Aw, da!" she protested.

Graeme carried on, eyes on the road.

"Thas my piggin dice, you lout!" One of the men shouted from behind them.

Beatrix swivelled and glanced behind her, peeking under her father's arm at the men playing dice. One of them had leapt to his feet and was standing aggressively over the other. The others had moved back to give them space.

"I'll give you lout, you unwashed scoundrel!" The other man spat back.

Graeme turned her head forward, as she heard a loud **smack** from behind. He kept her head forward as the men began fighting and wrestling in the dirt.

"Ohhh, lemme see, lemme see", Beatrix wailed.

In front of them, Cath flashed a look of disgust back at her daughter.

Beatrix stuck her tongue out as Cath turned away.

Graeme nudged her.

She looked up, and he shook his head. "Don't rile her now".

Beatrix rolled her eyes.

"Why hello, my pretty". They came to a stop, as a musky, heavily bearded man stepped into their path. His face was very close to Beatrix's, and he had an arm full of silver and gold necklaces. "Something to make you even more beautiful? The men in city will love this on you-"

Graeme's arm shot out automatically and caught the man by the scruff.

"Hey, get off, what do you think yer doin-".

Oof!

The man hit the dirt, landing on his behind.

Graeme kept walking, Beatrix in tow.

She turned back to grin at the man on the floor, who was cursing darkly and glaring at Graeme's back.

Cath flashed a coquettish look back at her husband, and Beatrix groaned. Gross.

Suddenly, Cath gestured to Graeme. "Here dear, it's here, the inn".

The Musky Muskrat, read the sign. There was a picture of a rather weird looking Muskrat in a hat, with what must be...stink lines...coming off it.

Cath frowned, and grimaced. "The Musky..." It was as if she couldn't finish the sentence, as if she found it too bizarre and distasteful. "Why would that man send us...here?"

"He didn't **send** us here, he jus mentioned the sister was near here", Graeme corrected his wife. Which was a mistake, because she scowled.

"But I agree, quite the fowl soundin place", Graeme said quickly.

Beatrix cackled. "The Musky...Muskrat. Ha!" She loved it.

"Behave yourself", Cath scolded.

Beatrix scoffed. Her mother was always so concerned with what people thought. She didn't care what people thought, least of all **men.**

"The sister won't tolerate a sinful girl", Cath warned.

"Who says I'm sinful?" Beatrix retorted.

"I do", Cath retorted.

"I do", Beatrix repeated mockingly under her breath.

"What was that?" Cath said sharply.

"Nothing", Beatrix said sweetly. "Now where's this sister, I'm thirsty. I could do with a drink".

Cath looked aghast.

"Well, if this is the inn, I guess it's jus up this hill then", Graeme interjected. "Off we go then".

He put his arm round his wife and started up the hill. He glanced back at Beatrix and beckoned her on with his head.

Beatrix followed just behind. Graeme glanced back every now and then to make sure she was ok. He seemed to think she was a bit safer in this part of the city, and Beatrix could see why.

There were no Musky Muskrats. And no loud men playing dice. No, this was the "good" part of town.

There were nobles and courtiers and merchants. Everyone was finely dressed, and they smelled fine too, which Beatrix found weird. She scrunched her nose up as she took in all the scents. Even the men! She found this strange. She'd never smelt a man who didn't smell like woodsmoke and sweat. Or beer. Always beer. These men were...what did her father call them? Dandies. That was it. Dandies. But not all of them. Not...this man.

She stopped and gazed dreamily at a tall man on a horse, picking his way carefully down the cobbled path of the hill. The stallion was about eighteen hands, and white as snow. The man was in plate armour like the sentries, but his was gold, and a chainmail coif sat around his neck. In the middle of his chest piece, was a blazing red lantern. A Torchbearer. But not just any, a knight.

There were swords, and shields, and lantern bearers, and then there were knights. Special soldiers blessed by the sisters and tasked with the duty of keeping the citizens safe from the dark ones, should they ever return.

The knight paused to address a young lady, who had approached his horse. She curtsied, then started fondling his reigns.

Cath tutted. She obviously found this sinful. "Shameful", she muttered.

The knights were supposed to be devout. They took an oath, forsaking all other earthly pleasures and diversions. Cath clearly found this knight to be lacking.

The knight seemed as if his mind was on anything but duty at that moment, as he twirled his blonde moustache that drooped either side of his wide mouth.

Beatrix couldn't stop looking at him. He had a broad, flat, face, with full lips and a sharp jaw. His hair was long and blonde, like his moustache, and was parted to either side. It sat handsomely beneath his ears.

Graeme snorted. He clearly didn't think much of this man.

Beatrix looked at her father, who stuck his tongue out her, like she so often did.

Beatrix giggled.

They walked away, past the knight who was still flirting with the lady.

As they walked up the hill, Beatrix glanced back over her shoulder. The knight was...looking at her.

At her?

He can't be.

She glanced around. There was no one else but her and her parents. Why was he looking at her?

The knight frowned, and a chill went through her, as his eyes became hard and piercing.

She turned her eyes quickly forward and didn't look back.

"Here we are", Cath said gleefully. "The Sacred Sisters".

Beatrix looked up at the daunting stone building. It looked like a cross between a church and a cathedral. It had a huge, daunting wooden door, with a gargoyle knocker.

Her mother stepped forward and knocked the gargoyle firmly, once, twice, three times. Then she stepped back and waited.

The door opened, and a severe woman stepped out. She looked like a nun. She was in a black robe with a white shawl wrapped around her head and neck. "Yes?"

"Sister". Cath stepped forward and curtsied respectfully, then bowed her head, holding it down for the required three seconds. "I bring you an offering, in thanks for your service, and for your vigilance". She began reciting the lines of the ritual. "She is pure, she is bright, and she is light".

Beatrix snorted. How silly it sounded.

Her mother's eyes flashed at her for a second, then returned to the sister. "She would be a Sacred Sister. Judge her worthy". Cath bowed her head again.

The sister looked seriously at Beatrix, standing just behind her mother and father. "This is the sister?"

Cath looked surprised, but also delighted, at how casually the sister had referred to her daughter as one of their own. She nodded.

"Come here girl, I would look at you". The sister beckoned Beatrix forward.

Beatrix sighed and trudged forward to stand before the sister.

"You would be a sister?" The sister asked.

"Yes", Beatrix said grudgingly.

The sister frowned and narrowed her eyes. "Why?"

Beatrix looked at her mother, who had a panicked look on her face.

"To...protect the light?" Beatrix volunteered hopefully, uttering the tritest thing she could think of.

The sister didn't say anything for a few moments, then nodded. "Come in". She stood aside and gestured that Beatrix should enter.

Cath moved forward, but the sister held up a hand to stop her. "This is for her, and her alone".

Graeme looked uncomfortable at this.

"Sister, are you sure?" Cath said.

"I am sure", the sister replied.

Beatrix looked at her mother, who looked a little deflated, and a little scared. "I'll be right here", she said feebly to Beatrix.

Beatrix nodded. She was a little scared now herself, now that it was here in front of her. She had found the whole idea rather funny, when her mother had first discussed it.

Her, a Sacred Sister. How hard could it be? They got to ride around in fancy carriages and eat fine food all day. And they lived in the city. And if she didn't like it?

Well, she'd just leave. Sneak out and be a barmaid. She had it all planned out. She wasn't worried in the slightest. **Hadn't** been worried in the slightest.

"I'll be back soon", Beatrix said.

"We'll be here", Graeme assured her.

The sister ushered Beatrix inside and closed the door behind her.

Outside, Cath stared at the door, face creased with worry.

"She'll be fine". Graeme's hand squeezed Cath's shoulder. She turned her head into his chest and wept.

*

When Beatrix returned, Graeme sprung to his feet happily. "Cath!" He cupped his hands around his mouth and called down the hill.

Cath came running, dress hitched up around her ankles so as not to dirty it. "Is she here? Is she here?" she asked breathlessly.

She saw Beatrix and smiled. "There you are". She ran over and gave Beatrix a warm hug.

"Ma, stop", Beatrix muttered into her mother's chest.

Cath looked down at her daughter. "Make me". She buried Beatrix back into her bosom and gave her a big squeeze.

"Ugh!" Beatrix protested. "Get off". She pushed half-heartedly at her mother, who was looking at her strangely. "What is it?"

"I'm just so proud of you!" Cath gushed, cupping Beatrix's face in her hands.

Beatrix shook her head. "Don't be. I stole her sherry". She pulled out a small bottle of sherry from her pocket and shook it insolently in her mother's face.

"Beatrix!" Cath hissed, whipping the bottle out of her daughter's hand and shoving it into the pocket of Graeme's jacket. She looked around quickly to see if anyone had seen. Thankfully no-one had.

"I don't know what to do with you", Cath despaired.

"Give me the sherry back?" Beatrix suggested hopefully.

Cath turned away and started walking down the hill, back stiff.

"Can't you leave her be, just once, girl?" Graeme said.

Beatrix shrugged. "I like sherry".

Graeme cuffed her lightly on the back of the head, and pushed her softly down the hill.

*

The ride home was a more sombre affair.

Cath was refusing to speak to Beatrix, and Graeme kept glancing awkwardly between the two of them. He'd been positioned in between them as a buffer.

When they got out, Cath stormed into the house ahead of them.

"Dramatic, much?" Beatrix mumbled.

Graeme raised his finger to his lips.

Beatrix went to go into the house, but Graeme stopped her.

"Wait, girl". He glanced behind to make sure the door was closed. "Your mother might be...rigid...but she means well. She loves you. She just wants a good life for you. There's nothin much here for you, you know that. The sisters is a good cause. It's..." He paused, searching for the right word. "Noble". He nodded.

Beatrix was irritated. They hadn't even asked her how it had gone. She had only visited the sister in the first place to make them happy. She'd had enough of this.

"And what's noble about being shipped off to a convent to live out my life as a nun?" Beatrix demanded.

"The sisters aren't nuns-" Graeme started.

But Beatrix interrupted him. "I don't want to be a sister. I want to be a barmaid. I want to move to the city and be a barmaid".

Graeme sighed. "I know, girl".

"Then why don't you stand up to her?" Beatrix asked.

"She's my wife", Graeme said feebly.

"And I'm your daughter. Shouldn't I get a say in the matter? It's my life after all".

Graeme went quiet. "Come on". He threw his arm around her and steered her into the house. This was always how it went. She'd rail at her father, and he'd go quiet, and nothing would ever be settled, and time marched on, and the time for choosing got closer.

Inside, her mother was waiting. She looked a little more settled now she was back in her own home. "Well?"

"Well, what", Beatrix shot back.

"How did it go?" Cath said eagerly, her irritation apparently forgotten.

"How'd what go?" Beatrix said sweetly.

"The sisters!" Cath gushed.

"Oh that", Beatrix said.

Cath stared expectantly at her daughter, clearly excited.

"It was fine", Beatrix said, noncommittally.

"Fine?" Cath turned to Graeme, then back to Beatrix. "Fine?"

"Mhm". Beatrix nodded her head, enjoying herself.

Cath took a deep, calming breath. "I expect you'll tell me properly, Beatrix Bellafonte".

"And why is that, Catherine Bellafonte?" Beatrix shot back.

Cath pursed her lips.

"Now, now, you two". Graeme intervened, as always, by placing a calming hand on his wife's arm.

Cath took another breath. "Please. Tell me".

Beatrix frowned. It rather took the fun out of it when she begged. It wasn't actual begging, but for Cath, it was basically lying prostrate on the floor.

Beatrix opened her mouth to begrudgingly oblige, when Cath frowned and moved quickly toward her.

"Wait, what is-" Cath reached for her daughter's face.

Beatrix batted her hand away. "Stop".

"What is-" Cath was persistent. "Bea, stop!"

"Ugh, fine, get it over with!" Beatrix groaned.

"Come here", Cath instructed. She pulled Beatrix over to the fire, which Graeme had lit while they were bickering.

She stared gravely at Beatrix, while she turned her head this way and that in the light of the fire. Suddenly, she gasped, and stepped backward, hands over her mouth.

"What? What is it?" Beatrix demanded. When her mother didn't respond, she continued. "What!"

"Your hair!" Cath gasped, stepping back further.

Graeme appeared behind Cath and caught her in his arms as she swooned.

"What about my hair?" Beatrix was bewildered.

Graeme guided Cath into her chair, then returned to his daughter by the fire.

He peered at her, then turned her head to the side. He swallowed audibly. "Your hair, girl...it's...it's...white".

Beatrix gaped, then ran from the room. She returned with her mirror and held it up in front of the fire, which was crackling aggressively in the grate.

She looked at her hair in the mirror. "Where? What are you talking about? I can't see any white".

But then she turned her head, and her stomach dropped. There. A small patch of white hair by her temple. Only three or four hairs. But there they were. Clear as day.

Graeme ran his hand over his mouth, then left the room. When he returned, he had a little silver pair of prongs that Cath used as tweezers.

Without saying a word, he grabbed Beatrix's head with one hand, and promptly plucked the hairs out with the other. He flicked them into the fire, where they sizzled and smoked. The smoke wasn't normal smoke, it was an aquamarine colour, and far too 'thin'. It was misty and ethereal. They both stared at it silently.

Beatrix was in shock. She didn't know what to say. She knew what this meant. Every girl did. White hair meant one thing.

It meant...she was dark one.

It meant...she was a witch.

Fire And Brimstone

Beatrix slept fitfully that night, tossing and turning, and annoying the heck out of Felix, who in the end got fed up and jumped down.

He curled up under the bed and started snoring contentedly within minutes.

Beatrix was not so lucky. She had strange dreams, in a half sleep. Vivid dreams. Waking dreams. She couldn't tell if she was awake or asleep for most of them. Those weird kinds of dreams where you feel like you're really in them.

She dreamt she was back in the castle, in front of the mysterious, misty door.

But this time, as she reached for the handle, she was thrown backwards.

She fell, and fell, and fell. She screamed, but no words came. Eventually, she fell forward and landed.

She was in the town square now, and everyone was screaming at her, and pelting her with rocks. Their eyes were red, and scary, and their faces blurred and twisted.

She scrunched her eyes and rolled over. She willed herself back to the castle.

She saw another face then. A handsome one. Beardless, with a mop of finely groomed blonde hair, parted smartly to one side.

Brilliant, blue eyes sparkled at her. They were the bluest eyes she'd ever seen. Like lightning striking through a blue sky, on a perfectly clear day.

The face smiled, and the man beckoned, his hand extended invitingly. She didn't fear the man, he looked friendly, and she reached for his hand.

Just as she took it, she woke up.

But she was really awake this time.

She heard the birds chirping outside, and Felix padding across the floor beneath her bed. She leaned over, and his face appeared looking up at her. "Come up", she mumbled.

Felix leapt nimbly up onto the bed and rubbed himself against her face. "Thank you". She rubbed his soft fur and enjoyed the emotional support.

She felt very scared, and very anxious. The dreams had left her in tatters. Perhaps Felix could sense that, for he started licking her nose. He didn't usually lick her face much.

"Love you", Beatrix whispered, holding Felix tightly.

Felix nuzzled her, then squirmed.

"Ok, ok", Beatrix said. She let him go and he meandered across the bed, then stood looking expectantly at the door.

She rolled out of bed and opened the door. Felix slipped out, and she closed the door and got back into bed. It was cold. Another cold morning.

She heard her father's rumbling snores. She didn't know how her mother slept with him. Sometimes he woke **her** up, and she wasn't even in the same room.

She lay and stared at the ceiling, thinking about the events of the day before. She ran her hand self-consciously through her hair. She wanted to check it, but she daren't. She was scared.

What would Lady Lysona do? She thought.

She'd be brave, that's what.

She pushed herself out of bed and sat down in front of her mirror. She refused to look at the mirror for a few moments, then looked at it, but scrunched her eyes shut.

Lady Lysona would look.

She opened her eyes and looked at her hair. There was nothing there. Phew. No white hair. Just her regular old black hair. Back to its curly self.

Its curly glory.

She smirked. She turned her head side to side, running her fingers through her hair. Not one strand of white hair.

Perhaps it was just a fluke. A freak occurrence. Perhaps it was something in the city air. Or the convent. Both were strange places, in their own ways.

Knock, knock.

She jumped in her seat, heart beating wildly.

What was that?

Knock, knock.

Again, the knocking.

It wasn't her door.

It must be the door to the cabin.

She got up and cracked her door.

She peaked through to see her mother stomping agitatedly toward the front door in her nightgown. She opened the door. "What is it?" She hissed.

"Cath, I'm sorry to wake ya dear, but it's urgent". It was Meggie, who was also in her nightgown.

"What is it?" Cath repeated, in an even tone this time.

"We just got word, Gatrick and me".

"Word of what?" Cath was impatient.

"It's The Mistress. She's coming. Today".

"What?" Cath was panicking now. "Back? Again?"

Meggie nodded gravely.

"Why?" Cath was whispering now.

Meggie shook her head. "No-one knows".

Cath didn't know what to say.

"But it must be serious...cause they never come back twice in one week. I've never known it to happen..."

Cath nodded automatically. "Yes...well...thanks for letting me know".

Meggie nodded and peered past Cath into the cabin.

Beatrix quickly closed her door and got back into bed, pulling the covers up over her head.

In the living room, she heard her mother and father whispering frantically.

*

When she left her bedroom, her mother and father were being particularly chipper.

"Hello darling", her mother said, rushing over and giving her a kiss on the forehead.

"Hello", Beatrix said suspiciously. She knew why they were being so chipper. But she didn't want to break the spell.

Perhaps if she pretended, and they pretended, it would all go away, and everything would be as it was.

"I made your favourite. Pancakes with fresh berries". Cath steered Beatrix to the table, and placed a plate loaded with pancakes and berries down in front of her.

"And..." Cath returned to the kitchen. "Fresh honey". She placed a pot of honey down on the table with a small spoon. "I know you like it sweet".

"Thank you". Beatrix was subdued, and picked up her knife and fork. She started cutting her pancakes and forking them into her mouth.

"Your honey". Cath hurried over and drizzled honey over the pancakes for her.

"Thanks", Beatrix said automatically.

Cath stood and watched her daughter, not sure what to do with herself. After a moment, she said, "Yes, well". She returned to the kitchen and Beatrix heard her doing the washing up in the bowl.

Felix hopped up onto the table beside Beatrix and started sniffing around her plate.

Without thinking, Beatrix picked a pancake up off the plate and gave it to Felix. He took it happily in his mouth and ambled away to the other end of the table, where he coiled himself comfortably down and sat chewing it.

Cath was so distracted that she didn't even notice. Usually, her senses were preternatural when it came to Felix.

Graeme ambled out of the bedroom he shared with Cath and plonked himself down in the chair opposite Beatrix. "Where's mine", he grumbled.

"You've had enough pancakes to last a lifetime", Cath snapped.

Graeme smacked his ample stomach. It was rather straining the belt of his trousers. "One more won't hurt". He winked at Beatrix. She smiled, glad for a break to the tension.

Cath tutted, but Beatrix heard her start cooking another pancake. She grinned at her father. Graeme grinned back.

The pancake was done in no time, and Graeme started eating hungrily. "Where's my honey?" He looked around blithely. "Oh, there it is". He pulled the pot toward him. "And me spoon?"

Beatrix handed him the spoon.

"Thank you kindly". He drizzled a liberal amount of honey onto his pancakes, watching it trickle down in swirls from the end of his spoon.

"You're such a child", Beatrix teased.

"There's a child in all of us", Graeme retorted.

"There's more than one in you", Beatrix said.

"Children are smart. Children like pancakes", Graeme retorted.

Beatrix giggled.

"What are you two giggling about?" Cath appeared around the corner from the kitchen nook, tea towel over her arm.

They looked at each other, then both said, "Nothing".

Cath rolled her eyes then went back to the washing up.

They finished their breakfast quickly, far too quickly for Beatrix's liking, and then it was time to get ready.

She pulled on her most modest dress and combed her hair neatly down her back. Felix hopped up onto her dressing table and arched his back for pets. She gave him some, then fixed a white ribbon in her hair.

When she came back into the living room, her mother and father were there, both in their best clothes.

Cath's mouth twitched, and she burst out, "Come here". She pulled Beatrix to her. Graeme joined in the hug, and they all stood in silence for a moment.

"You've done nothing wrong, you hear me?" Cath said to her.

Graeme nodded. "Your mothers right. Just go out there, say nothing, and do nothing, and she'll be gone. Then we can be on with it. And back to the pancakes".

Beatrix smiled tightly. It was a sign of how serious the situation was that Cath made no comment about the pancake jibe, she just squeezed Beatrix more tightly.

"Right", Cath brushed herself down, looking away. It looked like she had tears in her eyes, but Beatrix couldn't be sure, for she hurried away and began sweeping the floor.

After a few moments, she put the brush away and usher them toward the front door. "Let's go". She gave Beatrix a pained look as   she   opened   the   door. Outside, the villagers were already gathered, waiting.

They hurried toward them.

Her mother and father settled into the back, and Beatrix walked to the front row with the other boys and girls, as was expected.

In the distance, a carriage could be heard rumbling toward them.

The wait for it to arrive was tense.

Dullen was picking his nose again, but it didn't make Beatrix laugh this time.

Finally, the carriage rumbled to a halt, and The Mistress stepped down.

She strode over the assembled villagers.

This time, she wasn't alone.

The villagers gasped.

She was flanked by two Torchbearers. Knights. Beatrix's stomach fell out of her. One of them was the knight from Brightcastle. The man with the horse and moustache. He was staring at her. She lowered her eyes to the ground.

The Mistress stopped in front of them and addressed the assembled villagers. "You know by now, I am sure, why I am here".

Meggie shifted guiltily on her feet.

"So, I will waste no time", Mistress Madele continued.

The villagers held their breath.

"There has been...intelligence...that a dark one has been spotted...in this very village", Mistress Madele said.

The villagers gasped collectively and started muttering amongst themselves.

Mistress Madele raised her hand, and silence was instant.

"My noble brethren, Knight Gladius, has tracked the dark one...here. He is very skilled, Knight Gladius", Mistress Madele glanced admiringly at the knight behind her right side. "He is very talented...he is gifted. Yes. Gifted with The Sight".

One of the women in the crowd closed her eyes and made the sign of The Spirit.

Beatrix licked her lips. She stood statue still, afraid to breathe.

"The dark one came before him...and he saw. He saw...her...for what she really is. He saw her true self", Mistress Madele continued.

Knight Gladus raised his chin proudly and crossed his hands behind his back, puffing his chest out at the compliment.

The Mistress resumed her pacing, slowly, up and down in front of the group, hands still clasped behind her back, a thoughtful expression on her face. Her eyes were cast down to the ground, as if deep in thought. From time to time, she looked up to the sky, as if for guidance.

A bead of sweat started trickling down Beatrix's forehead.

In the crowd, Graeme shifted on his feet. His hands were bunched into fists at his sides. Cath gripped his arm, restraining him.

The woman who had superstitiously made the sign of The Spirit nodded fervently, holding a necklace tightly through the neckline of her dress.

"It has been almost two hundred years since this land has been blighted by a dark one...thanks in no small part to the work of The Sisters, and The Torchbearers". Mistress Madele bowed her head reverently at Knight Gladius, who nodded his own back in thanks. "We have worked tirelessly to root them from the land, as weeds from the field. And we have succeeded...we have succeeded".

People in the crowd were nodding now. They had been reared on the old tales of fire and brimstone. Fear of the dark ones had been passed down from mother to daughter, father to son, for generations. They knew it like breathing.

"Until now..." Mistress Madele said. She came to a stop before Beatrix. But she wasn't looking at Beatrix, she was looking overhead, into the eyes of the adults behind. "She stands before us, brazen, unashamed".

The superstitious woman tutted. "Shame", she whispered.

"Shame", a whisper came back from the crowd.

Beatrix was sweating freely now, and desperately wanted to wipe her forehead. She swallowed and licked her lips. She felt dizzy, like she was floating outside her body, looking down.

"Shame", Mistress Madele whispered. She turned and walked away a few paces, then swung back dramatically to face the crowd. "And the punishment for shame is death. By the flame of the fire, we shall **purify** them!" She seemed as if she was gripped by a frenzy, and threw her hands into the hair, pumping them wildly.

"Shame!" The superstitious woman screamed, knocking into the woman beside her, who stepped back, a look of terror on her face.

"Shame!" another woman moaned.

"Shame!" another voice joined.

"Shame!" And another. And another.

Some of the villagers looked terrified. Terrified that if they did not join the chant, they would be next for the fire, so they too joined the chanting, their faces painful and shamed, but guilty all the same.

Finally, only three voices abstained.

They belonged to Beatrix, Graeme, and Cath.

The villagers screamed.

Mistress Madele hung her hands by her sides, and stared malevolently at Graeme and Cath.

Beatrix glanced over her shoulder.

Graeme looked terrifying. His face was ever so dark. It was twitching, like he wanted to snarl and snap, like a feral dog. Like he wanted to rend and tear at The Mistress.

Cath's hand was still on his arm, but she too looked murderous.

The Mistress lowered her eyes to Beatrix and raised her hands for silence.

Beatrix stared back at The Mistress, too terrified to move.

"Beatrix...Bellafonte", Mistress Madele said quietly, each word dripping like honey.

The crowd went quiet as all eyes turned to Beatrix.

"The witch", Mistress Madele whispered ever so softly. But the whisper carried to all.

Complete silence fell on the village as The Mistress' words landed.

"Seize her", Mistress Madele said, breaking the silence.

"No!" Cath screamed. "No! Don't you touch her!" She burst through the crowd and wrapped herself around Beatrix. "Stay back!"

Beatrix was shaking with fear. "Ma", she moaned.

"Don't worry Bea", Cath whispered. "Everything will be alright".

"Take her", Mistress Madele repeated.

"No!" Cath pushed Beatrix behind her, and stood defiantly facing The Mistress and the knights, who had stepped forward. One of the knights, Knight Gladius' companion, reached for Cath to move her.

At that moment, a figure came hurtling from the back of the crowd and tackled the knight to the ground.

The knight landed with a crash, his plate armour rattling as it hit the ground. Graeme was on top of him. He lifted the knight and smashed him back down onto the ground, one, two, three times.

"Ugh", the knight grunted as the impact rocked him and knocked the lights out of him.

Knight Gladius stepped into action and kicked Graeme hard in the midsection.

Graeme cried out and went sprawling to the floor but pushed himself quickly to his feet.

Knight Gladius drew his sword and waited, his gaze challenging.

Graeme threw himself at him.

Knight Gladius nimbly sidestepped and brought the butt of his sword down hard on the back of Graeme's neck.

Graeme collapsed unconscious to the floor.

"Grame, no!" Cath ran forward and slapped Knight Gladius hard on the side of the face, leaving bright red weals where her fingers had struck.

He turned, and casually backhanded Cath to the floor with his gauntlet.

Cath moaned once and lay still.

"Prepare the fire", Mistress Madele instructed.

Knight Gladius nodded, and turned to the villagers. "You, men, gather wood". He addressed another group of villagers. "You, with me".

Before long, the village was a flurry of activity as the villagers set to building a pyre.

There would be a burning today.

A cleansing.

The pyre was built in no time at all, and Knight Gladius clicked his fingers at his companion, who bound Beatrix's hands with rope.

She had stood silent throughout it all, petrified, her eyes watching, unable to comprehend.

These were her friends, her family.

There was Dullen, her cousin, stacking wood against the pyre.

There was Meggie, her auntie, running back and forth for The Mistress gathering sticks.

She felt sick.

None of this felt real.

She gagged and retched, vomiting to the floor.

The knight holding her stepped back, but kept his hand on her arm. Otherwise, he showed no reaction, and kept his eyes straight ahead.

"Bring her", Mistress Madele said.

The words pierced vaguely through the fog of Beatrix's mind, and her eyes widened.

"No!" she screamed. "No! Get off me! I'm not a witch! You've made a mistake!"

"Not a witch?" Mistress Madele asked.

"No!" Beatrix pleaded. "I'm just a girl!"

Mistress Madele approached her. Her cold grey eyes were devoid of emotion, and full of judgment. Beatrix's stomach dropped.

"Then what is this?" The Mistress gripped Beatrix hard by the hair and pulled her head back.

"What! What!" Beatrix screamed in panic.

"This!" Mistress Madele hissed, turning Beatrix's head to the side so the villagers could see.

The villagers gasped.

"The mark", the superstitious woman whispered.

"The mark". Another whisper.

"She is marked!" The superstitious woman screamed. "She is marked!"

"What mark?" Beatrix pleaded.

Mistress Madele pinched a few strands of hair, and ripped them viciously out of her head.

"Ow!" Beatrix whimpered.

"This mark", Mistress Madele hissed. She was holding a clump of Beatrix's hair in her fingers, right in front of Beatrix's eyes. Beatrix looked. The hair was white.

"I'm sorry", Beatrix whispered, tears falling from her eyes.

"You're sorry?" Mistress Madele repeated. "She is sorry", she repeated for the benefit of the crowd. "Do we forgive her?"

"Never!" The superstitious woman hissed.

"Do we believe her?" Mistress Madele asked.

"The dark one speaks only lies!" The superstitious woman cried.

Mistress Madele nodded. "As it is written". She turned to Knight Gladius. "Take her to the pyre".

"NO!"

A growl caused them to turn.

Graeme's fist connected flush with the knight holding Beatrix.

The knight crumpled to the floor.

Graeme knelt and pulled the knight's sword from its sheath.

Knight Gladius looked at Graeme with interest, as if this was an unexpected and potentially fun diversion.

He unsheathed his own blade and walked slowly toward Graeme, stopping a few paces away.

He looked at Graeme expectantly and arched his eyebrow as if to say, "Come then, try me".

Graeme happily obliged and swung his sword hard at Knight Gladius' face.

Gladius parried the blow with ease, turning Graeme's blade, and using the momentum of his swing to take the blade out of his hand.

It spun through the air and clattered onto the floor a few feet away.

"Pitiful", Knight Gladius said, shaking his head and pressing his lips. He stepped forward and held his blade to Graeme's throat. He paused and looked to Mistress Madele, who nodded.

"No, wait!" Beatrix screamed. "I'm going". She began walking toward the pyre. "Take me, just don't hurt my da".

"How noble", Knight Gladius said, looking strangely at Beatrix, as if she were a particularly fine oil painting, that he just couldn't understand the beauty of.

Suddenly, he spun on his heel, and his elbow connected brutally with Graeme's chin, lifting him from his feet.

Graeme hit the floor with a thud and lay still.

Gladius looked at Beatrix, then back to Mistress Madele for guidance. She nodded, and he sheathed his sword.

He walked over to Beatrix and escorted her to the pyre, where two villagers carried her up and tied her.

A villager approached the pyre with an unlit brand. He paused and looked at The Mistress.

"The fire burns, the fire cleanses. May your soul know peace, free from its tether, free from its chains. Free from its darkness", Mistress Madele said gravely.

The villager lit the brand, then held it to the pyre, which started smoking.

Flames sprung up, dancing along the bottom of the pyre, hungrily licking at the wood and hay.

Before long, it was an inferno, and the flames reached high, and the smoke coiled thick and oily about Beatrix's face.

She squirmed and writhed as the heat pressed at her.

It was oppressive, and she was quickly drenched in sweat.

The villagers watched sombrely.

The Mistress stood in front of the fire, arms clasped behind her back, a pious look on her face.

Knight Gladius joined her and watched impassively.

Beatrix started to cough as the smoke filled her lungs. She was getting dizzy and finding it hard to breathe.

She swayed side to side as her eyes became tired.

The superstitious woman threw a rock at her. It hit her on the forehead, and she cried out weakly as a thin trail of blood dripped down her face.

She started to cry.

She was so scared. What had she done to deserve this? She wanted her ma. She wanted to wake up from this nightmare.

She wailed and choked as thick black smoke surged into her lungs.

She coughed wretchedly, as it wracked her.

"Please! Help me!" She screamed.

Adrenaline surged through her, and she panicked.

"Please! Please!" She looked around wildly, as the flames began to lick at her feet.

"Hey!" A sweet, high-pitched voice suddenly whispered in her ear.

"Hey, you!" The voice whispered again.

She blinked rapidly, looking side to side.

What was that?

Was she hallucinating?

"Hey!"

Her eyes focused on...a fairy?

A little fairy was fluttering in front of her! It had a forest green dress that looked as though it was crafted from pretty leaves and moss, and long, curly hair as red as the flames licking up around her feet.

The fairy was exquisitely beautiful, with skin that looked as if it never aged, and eyes that saw all.

The fairy reached toward her, and ran a tiny, soft hand down the side of her face.

She coughed and choked as more smoke entered her lungs.

She moaned as dizziness swept over, and her head swayed dangerously to the side.

"Hey!" The voice was insistent, hopeful, lilting.

Beatrix leant her head back against the pyre, trying desperately to focus on the fairy, who was shifting in and out of focus, as the world got dark around her.

"Don't worry", the fairy whispered in her mind. "He's coming!"

The Cottage In The Sea

"No!" Beatrix screamed, jolting upright. She was bathed in sweat, and her hair was stuck to her face.

"No, no, no!" She continued to wail piteously, thrashing about wildly. She was in a bed, and sprung out of it, glancing about wildly like a cornered doe.

She was in a room.

A stone room.

There, a door!

She lunged toward it, but a sound stopped her dead in her tracks. It was a creaky sound, like when a really old wooden door is opened. Someone was on the other side, and they were turning the handle!

She licked her lips and looked around.

The handle turned, and she dived behind the door.

The heavy wooden door opened with a loud creak, and footsteps sounded on the stone.

Step, step, step.

Someone was in the room with her.

All she could see was a pair of shoes. The rest of the "person" was still hidden.

"Beatrix?" A voice called into the room.

The person walked into the room, and Beatrix sunk back against the stone wall, hiding behind the door. She could see now it was a man. A tall man with shoulder length blonde hair.

"Beatrix? Are you here?" The voice sounded puzzled, and a little concerned.

Seizing her moment, she bolted forward and pushed the man hard in the back. He stumbled forward and fell onto the bed. She turned and dashed out of the room into the hallway.

She ran, and ran, and ran, her feet pounding the stone in panic and exhilaration. Her blood was pumping.

Where was she?

She rounded a corner and slowed. She frowned. It looked familiar. She shook her head and kept running. She wouldn't let them catch her.

She flew round another a corner and blistered down a high hallway. Halfway down the hallway, something caught her eye, and she stopped dead in her tracks.

Her mouth fell open as she stared out a window.

"It can't be", she gasped.

"Agh!" She screamed, and jumped back in shock, hand flying to her mouth, as a huge whale swam past the window.

If she'd been paying attention to her surroundings, she would have heard the man chasing after her. The sound of his feet hurriedly striking the stone floor, or his panicked, laboured breathing as he came puffing around the corner.

As it was, she didn't hear a thing, and didn't hear him when he slowed to a stop behind her either.

"Amazing, isn't it?" The man said.

"AGHHH!" Beatrix screamed in earnest this time, jumping back quickly and tripping over her feet. She scrambled backwards away from the man, staring up at him as if he were a dark one, come to get her in the night.

"It's alright, it's alright" The man assured her, raising his hands and walking toward her slowly. He was holding his hands out like he was scared of panicking her. As if she were a bomb, that might go off at any moment.

"Get back!" Beatrix hissed, anger taking over now.

"I-" The man began.

"I said get back!" Beatrix screamed, flinging her hand out wildly.

The man jumped back quickly, turning to the side, raising his hands and sucking his stomach in, as a vicious scythe of white lightning flew from Beatrix's hand.

It struck the stone wall behind the man and blew a hole right through it. The man's face paled, as he watched a bundle of bricks and dust topple to the floor.

Beatrix was panting and gasping, gazing at the hole in the wall with a look of disbelief on her face.

Suddenly, a green face with stubby, pointy ears appeared in the hole in the wall. "Erm...professor?"

The blonde man licked his lips and stepped gingerly toward the wall. "Nothing to worry about, Horace, just showing Beatrix here around the castle".

Another face appeared next to the green one. A girl's face. She swept a thick lock of white-blonde hair out of her eyes.

As she edged Horace out of the way, and stuck her head through the hole, Beatrice saw that her hair wasn't blonde, it was brown. It was just the hair at the front of her head that was white. It ran from her left temple, all the way down. A bit like a white stripe on an otherwise dark skunk.

The girl ran her tongue over her top teeth and arched her eyebrows, as if she was impressed. "Wow. You did this?" She looked up at Beatrice from the rubble on the floor. Behind her an excited muttering began.

Beatrice blushed.

"That will be quite enough, thank you", Horace said. "Back to your seat, Miss Cincesse".

The girl disappeared.

Horace gave the blonde man a sympathetic look, then he too disappeared.

The blonde man cleared his throat. "Yes, well, perhaps I'd better clear this up". He raised his hands, which started to glow. They didn't glow white like Beatrix's had, but a soft, gold colour. The rubble on the floor shook for a second. The man clapped his hands, and the rubble disappeared.

Beatrix gasped.

The bricks were flying off the floor and rearranging themselves in the wall, as they had been before she'd…damaged them.

In a moment, the wall was fixed, and the hole was gone.

The blonde man turned to her. He approached her slowly and dropped to his knees just in front of her, extending his hand. "Miss Bellafonte". He waggled his fingers.

She took his hand. What choice did she have? She didn't know where she was, or what she'd done, for that matter. And her panic had vanished. There was no mistress. And this wasn't the village. That much was certain.

He pulled her to her feet and patted her arms down gently. "There".

"Where am I?" Beatrix asked, dazed.

"Come with me", the blonde man said.

He turned and walked back the way they had came. He paused at the end of the hallway and beckoned her on with his head.

She followed.

They walked for a while, and passed the room Beatrix had woken in. Beatrix peered into the room, but the man kept walking.

After a while, they came to a crossroads. There were three passages. One going right, one straight ahead, one to the left. Beatrix looked right, and gasped. "It's..." She gravitated toward the passage to the right, but the man stopped her.

She looked crestfallen but allowed the man to steer her on.

At the end of the passage, was an opening. It looked a bit like an elevator.

Beatrix frowned and looked expectantly at the man, as if to say, what now? Why are you taking me into a dead-end? She was still a little wary and paused just before the opening.

The man stopped too and looked down at her. "I promise you, it's not much further now".

Beatrix narrowed her eyes.

The man smiled grimly. "No more of that, please. I have just remodelled".

The joke broke the tension, and Beatrix relaxed. She took a deep breath and stepped into the opening.

It was about seven feet high, and seven feet wide.

The man stepped in next to her and looked pleasantly back down the hallway.

"What n-" Beatrix began.

The floor began to shake, and she threw out her hand to steady herself.

The man smiled politely at her.

The next moment, the hallway disappeared, and everything went dark.

She could feel the floor rumbling. It felt like they were moving. No, falling!

"If you try to hurt me, I swear to god I'll kill you!" Beatrix hissed in the dark. Her hands started to glow white, and the man placed a comforting hand on her shoulder. She jumped back, and some sparks flew from her hands.

"Please, be calm. It is essential that you do not panic. If you panic, you will kill us both. I mean you no harm...I promise".

Beatrix licked her lips and took a deep breath. She kept her distance, back against the wall. She had no choice but to trust this strange man for now.

The ride down was uncomfortable and tense. Eventually, after what felt like a lifetime, but must have only been a few minutes, the rumbling stopped, and blue light flooded the...lift.

Beatrix gasped, and bubbles came out of her mouth. Her eyes widened and her hands flew to her throat as she saw that they were underwater.

"Do not panic", the man whispered into her mind.

"Do not panic?" she mouthed incredulously, but only bubbles came out of her mouth.

The man tapped her on the shoulder, and she felt a tingling sensation sweep through her body, like ice water dripping down her neck.

"Don't panic?" she repeated. This time, she could hear herself. The man smiled. It seemed like he could hear her too.

"That's right", the man said calmly. "Nothing to be gained from it". He clasped his hands behind his back and walked out of the lift, as if he were on a jaunt through his favourite park. He walked forward a few steps, then turned back to look at her over his shoulder. "Well?"

Beatrix scowled. "I'll give you well". She stormed out of the lift then stopped quickly. "Woah, woah, woah!" She looked down at her feet. It looked like they were resting on the bottom of the ocean.

She looked left and right. They were on a path, fenced in by high green reeds. Sea reeds. They were waving softly in the faint current of the ocean. "This is..."

The blonde man started whistling, which irritated Beatrix. She swallowed, and puffed her chest out, lifting her chin high.

The man was humming and whistling now, alternating between the two.

Beatrix focused her gaze on the back of the man, and kept walking, taking her steps gingerly, like a cat on a high beam.

After a few steps, she began to feel more comfortable. Initially she thought she would float away, with nothing to tether her to the floor, but it was as if her feet were stuck to the path like sticky glue. Every time she lifted a foot, it felt pulled back to the floor, by an unseen force. It wasn't a strong force, but she noticed that the higher she raised her foot, the stronger it became. She began enjoying herself and sunk down on her haunches.

The man turned to watch, as she jumped off from the floor as hard as she could.

"Woohoo!" Beatrix yelled.

The man smiled.

"Oof". Beatrix landed on the floor with a thump, and a bunch of dust shot up around her feet, drifting lazily up around her ankles.

"Oi!" An irritated voice yelled from her feet. "Watchu do that for?"

"Ah!" Beatrix jumped backward. "Who are you?"

"Oo am I? Oo are you!" The voice shot back. "Stompin around like you own the place".

Beatrix leant forward and squinted. The voice belonged to a tiny man with a pointy red hat, and a long, thick, red beard that came down to his stomach. He couldn't have been more than a foot tall. She could only see his head. It was quite off-putting. "Where's the rest of you?"

"Where's the…" The gnome shook its head, as if she had offended him greatly. He wiggled about in what looked like sand, then pushed his hands down hard, and popped himself out of the floor. "Is that a height joke?" He put his hands on his hips and glared at her angrily, like a pirate that had just been short changed. "Cause it better not be!"

Beatrix raised her eyebrows. She couldn't believe her eyes. "But you're…a gnome!"

The gnome turned to the blonde man. "Where'd you dig er up?" He looked at Beatrix as if she were slow.

"But…gnomes aren't real", Beatrix said wanly.

"News to me", the gnome said drily. He turned back to the blonde man. "Did you know, gnomes aren't real?"

The blonde man crossed his arms and chuckled softly.

Beatrix spun to face him. "And just what do **you** think is so funny?"

"Ooo", the gnome trilled. "Ark at er".

Beatrix whipped back to the gnome. "Watch it".

"I will if you do", the gnome retorted, then dived back into the ground, raising its hands above its head like it was springing off a diving board.

"Have you finished…making friends?" The blonde man asked.

"I wasn't-" Beatrix began.

"Wonderful", the man interrupted her, and turned his back on her, walking off down the path.

Beatrix scowled. She was beginning to dislike this man.

They walked for a few minutes in silence.

It was eerie.

The sea was heavy around them, like a blue-green blanket.

Suddenly, a building came into sight ahead.

A cottage, from the looks of it.

"A cottage in the sea", Beatrix mumbled.

The man turned and winked at her over his shoulder.

Beatrix sighed and rolled her eyes. "How dramatic".

The cottage was a light pink colour and had three windows and two chimneys. She didn't understand what business a chimney had being on a cottage under the sea, but then, she didn't understand any of this.

The man stopped and turned. "After you".

The door to the cottage swung open.

Inside, was darkness.

Beatrix looked dubiously at the open door.

The man raised an eyebrow, as if to say, "Really? After all this, you're scared by a door opening by itself?"

Beatrix huffed and walked into the cottage.

The man followed, and the door closed behind him. It was completely dark now, and Beatrix felt on edge again.

The man strolled forward and clicked his fingers. A sound rang out, like the **hiss** of a snake, and suddenly she could see.

There were lit candles, floating in the air above their heads. Beatrix frowned but said nothing. She'd just met a talking gnome who lived under the sea, after all. She was quickly acclimatising to her surroundings.

The cottage was simple. There was a kitchen to the left and what looked a like a bedroom next to it. There was a dining table with eight chairs in the centre of the room. At the back, was a fireplace. Either side of it were two windows.

"Have a seat". The man gestured to two comfy armchairs before a fireplace.

Beatrix sunk into one of the chairs, her eyes on the man all the while, as if watching him for any funny business.

The man sank into the other chair and moaned gratefully. "Ah, that is nice". He clicked his fingers, and a fire sprung up in the grate. It was at that moment she realised there was no water in the cottage. It was like a regular cottage, with air!

The man rubbed his hands appreciatively as the warmth of the fire hit him. "It does get rather cold down here".

Beatrix nodded. She didn't know what to say.

The man looked around searchingly and bit his lip. "Where did I..." He rubbed his chin. "Ah, yes".

He got up from his chair and dug something out from down the side of it. The something was a pipe, which he placed into his mouth.

He fished some tobacco out of his trouser pocket and sprinkled it into the pipe.

Beatrix waited for him to lean forward and light his pipe in the fire, but he did no such thing.

He made a fist, then held his index finger over the bottom of the pipe. Fire sprung out of his finger, which he held still as the pipe began to smoke.

He sucked on the pipe a few times, smacking his lips, then shook his finger, blowing on it as the fire went out. "Right", he said, in a business-like manner. "Beatrix".

"Yes?" Beatrix replied. She was rather at a loss, and now that she had sat down, she was beginning to feel tired, the weight of everything catching up with her.

"You are probably wondering", the man said, in-between more puffs on his pipe. "What you are doing here".

"Yes", Beatrix replied.

"Well, the answer is very simple. But it may be a hard one to swallow".

Beatrix nodded.

The man looked carefully at Beatrix, as if determining if she were ready to hear the truth or not. He nodded his head. "Beatrix".

She tensed.

"You are a witch...and you are in a cottage...in the sea".

Gregor Firewind

"Who are you?" Beatrix asked immediately.

"I am Gregor. Gregor Firewind".

"Firewind?" Beatrix looked as if she couldn't believe this was a real name. It sounded like something a bad writer had plucked out of a hat.

"Yes, I know", Gregor said apologetically. "Rather cliché, isn't it?"

Beatrix snorted. "Just a little".

Gregor arched an eyebrow. "And Bellafonte isn't?"

Beatrix narrowed one eye like a pirate. "Watch it, mister".

Gregor chuckled. "My mistake". He plugged his pipe with more tobacco.

"Do you have to? That's gross". Beatrix screwed up her face at the pipe.

"Yes, it is, but I am rather addicted unfortunately".

Beatrix didn't think much of this. "So why am I here?"

Gregor looked around, as if he wondered if there was something wrong with his cottage.

"I mean, here". Beatrix threw her arms out expansively. "Under the sea. In a castle".

Gregor opened his mouth to correct her.

"Cottage. Castle. Whatever!"

Gregor closed his mouth. "Do you remember what happened to you?"

Beatrix frowned. Flashes of red ran through her mind. Screaming voices. Snarling faces. She shook her head to free herself of the memories, then nodded. After a moment, she hung her head.

Gregor placed a hand on her shoulder and gave it a little squeeze. "You are safe now".

Beatrix's head shot up. "What about my family?"

Gregor grinned a toothy grin. His white teeth sparkled in the firelight. "They are fine".

Beatrix was not to be pacified. "Where are they?" She sprung to her feet. "Where is my father? He was battling that...knight. That arse, Gladius!"

"Your father is fine...we have...hidden him".

"Hidden him? Hidden him where?" Beatrix was interrogating Gregor thoroughly.

"Someplace safe...your mother too".

"But The Mistress...and the knights..."

"They are safe, I assure you".

"I don't believe you", Beatrix said haughtily. "Show me!" She demanded.

"I will...all in good time".

"Now!" Beatrix yelled.

The smile left Gregor's face. He raised his hand and made a lazy circle with his finger. The outline of the circle was a soft gold. After a moment, she could see something in the circle. At first it was blurry, but then, she could see it clearly. It was her mother and father. They were frolicking in a garden outside a cabin. But it wasn't their garden. In the background were mountains and high hills.

"Ma!" Beatrix yelled, bringing her face close to the circle. "Pa!"

"They cannot hear you", Gregor said quietly.

"Take me to them!"

"I cannot".

Beatrix went quiet then, and Gregor watched her carefully.

"Why not?" Beatrix asked.

"It is for their own safety".

"Rubbish".

"Right now, no one knows where they are, no one but me. If I were to take you to them, it would leave a trace. A trace that others could follow".

"Others?"

"Others".

Beatrix knew who he meant. But she wasn't sure if she believed him entirely. Before she could question him further, he spoke.

"Why would I lie to you?"

Beatrix thought about it. He had a point. He had rescued her after all. "How did I get here? How did you get me away...from The Mistress...and the knights".

"Much the same way you made a hole in the wall".

"You killed them?" Beatrix looked impressed.

Gregor shook his head. "Not quite".

"Then how?"

"Magic".

Beatrix looked confused.

"Not all magic is…destructive".

Beatrix blushed. For some reason she felt stupid. Like she was rather inexperienced, and didn't know what she was doing, which was of course entirely the case. She nodded.

Gregor smiled again, and the mood lightened. They sat quietly for a few minutes, both digesting the events that had brought them together.

"Was that really a gnome?" Beatrix asked suddenly.

"Yes", Gregor replied, a mischievous twinkle in his eye.

"Under the sea?"

"Is it really so hard to believe, after everything you've seen, everything you've witnessed, these past twenty-four hours?"

"Twenty-four hours?" Beatrix looked panicked.

"Yes".

"I've been here that long?"

"Yes, you were rather tired after the…events that transpired in your village".

Beatrix nodded. She still felt tired. "Back in the castle…what did I do…to the wall?"

"Well, you rather blasted it…blasted it to smithereens in fact".

Beatrix giggled. "I did, didn't I? Sorry".

"It is quite alright...I reacted rather the same when I first learned of my...situation".

Beatrix frowned.

"When I first learned I was a wizard", Gregor clarified.

"Ah".

"It was rather a larger hole, in fact". Gregor looked thoughtful, and his mouth was twitching mischievously.

Beatrix opened her mouth to question him further, but he raised his hand, as if to say, that's enough for now. She let it lie.

After a while, she asked, "In the castle, I saw another girl. Is she like me? Are there others...like me?"

"Oh yes", Gregor confirmed. "Quite".

Beatrix brightened. "I can't wait to meet them".

"And I am sure they feel entirely the same, after your rather flamboyant entrance".

Beatrix grinned a toothy grin. "Sorry".

"Quite alright, quite alright..."

"So...what am I going to do here? In the village I had to the washing with Fiona and the other girls, but I bloody hated it to be honest".

Gregor raised his eyebrows.

"What? You try doing the washing for a village-full of clumsy, messy men. It ain't a walk in the park you know? You know how hard it is to get a beer stain outta a linen shirt?"

Gregor nodded thoughtfully. "No, I do not".

"So, what am I gonna be doing here? Hopefully it's something better than the washing..."

"There are no chores for you here, at least, not yet".

Beatrix darkened.

"The older girls mop the floors and dust the corridors, but we have help with most things".

"So, what am I gonna be doing then?"

"Learning, mostly".

"Learning what?"

"To control yourself".

"Oi, what's that supposed to mean". Beatrix bristled.

"Your magic".

"Oh. Why didn't you say in the first place".

Gregor continued as if nothing had happened. "Once you learn to control yourself, the real fun can begin".

"Real fun?"

Gregor got up and walked into the kitchen. "Tea?"

"Yes", Beatrice said absentmindedly. "But more about this fun".

"All in due course".

Beatrix tutted. "You old people and your 'due course'. You sound just like my mother".

"Old people?" Gregor looked aghast. "I am forty-three!"

"Forty-three?" Beatrix exclaimed. "Wow, you're older than I thought. The hair makes you look younger".

Gregor grimaced and went back into the kitchen. She heard him muttering to himself, "I think I look very good for my age, thank you very much".

She looked back over her shoulder and saw Gregor running his hand softly down his face. She chuckled. "I was only joking. I've seen worse".

"Oh, thank-you, that makes it so much better", Gregor said sarcastically. He placed a tray with two cups on a small, low table that sat in front of the two chairs.

Beatrix leaned forward and grabbed hers, taking a big gulp from it. "Ow!" she said thickly. "Ot!"

"I would imagine it is", Gregor said wryly.

"Ooo did that on purpose!"

"I did not. And I am not **that** old, yet".

"Fair pway", Beatrix said thickly. This man was pretty quick on his feet. Usually, her pa got himself all tongue tied and barked for her ma when she was being sassy and argumentative.

"How is it?" Gregor asked politely.

Beatrix blew on her tea then took a sip. "Good".

Gregor nodded. He looked pleased with himself. He took a sip from his own tea. "I do love a good cup of tea".

"Me too". Beatrix felt rather adult, sat there with Gregor, drinking her tea before the fire. It reminded her of her ma and da. They'd drink tea before the fire in the evenings sometimes, when she was out climbing trees, or making a nuisance of herself with Felix.

"Felix!" she cried suddenly, remembering her cat and jolted forward. "OWWW!" She yelped as she spilled tea all down her legs. "Hot, hot, hot!" She jumped up and stomped her feet, shaking her hands in a weird dance.

"What are you doing?" Gregor cried. "My rug! My precious rug!" He fell to his knees and began delicately dabbing at the tea stains on a cream-coloured rug.

Beatrix stopped hopping and winced against the pain. "Sorry!" She felt bad, even through the pain of the hot tea stinging her legs.

"Ohh", Gregor moaned.

"Hey, wait, can't you just use magic or something to clean it up?"

Gregor stopped dabbing. "Oh...yes" He looked rather embarrassed. He joined his hands together, like he was mimicking a bird in flight, then shook them out to the sides. The stain disappeared. He flicked a hand at Beatrix, and her legs stopped stinging.

"Thanks", Beatrix said gratefully. Her cup was hanging in her hand, and she noticed Gregor's eyes were on it. "Oh!" She noticed the cup was full of tea again. It should have been spilling out onto the floor, but it was held in place by some unseen force.

She righted the cup and put it down on the table.

Gregor took his eyes off the cup, and steam started to waft lazily up from the tea, as if it had been reanimated.

"Best if you don't tell anyone up at the castle about that".

"About what?"

"The, err, mopping of the tea".

Beatrix looked blankly at him.

"Forgetting I was a wizard!"

"Oh, yeah. Course".

"Thank you", Gregor said politely.

"Holy macaroni!" Beatrix cried suddenly, skidding backward in her chair. "What is that?"

"**Who** is that", Gregor corrected her.

Floating in the window to the right of the fire, was a merman. As blue as the sea around him, he had gills on his neck and was wearing a pristine white toga over his top half. In his hand he had a barbed trident.

He leaned forward and pressed his face against the glass, distorting it weirdly. His eyes were an electric blue, contrasting against the dark, murky blue of his skin.

Suddenly, the merman knocked loudly on the window. "Professor". The merman was peering into the cottage as if he couldn't see anything.

"Sorry", Gregor said to Beatrix. "His eyesight isn't what it used to be".

Gregor walked forward, close to the window. "Hello, Dimitri".

Dimitri grinned a childish grin as he saw Gregor. "Ah, professor, there you are!"

"Here I am", Gregor conceded.

"I was looking for you".

"That much I gathered".

Beatrix smiled.

"It's the swordfish again...they've chewed through my fence, and eaten up half of my pumpkins...I was wondering if you could have a word?"

"Certainly".

Dimitri put his hands together gratefully. "Thanks professor. I'll see you at dinner!" He turned and swam away into the depths of the ocean, his lower half propelling him easily through the water, waggling gracefully side to side.

"Rather unruly bunch", Gregor said to Beatrix.

"The swordfish?" Beatrix found this very amusing for some reason.

Gregor nodded, as if this was completely normal. "Always harassing Dimitri. Eating his vegetables. Blocking his chimney with seaweed. Generally being rather unsociable little things. You know, the usual".

"No, actually, I don't".

"Oh yes, how silly of me. Well, you will, soon enough".

Beatrix's stomach growled. "Uh, professor?" She'd heard a bunch of people call Gregor 'professor' so far, and she figured the best way to fill her stomach was to stroke his ego a little and do the same.

"Yes?"

"The merman...Dimitri...he said about dinner?" Her stomach growled again, and Gregor hopped to his feet.

"You must be starving".

"A little", Beatrix admitted.

"Come on then. Back to the castle with you".

Gregor strode to the door, and it swung open. "After you".

Beatrix rolled her eyes, but she was too hungry to argue. "There better be potatoes. I **love** potatoes. And gravy. No point having potatoes without gravy".

Gregor smiled widely as he watched Beatrix stroll down the path toward the lift, as if she had not a care in the world.

Lots Of Potatoes

"Well, I will leave you here", Gregor said, a little awkwardly.

"Thanks", Beatrix replied, equally as awkwardly.

Gregor had taken her back up to the castle, and deposited her in a grand hall, with a high arching ceiling and four long trestle tables.

"Gwinny". Gregor beckoned a girl sat at one of the tables.

She got up and came over to join them. "Yes?"

"Can you look after Beatrix for me? Make sure she gets fed. And plenty of potatoes".

Beatrix snorted, and Gwinny gave her a strange look. "Alright".

Gregor smiled at Beatrix, then walked away to a table at the back of hall. There were adults there, who Beatrix assumed were the other 'professors'.

"Come on". Gwinny led Beatrix by the hand back to the table. "Move up". A girl with a round face scowled at Gwinny but shuffled up to create space.

"Thanks", Beatrix said shyly, plonking herself between Gwinny and the other girl.

"So, you're his new pet", the round-faced girl chimed immediately.

Beatrix frowned. She was a bit off balance. She hadn't even located the potatoes yet! But she knew one thing, she was nobody's pet. "I beg your pardon?"

The girl looked taken aback. "His new **project**".

"I don't know anything about that". Beatrix shrugged. "I just came here yesterday".

The girl tutted. "Well yes, I know that, but-"

"Leave her alone, Edni, can't you see she's just trying to get settled? I swear you have no social skills whatsoever". It was the girl who'd stuck her head through the hole in the wall earlier. She was sitting a few seats along from them.

Beatrix blushed and smiled shyly at her, grateful of the reprieve, but she'd already turned her attention back to her food.

Beatrix looked up and down the table. There was lots of food. Chicken and hams and vegetables. And potatoes! "Ooh, roasted potatoes!" She hungrily grabbed a platter of potatoes and scooped a bunch onto the plate in front of her.

"Careful of the tablecloth", Gwinny muttered to her.

"Oh, sorry". Beatrix straightened the tablecloth, which had come unstuck and was in dangerous proximity to the gravy tureen in her hand.

The tablecloth was frilly and flowery in the colours of the forest. Greens and yellows and reds and pinks.

It was a little old fashioned, Beatrix thought. One of the other tables had a vivid pink and red tablecloth. It made her think of wild berries and thorns.

"Madame is very particular about her tablecloths", Gwinny continued to mutter.

"Madame?" Beatrix frowned.

Gwinny nodded her head toward the table at the back of the room.

Beatrix squinted.

"See if you can guess", Gwinny muttered.

Beatrix looked at the people sat at the table. She noticed they were mostly women, but there were two or three men, Gregor being one, and the green man she had met earlier another. Her eyes settled on a woman sat in the centre of the table and she gasped.

Gwinny grinned. "That's her".

"She's beautiful". Beatrix thought the woman looked terribly intriguing. She had high cheeks, curt lips, and a strong chin. She looked a bit like a queen.

It was her hair that Beatrix found fascinating, though. It was snow white. But it wasn't fuzzy or frayed, like an old person's hair. It was sleek and shiny, and seemed to move a little, like it was blowing gently in the wind. Or maybe, she was just imagining it.

Gwinny nodded. "That's Madame".

"**Who is she?**" Beatrix said breathlessly.

"Madame Tempest, the headmistress".

"Headmistress?" Beatrix paused, fork full of potato hanging in front of her mouth. "But I thought Gregor was the...headmaster?"

Gwinny snorted. "Oh, no. Don't be silly. Though he is rather powerful".

Beatrix frowned. "But he has a...cottage in the sea".

Edni cackled. "Ooh, a cottage in the sea!" She seemed to find this ever so amusing.

"Shut up Edni". It was Gwinny's turn to tell Edni off.

"Gregor is rather important to the school...so I can see why you thought that. Don't feel silly. He's often the first-person people meet when they...come here". She turned away, as if she were remembering a rather painful memory.

Beatrix put a comforting hand on her arm.

Gwinny smiled thankfully, then took a deep breath. "This is a witches school after all".

Beatrix thought this sounded strange. "What do you mean by that?"

"Well, the boys have their own, don't they?" Gwinny said.

"They **do?**" Beatrix was amazed.

"Oh, yes you just got here. Sorry, I'm quite hungry today, it's rather clouded my judgement a little".

"It's rather clouded my judgement a little", Edni sneered.

Gwinny threw her a dark look. "Ignore her", she said to Beatrix. "She's just sore that I pasted her at channelling today".

"Am not", Edni shot back.

Gwinny rolled her eyes at Beatrix.

"So, there's...a wizard's school too?" Beatrix asked, uninterested in the petty squabbling, but very interested in learning more about this boy's school.

"Oh, yes. The boys have their school, much as we do". Gwinny nodded.

"Fat lot of good it does them", Edni scoffed.

"You really are insufferable today", Gwinny replied.

Edni stuck her tongue out, which was covered in gravy.

Gwinny looked disgusted, but Beatrix laughed.

Edni seemed taken aback and raised her eyebrows. She quickly went back to shovelling roast chicken into her mouth like it was a wheelbarrow for meat and gravy.

"What do you mean?" Beatrix was intrigued now.

"Well-" Edni began through a mouthful of chicken.

"Finish your mouthful before you speak!" This seemed to really irritate Gwinny, who had closed her eyes and gritted her jaw.

Edni took an epic swallow, then continued. "They're not very good, are they? Boys, I mean. Useless, rather, most of them".

"Are they?" Beatrix was fascinated and leant her head forward on her hand.

Edni nodded. "Doesn't come naturally to them, like it does us".

"But what about Gregor?" Beatrix asked. "I get the impression he's pretty powerful!"

Edni rolled her eyes. "That's Gregor". She said this as if it explained everything.

"Gregor is...different". Gwinny didn't seem to know how to explain it.

"But what about..." Beatrix paused, as if not sure how to diplomatically explain it.

"Horace and Dimitri?" Gwinny seemed to have an answer for everything.

"Yes", Beatrix replied.

"Well, they're not human, are they?" Gwinny said.

"No..." Beatrix said slowly.

"Horace is a goblin, and-" Gwinny began.

"**Greenling**", Edni interjected, spraying a little chicken and potato to the tablecloth in front of her. She hurriedly cleaned it up, as Gwinny looked to the heavens.

"Yes, sorry, greenling", Gwinny continued, ignoring Edni's lack of table manners. "And Dimitri is a merman".

"Why does that mean they can do magic, but boys can't?" Beatrix was confused. It was all so much to take in.

"Well, it's not that boys **can't**, it's just, they're not very good at it. Most of them. There are some exceptions of course, like Gregor, and some of the boys in the wizards school". Gwinny seemed thoughtful.

"You say the school...where is it? They're not here?" Beatrix seemed disappointed.

"Yes, rather a letdown, isn't it?" Gwinny said.

Edni scowled. "I miss boys!"

The girl from the wall overheard and chimed in from further down the table. "Yeah? Well, they don't miss you!"

The girls along the table cackled and Edni narrowed her eyes threateningly. Beatrix burst out laughing too but felt rather guilty about it. "Sorry", she said to Edni.

"Oh, don't be", Gwinny said. "She is rather a menace".

Edni shrugged. She'd gone a little red.

Beatrix thought the girl from the wall was perhaps a little cruel. But then, she got the impression that Edni could be too. She didn't know what to make of them both so far.

"So where is it? This wizard's school", Beatrix said persistently.

"Why? Are you going to climb up there along some rope?" Edni mocked.

"You'll need a rather long rope", Gwinny said drily.

From the corner of her eye, Beatrix caught the girl from the wall watching her. The girl quickly turned away, pretending she hadn't been looking. For some reason this made Beatrix feel good.

"Why? Oh, come on, stop teasing me", Beatrix pleaded.

"Shall we tell her?" Gwinny asked Edni.

Edni seemed to ponder this.

"Yes, you shall!" Beatrix was getting impatient now.

"Ooh", Gwinny teased. "Fiery one, this".

Edni nodded. She looked surprised, but like she agreed with the assessment.

"Why would I need a rope, damn-it?" Beatrix demanded.

Gwinny frowned, as if this was a silly question. "Well, because it's in the sky, of course".

Where's My Damn Cat?

Beatrix was sufficiently fed and watered, and now felt gloriously at peace. She thought of her parents and felt guilt creep into her stomach. They're safe for now, she reminded herself.

Gwinny had taken her upstairs to their living quarters, that they called The Witches Den. It did look a little like a den. There was a fireplace, and some chaise-longue's and some comfy armchairs. It was very cosy. There was pink and fuchsia and lots of girly colours, which Beatrix didn't think much of, but she had to admit, it was nice to be in a space just for girls. And not a mug of beer in sight.

She gazed out of a big cathedral style window, that looked out onto the sea. It was strange, she felt like she was high up in a building, but she knew was deep, deep in the sea. It was an odd feeling. Being high up in the castle, yet still very low in the grand scheme of things.

A dolphin swam past, and she jumped excitedly. "Gwinny! Gwinny!"

Gwinny strode over. "What?"

"A dolphin, look! It's a dolphin!" Beatrix was like a kid at Christmas.

"Yes, I like them", Gwinny agreed.

"What did you expect? Turtles?" Edni scoffed.

"Oh, behave", Gwinny said.

Edni joined them at the window. "I suppose they are rather beautiful". She seemed in a better mood now she had eaten. And perhaps she **had** been sore about losing at channelling, whatever that was.

"They're the most beautiful things I've ever seen!" Beatrix watched, enthralled, as a pair of dolphins did spins and turns, and spiralled upward, entwined around each other. "Do you think they love one another?"

"I expect so", Edni said quietly.

Beatrix turned to look at her, but she walked away and sat down in front of the fire. She was reading something. "Is she ok?"

"She's fine", Gwinny said.

Beatrix felt something soft wrap itself around her legs. She glanced down. "What is...oh!" She jumped. "A cat!" She immediately bent down to pat the cat. It was a white ragdoll with baby blue eyes. "Hello, you". Beatrix ran her hand across the cat's soft fur. The cat closed its eyes and revelled in the attention.

"I think she likes you", Gwinny said.

"I think so too", Beatrix agreed.

"Trudy likes most people", Gwinny said.

Beatrix felt a little deflated. "Oh".

"But I think she really likes you", Gwinny said.

Beatrix felt a little of her previous goodwill return. "Oh, really?"

"Mhm", Gwinny said. "Usually, she's a little more cautious. She likes to make people work for it. Her affections, that is".

"Oh, well, it's an honour, Madame Trudy", Beatrix said.

Gwinny smiled. "That's cute...Madame Trudy".

"She certainly is a madame", Edni muttered from the fire.

"Edni doesn't like Trudy. She doesn't get on with her with cat", Gwinny explained.

"Her cat?" Beatrix asked.

Gwinny opened her mouth to speak, but Beatrix had a look on her face like she'd forgotten her most prized possession, just after embarking on a long trip.

She clapped her hand to her head. "Oh my god! Felix!" She looked around in a panic, then strode across the room frantically. "Felix!"

Gwinny followed her, trying to keep up. "What is it? What's the matter?"

Beatrix ignored her and started looking under the chaise-longues. She seemed really upset.

"What are you looking for?" Gwinny asked.

Edni had put her book down and was watching Beatrix with curious fascination.

"FELIX!" Beatrix yelled.

"Stop!" Gwinny grabbed her arm.

"Get off me!" Beatrix shook Gwinny's hand off roughly. "Felix!"

Gwinny seemed at a loss.

"AGHHH! That bloody blonde man. Brought me here to this god-forsaken place, stole my parents, and forgot my cat". She stopped pacing. "Where is my damn cat!"

"Right here", a voice chimed in her mind.

It scared her so much she fell over backwards, right into Edni's lap.

"Hey!" Edni spluttered. "What the hell are you doing?"

Beatrix ignored her, and pushed herself to her feet, using Edni as a springboard.

"Owwwwch!" Edni wailed. "What is wrong with you?"

But Beatrix only had ears for the voice in her head. "Felix? Felix? Is that you?"

She strode around the room, looking under cushions, checking behind the fireplace, she even checked the windowsills.

"She's lost her mind", Edni said to Gwinny. They were both watching Beatrix from by the fire now.

Gwinny frowned.

"Will you keep it down? I'm trying to sleep". The voice rang out in her mind again. It was a male voice. A silky, smooth voice, with a deep timbre. Like a smooth-talking poet, or a musician.

Beatrix stopped. "Sleep?" Suddenly, she knew exactly where to look. She went back over to Edni's armchair and dropped to her knees. "Felix!"

Felix was curled up contentedly under the armchair, eyes closed. He looked completely unbothered, and completely uninterested in the chaos that had been unfolding around him.

Beatrix reached under the chair and picked him up. She cuddled him immediately and rubbed her face against him.

Felix purred.

"Is that what you were looking for?" Gwinny asked.

"Yes", Beatrix said meekly.

"Why didn't you just say?" Gwinny said. "He's been there all day. I think it's his favourite spot. He must like the warmth from the fire".

Edni looked appraisingly at Felix. "Nice cat. He's rather handsome, isn't he?"

"Yes", Beatrix said proudly, rubbing Felix. Her face changed again, panic sweeping across it. "But how can I hear him? Am I losing my mind?"

She almost dropped Felix, and he gave an agitated meow. "Sorry". She petted him apologetically. "But cats don't talk". She looked to Gwinny and Edni for clarification.

"That's news to me", Edni said.

"Oh, but they do", Gwinny said.

"They do?" Beatrix asked.

Gwinny nodded. "But most people can't hear it. You can hear it because you're a witch".

"But why couldn't I hear it before?" Beatrix asked.

"You weren't a witch before", Gwinny said.

"I don't..." Beatrix shook her head.

"It's a lot to take in...I know". Gwinny placed a sympathetic hand on Beatrix's arm.

Felix opened one eye and stretched his head toward Gwinny. Gwinny rubbed his head. He seemed to like this. Gwinny and Beatrix shared a smile.

"Didn't Gregor explain all this?" Gwinny asked.

"No...well...some of it. There was a gnome. And Dimitri. And we mostly just drank tea. And then I spilled some on his rug and he got upset". Beatrix tried to think if there was any more.

"Him and that bloody rug", Edni moaned.

"He does rather like it", Gwinny confirmed. "And you spilt tea on it?"

"Yeah...but I didn't mean to!" Beatrix defended herself.

Edni cackled.

"What?" Beatrix rounded on Edni.

"It's funny", Edni said.

Gwinny smiled. "It is a little.

"Whatever. I don't care about the rug. How come I can speak to Felix?" Beatrix was not to be deterred.

"When your...hair turned white". Gwinny's eyes darted to the patch of white in Beatrix's hair. "That was your power awakening".

"My power?" Beatrix asked.

Gwinny nodded. "The latent witch's power in you. We all have it. From birth. But it doesn't awaken until later. Usually when we're ten or eleven".

"I'm thirteen", Beatrix said.

Gwinny frowned. "Maybe you're a late bloomer".

This made Beatrix feel inferior. "Maybe I'm no good!"

"I don't think so", Gwinny replied.

"Why'd you say that" Beatrix asked.

"We all saw what you did to that wall", Gwinny replied.

"That? I didn't even know what I was doing!" Beatrix wailed. She was clearly an awful witch.

"Wow!" another girl replied from across the room, snapping shut a large book she had been lost in. She was a little blonde girl who only looked to be ten or eleven. "You did it without channelling?" She was staring excitedly at Beatrix.

"What? Channelling?" Beatrix was dumbfounded. "What do you mean?"

The little blonde girl looked confused.

"She means you did it without meaning to", Gwinny interjected. "Without channelling the spell".

"What?" Beatrix felt like one of the village drunks, like she couldn't comprehend anything that was being said to her. It was all flying right over her head.

"All spells have to be channelled", Gwinny said. "They don't just **happen**, for the most part".

"Channelling? What do you mean?" Beatrix asked.

The little blonde girl walked over to join them, settling herself into the armchair beside Edni.

Edni gave her a distrusting look, but the girl was so fascinated by Beatrix that she didn't see. Or perhaps she just didn't care.

"Channelling". Gwinny looked at Beatrix to see if this triggered any recognition. "Focusing your spirit and mind to channel the power of the elements. That's what magic is. Fire, water, air, earth. All magic comes from the elements. For the most part. Of course, it's not quite as simple as that..."

Edni yawned. "She doesn't need a Magical Theory lesson, Gwin. She just wants to know how she shot lightning from her fingers".

"Was it lightning?" Beatrix looked impressed. "Wow".

The little blonde girl seemed to agree. "Wow". She was gazing at Beatrix like she was some kind of celebrity. "And you really did it without channelling? Not even a little bit?"

"I guess..." Beatrix said.

The door to The Witches Den opened. "Right, that's it ladies, enough. Time for bed". It was a stern woman with a severe haircut.

Edni grumbled.

"Come on", Gwinny took Beatrix by the hand and led her away up a winding stone staircase. At the top was a bedroom with a bunch of four poster beds. "Well, what do you think?"

"I think it's great!" Beatrix said excitedly, picking a bed and springing onto it.

"Hey! Get your own bed!" Edni called.

"Oh, sorry". Beatrix stood up gingerly.

"This one's free!" The little blonde girl called. She was pointing at a bed at the end of the room, by two big windows with a sea view. The bed was directly opposite the little blonde girl. Gwinny got into the bed next to it. Taking it as a sign, Beatrix sat down on the bed. There were fresh pyjamas on the pillow.

"Well, goodnight!" Gwinny called cheerfully to the room, drawing the drapes around her bed.

"Goodnight", Beatrix replied softly.

"I'm Lucrecia, by the way". The little blonde girl waved at Beatrix, then she too disappeared behind the drapes of her bed.

"I'm Beatrix", Beatrix whispered.

"Nice to meet you", Lucrecia whispered back.

"Go to sleep!" Edni moaned grumpily.

Felix padded into the room and hopped up into the bed with her. She drew the drapes closed around them, and it felt like they were in their own comfy little world. Slipping into the pyjamas, she sunk under the blankets with Felix curled up next to her face.

"Night, Felix", Beatrix whispered, ever so softly, so that only Felix would hear.

Felix gave a little purr, then went to sleep.

A Spell Or Two

Beatrix was the first to wake, and she was excited. Excited to start her day. Excited to start her new life as a witch. She didn't know what that meant yet, but thoughts of the city and her life as barmaid were far from her mind this morning.

She lay quietly in the bedroom she shared with her new friends. Beside her, Felix opened his eyes.

"Really? This early?" His voice chimed through her mind.

"Sorry", she whispered back.

"You know I can hear you, you don't have to whisper", Felix replied.

"What?" Beatrix looked confused.

"Your thoughts", Felix replied with his mind voice.

"You can hear my...thoughts?" Beatrix asked

"Of course...how do you think you can hear mine?" Felix asked.

"I thought you were speaking to me...in my mind", Beatrix replied

"Don't be silly", Felix replied.

"Oh, that's silly", Beatrix whispered sarcastically. "But a castle in the sea is not. What's that. Just totally **normal** I suppose?"

Across the room, Lucrecia moaned softly.

"Quiet!" Felix hissed through Beatrix's mind.

"You be quiet!" Beatrix hissed back, this time with her mind. She grinned, as she realised what she'd done.

"Don't look too pleased with yourself, technically **I'm** the smart one for reading **your** thoughts", Felix thought.

Beatrix mouth dropped open. "You are so cheeky. Have you always been such a cheeky cat?"

"Where do you think I learned it all?" Felix replied drily.

At that moment, a ginger tabby-cat padded softly over to the side of the bed. It sat down and stared up at Felix, who had turned over to watch it.

"What do you want?" Beatrix heard Felix enquire.

"Oh, is that so?" Felix thought.

"What, what is it?" Beatrix thought.

"She says she wants to play with me", Felix thought.

"Play...with you?" Beatrix thought.

"Oh, don't be so droll", Felix thought, waving his tail lazily. "Well, bye then". And with that, Felix hopped off the bed and sauntered away with the ginger tabby-cat, their tails rubbing softly against each other.

Beatrix lay back in bed, thinking. "Why couldn't I hear the other cat?" she mumbled softly to herself.

She heard a thud, and a pitter patter on the floor. Before she could sit up, she felt a weight in the bed next to her.

"Because you can only hear what your cat is thinking". It was Lucrecia, and she was gently pulling the blanket across, so it covered her too.

"Umm". Beatrix didn't know what to say. She barely knew this girl, and she had gotten into bed with her.

"It's quite normal..." Lucrecia went quiet and stared at the ceiling. After a while, she turned into Beatrix and rested her head on Beatrix's shoulder. "I like your cat".

"I like him too", Beatrix said.

"He's cheeky", Lucrecia said.

"What, how do you know...I thought you said witches could only hear their own cat's thoughts?" Beatrix said.

"That's right...but you can just tell...he has real cheeky energy", Lucrecia mused. "They say cats take after their owners". Lucrecia stared into Beatrix's eyes.

"What's that supposed to mean?" Beatrix said.

"Nothing", Lucrecia said.

Beatrix frowned, in a rather bemused fashion. "You're weird".

"I know", Lucrecia admitted.

Beatrix felt a little bad. "In a good way".

Lucrecia beamed. "Thank you..."

They lay quietly in bed, enjoying the warmth from each other's bodies. Eventually, the rest of the girls began to rise.

"Mmm, what a sleep!" Edni stretched, then pulled herself up against the headboard.

"Rather", Gwinni agreed. She was already sitting up looking rather content and serene. She was knitting something out of plum red wool.

"What are you making?" Beatrix asked.

"Mittens", Gwinni said. "You can never have too many mittens. Or socks".

Edni cackled.

"What?" Gwinni said. "You can't".

"I'd rather have some evening wear", Edni said, stretching her leg rather provocatively out from under her blanket.

Gwinni scowled. "You are incorrigible".

"Ooh, incorrigible", Edni teased. "What a **big** word".

"Give it a rest you two", Beatrix said.

Both Edni and Gwinni looked surprised. Beatrix had only been there one night, and she was already interjecting herself into their arguments.

Edni stuck her tongue out at Beatrix and got out of bed to get dressed. Gwinni watched her a moment, then did the same.

"Time for breakfast", Lucrecia said brightly.

"I hope there's potatoes", Beatrix said automatically.

"For breakfast?" Lucrecia looked aghast.

"For every meal! What's better than roasted potatoes?" Beatrix asked.

"You're weird", Edni said.

Beatrix narrowed her eyes and Edni hastily left the room.

"I like bacon. And sausages", Lucrecia said politely. "And eggs, but not so much. I have chickens at home. They make big eggs".

"That's nice. We had chickens in the village. I didn't have any myself...but Felix likes to chase them around the coup. Sometimes he breaks in and...well, he's a bit of a nuisance. He doesn't hurt them. I think he just enjoys playing with them". Beatrix trailed off.

Lucrecia was nodding and listening intently. "I can see that. Well, shall we go?"

"Let's".

The two of them went down to the great hall, where breakfast was being served.

The brown-haired girl from the hole in the wall was already there, chatting animatedly to a group of girls who were hanging on her every word.

Beatrix and Lucrecia sat down together.

"Who is that girl, Luce?" Beatrix asked Lucrecia, her eyes still on the brown-haired girl.

"Luce?" Lucrecia replied.

"Oh...sorry". Beatrix had been distracted. She hadn't realised she'd given her a new friend a nickname without even realising. "Lucrecia".

Lucrecia frowned. "No-one's called me Luce before".

"I'm sorry, it's a nickname...it's just easier", Beatrix said. "Sometimes people call me Bea".

"Luce". Lucrecia sounded it out then smiled brightly. "I like it. I've never had a nickname".

"Really?" Beatrix's attention was fully on Lucrecia now. She realised the girl was a little fae, and maybe she didn't have many friends. "Well, you're still young. What are you, ten? I'll be fourteen soon".

"I'm ten, yes", Lucrecia replied politely.

"Plenty of time for nicknames, besides, I just gave you one, Lucey Luce!" Beatrix said.

Lucrecia's eyes widened.

Beatrix worried she'd gone too far, been too overfamiliar, but Lucrecia grinned. "Oh, I love it!"

Beatrix grinned back. "Good! Cause it's your name now, Luce".

Lucrecia beamed.

"Now pass me those tatoes". Beatrix pointed to a large tureen of roasted potatoes.

"For breakfast, really?" Edni said, sitting down opposite.

Beatrix glared at her, and she dropped it.

"Have some sausage, it's very good". Lucrecia offered Beatrix a platter of thick, well-cooked sausages.

Beatrix wasn't overly fond of sausages, but she forked a couple onto her plate. She didn't want to upset Lucrecia.

"Give it here". Edni grabbed for the sausage platter, which was now in Lucrecia's hands.

Beatrix gave her a warning look, and she waited until Lucrecia was finished.

"Thanks", Edni said, taking the sausages.

"I hope you're not eating all of **my** sausages". Beatrix looked up from her plate. It was the brown-haired girl. She was standing behind Edni, flanked by two other girls. They looked rather pompous.

"Who says their yours?" Edni said warily.

"I do", the brown-haired girl replied. "My father is the reason you **have** sausages, so it is only fair you leave some for me and my girls".

"Your girls?" Edni sniggered.

"Think that's funny, do you?" The brown-haired girl replied coldly. "If you had any friends, you'd know the feeling".

Edni stopped sniggering and looked down at her plate.

"She has plenty of friends", Beatrix said defiantly. She had initially liked this spunky brown-haired girl, but now she wasn't so sure. She didn't like bullies.

"Is that so?" The brown-haired girl looked her up and down. Beatrix felt as if she was being appraised by an auctioneer.

"Yes", Beatrix replied, lifting her chin and holding the girl's eyes. The girl's cronies were appraising Beatrix too. It felt like they were waiting to see what might happen.

The brown-haired girl didn't say anything else. She just walked away with the sausages. Her two friends stared at Beatrix a moment longer, then followed.

"Who was **that?**" Beatrix asked distastefully.

"Cincesse", Gwinni replied.

"**Cincesse?**" Beatrix scoffed. "What a silly name".

"You shouldn't talk back to her", Edni warned.

"You did", Beatrix replied. "And why not? I'm not scared of her".

"You should be", Edni said.

Beatrix didn't think much of this. "Whatever".

Edni looked impressed.

"I don't care about any of this. I'm just here for a spell or two. Then I'll be on my way", Beatrix said airily.

"A spell or two?" Gwinni enquired.

"Right. Once I learn enough to burn those blasted sisters to cinders, I'll be out of here". Beatrix looked vengeful.

Gwinni gasped. "You don't mean...The Sacred Sisters?"

"Course I do. Who else?" Beatrix replied brashly. "They tried to bloody kill me!"

"Shh", Gwinni replied. "Keep your voice down".

"Why?" Beatrix asked.

"We're not really supposed to speak about them", Gwinni informed her.

"And why not?" Beatrix asked.

"It might upset some of the...younger students", Gwinni replied. She widened her eyes and nodded subtly at Lucrecia, who was eating quietly with her eyes fixed on her plate.

"Oh, sorry". Beatrix felt bad. Again, with her big mouth.

"Not everyone takes it as...well...as you have", Gwinni continued.

"I didn't take it well, I-" Beatrix stopped and stared at Lucrecia. "Forget it".

They ate in silence then.

After a while, Beatrix asked, "So when do I get to learn some spells? Some magic?"

"Well...I doubt you'll be learning any **spells** for a while...but your first class is after breakfast". Gwinni looked as if she wasn't sure what to make of Beatrix still.

"Wicked! I can't wait". Beatrix's face lit up with excitement.

Further down the table, Cincesse's eyes strayed to Beatrix every now and then.

"I think you've caught her attention", Edni mumbled to Beatrix.

"Who?" Beatrix replied.

Edni glanced pointedly at Cincesse.

Beatrix casually peered down the table, as if to see if there was any more food. She caught Cincesse watching her, from the corner of her eyes.

Beatrix smirked. "Good".

When they were finished with breakfast, Madame Tempest stood at the head of the teacher's table. A quiet fell on the room immediately.

"Good morning, ladies". She waited expectantly.

"Good morning, madame", they all replied.

"We have a new student with us". Madame Tempest paused, as every head at once turned to stare at Beatrix.

"I expect you to make her welcome". It was not an order, but it sounded like one, nonetheless. "I am sure you all remember your first night here...and your first week". She allowed a silence to build, as the girls each thought back to their own arrival at the castle, and the trauma preceding it.

As if deciding nothing more need be said about this, she continued speaking in a brighter, airier voice. "Now, I have a few announcements. Professor Dimitri has asked that you please do not go near his greenhouse or his vegetable garden for the foreseeable future. He is experiencing some issues with...the

·swordfish…and is engaged in an ongoing battle to reclaim his land, and his vegetables. Please stay away, for your own safety".

Some of the girls sniggered.

Professor Dimitri, who was floating above a chair further down the table, blushed.

"Professor Gregor has asked me to remind you that magic in the corridors is prohibited, regardless of how hard you are pushed, or how 'viciously' your outfit is insulted". Madame Tempest stared at Cincesse as she said this last. Cincesse smirked and her cronies giggled.

"Finally, for the benefit of our new student, please remember that your assignation is for your own safety, and the safety of your fellow students. Please do not attempt to take classes outside of your assignation, until you are graded ready by Professor Gregor".

"Assignation?" Beatrix whispered.

Gwinni raised a finger to her lips, signalling hush. She looked rather irritated.

Beatrix rolled her eyes.

"Unless told otherwise, new students enter our school with the assignation, Novus". Madame Tempest looked directly at Beatrix, who shivered as she felt a chill go through her.

"That is all, thank you". Madame Tempest sat back down, as if she had just delivered a rather important meeting. She was already talking to a woman to her left about something or other.

"Novus?" Beatrix looked dumbfounded. "What's that?"

"Come on". Gwinni took her arm and led her out of the great hall. "There are three assignations in the school. Novus, Vetus and Domini".

Beatrix looked blankly at her.

"All students start as Novi, with an assignation of Novus", Gwinni continued, as they walked toward the Witches Den.

"Right". Beatrix looked like she was getting it but finding it rather weird.

"Once you are deemed worthy, you advance to Vetus, and you're then a Veti".

"Right".

"It's a bit like beginner and advanced".

"That makes more sense".

Gwinni nodded and smiled at a group of older girls going the other way, already in their uniforms. Gwinni and Beatrix were still in their pyjamas.

"So, what about the other one...the dommy thing", Beatrix said.

Gwinni giggled. "Domini".

"Domini, right".

"You don't have to worry about that for a while".

"Why's that?"

"Domini is the highest assignation. Domi are rare".

"Why?"

"It's hard...very hard to get assigned Domini".

"But why?"

"It just...is". Gwinni looked a little awkward. "Not many achieve it".

"Really?"

Gwinni nodded.

"So do you stay here forever then, until you get it?"

"Oh, goodness no". Gwinni looked flustered. "No, no".

"Oh".

"Most girls stay here until they are of age. Or until they learn to control their magic. Everyone's different".

"Of age?"

"Seventeen".

"Oh, that's not long". Beatrix seemed disappointed.

Gwinni smiled. "You are rather excited, aren't you?"

"Weren't you?"

Gwinni smiled thoughtfully and looked up at the ceiling. "Why, yes, I suppose I was".

Beatrix didn't push it. She didn't want to pry into Gwinni's past, not after what she'd learned at breakfast.

"Come on, let's get dressed".

Beatrix looked at the uniform on her bed. She grimaced. She didn't like it very much. It was very...girly. She pulled the pinafore on and picked up the ribbon gingerly.

"Here, let me help". Gwinni threaded it through her hair. "There. You look wonderful". She stepped back, admiring her handiwork.

"Thanks". Beatrix blushed. She wasn't comfortable with compliments. She slipped her smart shoes on and stared at herself in the big full-length mirror that stood between the two windows.

"Ain't she a picture, Grae?" Her mothers voice ran through her mind, and she frowned.

"What is it? Are you alright?" Gwinni asked. She sensed a change in her new friend's mood and came over to put her arm around her. "You do look rather wonderful in the uniform".

This cheered Beatrix up a little bit. She sniffed and rubbed her eyes. "Thanks".

"Come on, let's go, Gregor is rather precious about being on time". Gwinni took her arm and led her toward the door.

As she left, Beatrix turned and looked back over her shoulder at the mirror.

"Proud of you, kid", Graeme's voice whispered in her mind.

Brightcastle

King Wallace stood naked in front of his balcony, hidden behind the frilly white drapes that guarded it from any prying eyes outside.

He gazed down at his city. Brightcastle. Already it was stirring. In the distance he could see merchants carting their wares down the cobbled streets, and faintly hear the cursing and grumbling of the morning workers.

Oh, he loved it so. He sighed contentedly and walked to the mirror opposite his bed. He gazed at his reflection and sighed again, without content this time. He pulled at his cheeks and pawed at the lines that had appeared beneath his eyes.

"Bleugh". He slapped his belly, though there wasn't much of one. His stomach was still mostly taut and well-muscled, but there was a little more than he would like around the sides.

He was getting old. In his forties now. He was still young, of course, but he was getting there. It now dominated his thoughts a lot more than he'd have liked.

"Come back to bed". A sleepy voice called from across the room.

He grimaced, then turned as the voice stirred something in him, as it always did. "And why is that?" He replied huskily.

"Because I deign it", the woman replied. "And I am a queen".

"Can't argue with that". Wallace strode across the room and quickly climbed into bed with his wife.

He kissed her neck from behind, and she smiled lasciviously.

He kissed it again.

She blushed and turned to face him.

When they were done, they lay together peacefully in the bed, The Queen's head atop Wallace's chest.

"What are you going to do about it?" The Queen asked suddenly.

"About what?" Wallace replied.

"You know what..."

"Oh, that..."

The truth was, Wallace knew what his wife was talking about, he just didn't want to talk about it. It was dominating his thoughts, and his dreams. He'd tossed and turned and spent many a sleepless night since it had happened.

"You cannot allow it", The Queen said.

"I know", Wallace replied.

"Do you?"

Wallace sat up. "What's that supposed to mean?"

"You know that it means". The Queen had a hard edge to her eyes.

"I don't want to hear this". Wallace got out of bed and began to dress himself.

"You can't run from it", The Queen said from the bed.

"I'm not running from it", Wallace replied, pulling on his trousers.

The Queen said nothing.

Wallace paused at the door and forced a smile. "I'll see you downstairs".

The Queen watched him go, and her face darkened.

Outside the room, The King's guards snapped to attention, their spears clanking against their golden plate armour.

"Lads". Wallace nodded at them as he passed.

His mind was elsewhere as he padded along the plush red and gold carpet. He nodded absentmindedly at retainers and servants as he descended the stairs and headed to the dining room.

Well, it wasn't the official dining room, but it was his favourite place to eat his breakfast. The servants now referred to it as The King's Room. To be fair, he did spend a lot of time there. And who could blame him? It was beautiful, with a large open terrace that looked out onto The Royal Gardens.

The King liked to eat his breakfast on the terrace. Sometimes his retainers brought him news or scrolls to read. Sometimes they left him alone. This morning, they left him alone.

He ate his breakfast quietly, and listened to the sounds of the city, enjoying the fresh morning air.

"Sire".

Wallace jumped. He hadn't heard his manservant, Humphrey, approach.

"Announce yourself man, whisht, I almost filled my britches". King Wallace looked aggrieved.

"Apologies, sire, I will make a note of it", Humphrey replied with a totally straight face.

Wallace sighed. He missed Caelech, his old manservant. But The Queen hadn't liked him and had accused him of being discourteous.

She'd arranged for his dismissal from the palace, behind Wallace's back. When he'd found out he'd been furious, but she got her way, and managed to appease him, as she always did.

"What is it, let me have it", Wallace said wearily.

"There have been a further three revolts quelled this week, sire", Humphrey informed him.

"Three!" Wallace rocked in his chair. "But that's…"

"Fifteen this month, sire", Humphrey replied.

"Fifteen villages with no mistress", Wallace mused.

"Indeed sire", Humphrey said.

Since the events with the Bellafonte girl, Beatrix, there had been nothing but trouble. Numerous villages had revolted and expelled their mistresses, turning their back on The Sacred Sisters, and the order they had worked so tirelessly to instil.

Some of the mistresses had been peacefully expelled, some of them…

Wallace sighed. "Send Gladius".

"Sire".

"And a detachment of knights".

"How many, sire?"

"A full Order".

"That many, sire?"

"I want an end to this, it can't continue".

"Sire". Humphrey bowed obediently and left.

Wallace chewed his lip. He wasn't relaxed now, and the sounds of the city grated.

"Good morning, papa". His daughter, Loresia, draped herself across him, sitting down in his lap.

"Oh". Wallace grunted. "Morning princess".

"What's the matter?" Loresia enquired.

"You're getting big. You're not a little girl anymore".

Loresia looked like she couldn't quite decide whether to get offended that he'd called her big, or excited that he'd suggested she was almost a woman. She opted for the latter. "I'm a young woman now, papa".

"You are indeed". Wallace beamed at his daughter. She was the spitting image of her mother. But that was where the similarities ended, something he was grateful for.

"Where's mama?" Loresia asked innocently. She knew full well her parents had probably argued again. It was all they had done these past weeks.

"Upstairs", Wallace grunted.

Oh..."

Wallace took a bite of his orange that had been perfectly peeled. It looked like he wasn't enjoying it.

"I miss her..." Loresia said suddenly, looking off into the distance.

Wallace said nothing for a moment. He swallowed his orange. "I miss her too".

"Will she be ok?" Loresia looked worried.

"She'll be fine". Wallace wasn't sure, but he couldn't tell his daughter that. He sure hoped he was right.

"Are you sure?"

"I'm sure, girl".

"Where is she?"

"She's someplace safe…"

"But-"

"You know I can't tell you…"

"I know…"

"S'for your own good, girl. If one of them fanatics were to get a hold of you…"

"I know, I know". Loresia didn't like the situation at all. It was positively wretched, and she missed her sister. She just wanted her back. "I hate them!" She said suddenly. "I hate them all!"

"Don't say that".

"Why not? It's their fault! Because of them my sister had to go away".

"They're just scared…they're good people mostly".

"No, they aren't, and I hate them all!"

"They're just like you and me, girl".

"No, they aren't! And I won't hear of it!" Lucresia sprung up and stormed off.

Wallace looked dejected. He knew his daughter didn't mean it. She was just scared. He didn't blame her. He was scared too. These were scary times.

The Sacred Sisters were growing more powerful by the day. What had started as a quasi-religious order to root out witches had morphed into something else. Something dangerous. Something virulent. They worried him.

The Knights worried him too. Were they still loyal to him? To The Crown? Sometimes he wondered. They were too close to The Sacred Sisters. He'd have to do something about it. If he could. If he hadn't left it too late.

Wallace looked up at the sky. "What would you do, pa? You'd know what to do, surely you would".

He didn't like being a king.

He'd liked things much better before.

Back when the only things he had to worry about were chasing girls and hunting.

Responsibility didn't sit well with him. He didn't like bossing people about. And he didn't like the seriousness. The decision making. And he hated the discipline.

Wallace was not a serious man. His wife would be the first to tell him that. And she did. She brought it up regularly, along with all his other flaws when they argued.

Sometimes he wondered if he'd been born into the wrong family by accident, or if he was adopted. Perhaps they'd swapped the babes at birth. Some mischievous midwifery.

The Royals were not popular with the folk of Brightcastle. Well, that wasn't entirely truthful. They'd loved his father. GoldHammer. GoldHammer The Great.

GoldHammer who'd built a kingdom and turned back the barbarians at the gates. At the walls. GoldHammer who'd seen off two invasions and one rebellion.

Could he ever live up to his father's name? He doubted it.

"Stop with the self-pity, man", Wallace mumbled. "Think of your daughter".

"I hope he's keeping yer safe, girl, wherever you are". Wallace turned his gaze once more to the sky.

Novi

They were gathered in the courtyard, waiting for Madame. The courtyard was enchanting. Beatrix felt like she was in a bubble of magic.

There was grass, real grass, and the sky was blue with clouds and there were even birds chirping and singing.

She had asked Gwinni how this was possible, and Gwinni had told her it was enchanted. She didn't know it worked, but she loved it, nonetheless.

Beatrix was terribly excited. This was to be her first magic lesson. She was to be a witch!

As a child she had feared them. The witches. The dark ones. She'd been fed stories of them from the cradle on. Of their evil, their darkness, their wrongdoing.

She knew now that was all rubbish. Nonsense and fearmongering spread by frightened men, desperate to oppress her, lest she rise up and strike them down.

She was a witch!

And they were witches too!

She gazed blissfully around the courtyard, at her friends, at the other girls.

Some girls looked scared.

Some looked nervous.

Some looked excited.

Cincesse entered the courtyard flanked by her two cronies, and the mood changed.

Many girls looked nervous now.

Cincesse carried herself like a queen. Who did she think she was? She positively strutted.

The other girls were waiting patiently in a line, and Cincesse walked to the centre of the line. The two girls in the centre shuffled awkwardly to the side, making room for Cincesse and 'her girls'.

Not long after that, smart shoes on stone rang out from the castle behind them, where the big double wooden doors were wide open.

Madame Tempest arrived and walked briskly out into the courtyard. A hushed whispering broke out immediately.

"Why is she here?"

"She never teaches Novi!"

"What's she doing?"

She stopped ten paces or so away from them and turned to face them. "Good morning, ladies".

The whispering stopped, and they all responded. "Good morning, madame".

"I am here today, to teach you about **control**". She placed emphasis on this last word.

Beatrix frowned. This didn't sound very fun.

"You may think that magic is all casting spells, fancy hand movements, and flying about with your cats-"

"Flying?" Beatrix whispered to Gwinni, who was beside her.

"Shh", Gwinni whispered back. She was listening intently to Madame Tempest.

"-but I can assure you, it is **not**". Madame Tempest looked around at them severely. "And anyone who thinks otherwise, will not last long at this school". Her eyes fell on Beatrix.

Beatrix stared defiantly back.

"Now, I need two volunteers", Madame said.

The girls went quiet. There was no excitement, no whispering now. No one wanted to be the first to look stupid in front of their peers.

"No? Then I will pick for you", Madame said. "Cincesse". She beckoned imperiously. "And..." She looked around the girls. Her eyes stopped on Beatrix again. "Miss Bellafonte".

Beatrix's stomach jolted. "Me?"

"You", Madame repeated.

Beatrix stood still.

"Is there a problem?" Madame asked.

"No", Beatrix said quietly. She didn't feel so confident suddenly.

She joined Madame, and Cincesse, who smirked at her. Madame led them away from the girls to the centre of the grass.

"Now, listen carefully", Madame began. "Magic comes from within. It may involve the channelling of the elements, but if it didn't require an innate affinity for air, and wind, and fire and earth, anyone would be able to do it. Even men". The girls laughed.

"**Witches** channel these elements. They harness them and use them for their bidding. This is a gift. A great gift, a **precious** gift. The elements are not to be trifled with. They are powerful. Far more powerful than any witch. And they will consume you, if you attempt to abuse them. Treat them with respect. Cherish them. Pay homage to them". She bowed her head.

Beatrix frowned.

"Be thankful for them". Madame raised her head. "Now". She clapped her hands. "Face each other".

Cincesse and Beatrix walked a few paces apart, then faced each other. Beatrix was pleased to see that Cinesse also looked a little nervous, though she was trying hard not to show it, flashing little smirks to her cronies every now and then.

"Today, I want you to try and blow each other over", Madame said.

There was stunned silence at this.

Usually in these lessons, they tried to calm the mind and find The Place. An emptiness, a oneness, required to channel the elements. Sometimes, they accessed the elements. Connecting to them and allowing them to briefly flow through the body before dissipating. Never had they channelled them in such a way.

Cincesse might be able to muster up a light breeze, but Beatrix? She didn't even know how to find The Place! It was pointless. Did Madame mean to humiliate her?

"But, Madame-" Gwinni started.

Madame raised a hand without turning and Gwinni went quiet.

"What do I-?" Beatrix started.

Madame raised her hand again, in the same final manner. "Begin".

Immediately, Cincesse tensed, then closed her eyes.

Beatrix stared stupidly, not sure what she was supposed to do.

She looked back at Gwinni, who gestured frantically that she should pay attention. Even Edni had nothing to say, and was watching, eyes wide, mouth firmly shut.

Beatrix turned back to Cincesse. She blew at her and giggled to herself.

"I'd take it seriously, if I were you", Madame said.

Beatrix opened her mouth for a smart remark, then gasped.

Cincesse's hair was floating around her face, like she was underwater.

"What?"

Cincesse began to float a few inches off the floor.

Beatrix stepped backwards.

Her heart was beating hard in her chest.

For some reason, she felt scared.

On a deep, primal level.

Something about this terrified her.

"Stop it", Beatrix pleaded.

Cincesse's cronies giggled.

Cincesse floated a few inches higher off the floor.

Beatrix closed her eyes as a flash of fire burst through her mind. "Stop it!" she said more forcefully.

Madame said nothing.

"Madame!" Gwinni called. She was worried about her friend.

Madame silenced her with a wave of her hand.

A fire had taken root in Beatrix's mind, and she began to rock back and forth. "No", she moaned. "Stop!" Red lightning shot through her mind, cracking and shrieking.

"Madame, please!" Gwinni called.

"Enough!" Madame snapped curtly.

Cincesse moaned, as if the effort to hold herself in this state was costing her. Suddenly, she cried out and threw her hand toward Beatrix.

A gust of wind flew across the grass and hit Beatrix.

"Ugh!" Beatrix slid backwards a few feet, then stopped. She was shaking now, like she was fighting an unseen force.

The wind continued to come from Cincesse's hand. It wasn't very strong, but it was persistent.

Cincesse moaned and scrunched her face up in concentration.

Beatrix tried to close her eyes again, but the wind was too strong. "Stop it! Please!"

Cincesse smirked. She seemed to be gaining control of herself, and the cries of her peer were encouraging her to greater heights. "Perhaps I will. If you ask nicely".

Her cronies cackled.

"Really, Madame, please, we shouldn't!" Gwinni yelled.

Madame turned and pointed her finger at Gwinni, who's cries were cut off sharply. Gwinni's hand flew to her mouth. It was if she couldn't speak anymore.

Beatrix had her hands stretched out, as if trying to shield herself from the wind, or perhaps trying to push it away from her.

She was vibrating as the wind continued to buffet her. It seemed to be gaining momentum, and she slid back a bit further on the grass, toward the stone pillar behind her. "Please", she whispered.

Cincesse seemed to think about it for a moment, then said, "No". She threw her other hand out, and the intensity of the wind increased.

Beatrix saw a woman's face then, in her mind. It was perfectly formed, but all she could focus on were the eyes. The pupils were dilated, like a cat's.

"Try. Harder!" The voice screamed in her mind.

Something in her broke, and she shrieked. "**NO!**" She lashed out savagely with her hand, and a tremendous gale ripped through the courtyard.

It hit Cincesse, who fell to her back a few feet away. It blew right past her into the stone pillar behind, which disintegrated into dust. Rocks from above the pillar tumbled to the floor.

There was silence in the courtyard now.

Madame looked shocked.

Beatrix was breathing heavily from her knees.

Gwinni ran to her and hugged her. "I told you!" She shouted up at Madame.

Madame said nothing.

"Are you ok, Bea?" Gwinni asked quietly.

Beatrix shook her head.

Madame Tempest turned to the rest of the class. "That will be all. Dismissed".

Edni looked like she wanted to stay, so did Lucrecia, but Madame stood her ground and gave them dark looks, as if to say, don't you dare disobey me.

As the girls trooped out of the courtyard, Madame turned to Beatrix and Gwinni.

"Gwinni, take Beatrix upstairs and get her some water. You are excused from second period". With that, she walked away.

Beatrix looked up at Madame as she left. There was hate in her eyes.

"Come on", Gwinni said, helping Beatrix to her feet. "Let's get you some water".

Settling In

Lunch was a stressful affair, and honestly, Beatrix just wanted to go to bed. She was awfully tired. Whatever she'd done in the courtyard had really taken it out of her.

The other girls were giving her a wide berth, and there was lots of whispering and pointing when she first arrived in the great hall.

"You sure know how to make an entrance", Edni said, thumping herself down into the seat next to Beatrix. "Oh, excellent, ham".

Edni seemed in high spirits.

"You could be a little more understanding, you know", Gwinni scolded her.

"About what?" Edni asked.

"Beatrix". Gwinni widened her eyes at Edni.

"What about her?" Edni asked.

"She's still a little shaken from this morning, obviously! God, you are terrible, I don't know why I bother sometimes", Gwinni despaired.

"Oh, that? Are you still going on about that? I thought it was wicked cool", Edni admitted.

Beatrix smiled weakly.

"About time someone put her on her arse", Edni continued. "Prim cow". She cackled with glee and looked down the table at Cincesse, who was unusually subdued.

"You could try a little **tact**", Gwinni said.

"It's fine...thanks Gwin", Beatrix said.

"Gwin? Bea?" Edni made a face like she'd smelt gone off eggs. "Gross".

"Shut up", Gwinni said.

"You two made friends pretty bloody quickly", Edni said.

"You're just jealous", Gwinni shot back haughtily.

"Don't think so", Edni mumbled, through a huge mouthful of ham sandwich.

"Yes, you are", Gwinni said.

Edni swallowed. "Am not. Why would I be?"

"Oh, you are just awful!" Gwinni seemed rather flustered and jumped to her feet. She stormed off without a backward glance.

"What was that about?" Edni asked, after swallowing another gargantuan bite of ham sandwich.

Beatrix shrugged.

She didn't want to get in the middle of whatever it was between those two.

"How are you feeling?" A sweet voice asked from her right.

Beatrix smiled at Lucrecia. "I'm fine now, thanks".

"That was quite the feat". Lucrecia's eyes were sparkling with admiration.

"Thanks", Beatrix mumbled.

"I didn't know you could do that. Channel the wind, that is", Lucrecia said.

"Neither did I", Beatrix admitted.

"It wasn't **really** channelling the wind", Edni interjected. "You should see what Madame can do".

"But she's a **professor**", Lucrecia said. She was looking at Edni as if she was a rather uncivilized lout that had snuck in the backdoor.

Edni shrugged. "She's still way more powerful".

"She would be". Lucrecia now looked as if she were talking to an idiot.

Edni shrugged again. "Whatever. It was still pretty cool". She eyed Beatrix appraisingly. "Sure you haven't practiced magic before?"

Beatrix shook her head.

Edni nodded and raised her eyebrows. "Impressive. You could be a natural".

Lucrecia nodded. She seemingly agreed with this statement at least.

Beatrix didn't know what to say, so started eating.

As she was finishing her lunch, a muttering reached her ears. She looked up. Cincesse was standing behind her. Her cronies weren't with her.

Edni paused with a ham sandwich inches from her mouth, watching.

Beatrix turned to look at Cincesse better.

"Um". Cincesse seemed unsure of herself.

Beatrix waited.

"I just wanted to say. I'm sorry. For earlier", Cincesse said.

Beatrix arched an eyebrow.

"It wasn't right...what Madame did", Cincesse said.

Beatrix opened her mouth, then closed it.

"And I just wanted to say, I'm sorry". Cincesse was playing with her hands now.

"Thanks", Beatrix said.

Cincesse nodded.

They held one another's eyes for a moment, then Cincesse walked back to her friends, who immediately leaned in to get the gossip.

Cincesse shook her head and carried on eating.

Her friends looked disappointed.

"Well, I'll be damned", Edni said bluntly.

"What?" Beatrix said.

"I never thought I'd see the day", Edni continued.

"WHAT!" Beatrix demanded.

Edni seemed unfazed. "You just got an apology out of Cincesse. **Cincesse**". She seemed to find this awfully impressive.

"And?" Beatrix shot back.

"And?" Edni replied. "It's **Cincesse**. She's school royalty. That's like getting an apology from The Queen".

"Oh, behave", Beatrix said.

Lucrecia nodded.

"You agree with her?" Beatrix asked Lucrecia.

"She does have a point. Cincesse is not known for showing contrition, or remorse", Lucrecia said.

Beatrix didn't know what to say.

"Or brain cells", Edni interjected.

Lucrecia frowned, as if this was rather rude.

Beatrix glanced at Cincesse, who was watching her. Cincesse looked away quickly. It was becoming something of a habit.

Beatrix watched Cincesse a moment longer.

"Oi", Edni said.

"Hmm?" Beatrix turned back to Edni.

"I said, what have you got after lunch?" Edni asked.

"Oh, I don't know", Beatrix said.

"Then you better go find Gwinny", Edni instructed. "She'll know. And you're both Novi, so you'll have the same classes".

"You're not a Novi?" Beatrix asked.

Edni scoffed. "No. Course not".

"Oh", Beatrix said. She was surprised. She hadn't thought much of Edni. She thought she was all bark and no bite, as her pa used to say. Perhaps there was more to her than met the eye.

"Wait a minute. Then why were you there this morning, in the courtyard, with the other Novi?" Beatrix asked.

"You think I'd miss your first lesson, after you blew a hole in the wall within five minutes of setting foot in the castle?" Edni cackled. "Not a chance!"

Beatrix was speechless. Perhaps she had really misjudged Edni. "But, won't get you get in trouble?"

"Nah", Edni said. "Besides, Horace will be glad of a break from me. He's sick of the sight of me". She said it so matter-of-factly, that Beatrix couldn't help but laugh.

"You're crazy!" Beatrix said.

Edni laughed too. "I know".

"Well, I better go". Beatrix paused. "Thanks".

Edni looked up. "For what?"

"For making me laugh".

Edni looked touched. She watched Beatrix leave the hall and looked thoughtful as she left.

"That was very nice of you". Lucrecia sat herself gracefully next to Edni.

"Shut it", Edni said.

Lucrecia looked taken aback.

Edni smiled at her.

Upstairs, Beatrix braced herself outside The Witches Den. For some reason, the thought of seeing Gwinni again made her nervous.

She knocked on the door and entered.

Gwinni was standing in front of the fire, nose buried in a book. She looked up as Beatrix entered. "Oh, hello. Are you feeling ok?"

Beatrix nodded. "Thank you for looking after me".

"It's quite alright". Gwinni snapped the book shut. "Let me look at you". She approached Beatrix and put her hands either side of her face. "You still look pale. You should have some mead".

"I'm fine, really".

"Are you sure?"

"Mhm".

"Well, alright".

Beatrix cleared her throat. "Edni said you'd know what I have next...you know...my schedule".

"Oh, of course!" Gwinni clapped her hand to her head. "Have they not given you a timetable yet?"

Beatrix shook her hand.

"Typical".

"What is?"

"Well, Madame is in charge of the timetables".

"Oh".

"Don't take it personally. Madame doesn't like most students".

"Then why is she in charge?" Beatrix was beginning to seriously dislike this Madame Tempest woman. She felt defiant. She never thought she'd see the day she'd champion a man over a woman, but she wished Gregor was in charge at that moment.

Gwinni shrugged awkwardly. "She's very powerful".

"What about Gregor? Isn't he also powerful?"

"Oh yes, most certainly...but Madame..."

"What?"

"She's a Domi".

"So? Aren't some of the students?"

"Not really...no"

"But Edni said..."

"Edni says a lot of things...there's really only a few Domi out there...Madame is one...Gregor is another".

"Then why did Edni say-?"

Gwinni cut her off. "There are **Domi** and then there are **Domi**".

"I don't understand..."

"A few students have been granted the assignation over the years, sure, but..."

"But what?"

"There's politics involved..."

"Politics?" Beatrix looked baffled. "What do you mean?"

"Favourites. Nepotism..." Gwinni looked uncomfortable.

"What..." Beatrix looked at a loss. She didn't understand anything about politics or nepotism. She lived in a small village. They all got by and pulled their weight.

"There is more than one way to achieve Domini assignation, let's put it that way", Gwinni said primly. She looked rather perturbed by this.

Beatrix nodded. She was started to get an inkling of what Gwinni meant.

"But there are **really** only two Domi that I know of. Gregor. And Madame Tempest. The others..." She waved her hand dismissively as if they didn't count.

Beatrix nodded. "So why can't Gregor be in charge, if he's also a Domi?"

"Madame is more powerful", Gwinni said.

"How do you know?"

"They duelled, of course".

"What?" Beatrix was aghast.

"Mhm. Almost destroyed the castle".

"You're joking!"

"Oh, no. No". Gwinni looked grave.

"Come to think of it...Gregor did make some comment about remodelling recently...though I thought he was just making a bad joke".

"He does like to do that. But no, he is rather sore about it. There's bad blood between them".

"Bad blood?"

"Mhm. And not for the first time".

"No?"

"Well, no, of c-" Gwinni stopped herself. "I must stop that".

"What?"

"Forgetting that you are new".

"It's alright". Beatrix waved her hand impatiently. "What's that about bad blood".

"Oh. Well, I thought you knew. I thought he'd told you that much at least?"

"Told me what?" Beatrix was beginning to see why Gwinni and Edni were constantly bickering. Gwinni did have a flair for the dramatic, and loved knowing something you didn't.

Gwinni smiled dramatically, a little twinkle in her eyes.

"Out with it!" Beatrix barked, in a manner reminiscent of her father.

"They were married".

The Pub

The next weeks passed in a blur, and before long, Beatrix felt quite at home.

Her days were filled with lessons, reading and exercise. The girls loved to exercise, as she quickly, and painfully, found out.

Lessons were rather more uneventful. Madame Tempest hadn't appeared in any more of them, thankfully, and Beatrix continued learning how to find The Place, and after that, how to find the elements.

She was learning quickly, and could find water, air and earth now. For some reason, she felt a block around fire, and hadn't been able to find it, no matter how hard she tried.

Gwinni told her not to worry. That it was completely normal, and she was miles ahead of where she should be. She said it usually took students months to even find The Place, let alone locate three of the core elements. This made Beatrix feel rather proud.

She had settled into an uneasy truce with Cincesse and her two friends. She'd later learned the friends were called Eli and Clio. Cincesse had taken to avoiding her or being very polite in her presence. Beatrix was glad for the peace. She didn't want to fight with anyone.

And so, the days flew by, and the nights with them. Felix seemed to be enjoying himself, and often, she saw him gallivanting around the grounds with the ginger tabby, Katy. She'd later learned the cat belonged to Lucrecia.

She didn't know why Lucrecia hadn't said sooner. When she'd asked her why she hadn't, she said, "Does anyone really own anything?" Beatrix thought it was an odd answer, but let it lie.

And so it was, on this late spring morning, we find Beatrix in the great hall, enjoying breakfast with her friends.

"Brr, it's cold", Lucrecia said, hugging her cloak about her.

"You don't say?" Edni said drily.

"It really is". Gwinni shivered.

"I like it", Edni said.

Gwinni tutted.

"What?" Edni said.

"You're not normal", Gwinni said.

"Just because I like winter?" Edni asked.

"**I** like winter. But I **hate** the cold", Gwinni said.

"That doesn't even make any sense", Edni replied.

Beatrix rolled her eyes at Lucrecia as if to say, here they go again.

"Yes, it does. I like winter. I don't like the cold. What part of it don't you understand?" Gwinni asked.

"All of it", Edni replied.

Beatrix zoned them out and looked down the table.

Cincesse looked cold too, her cloak was fastened at her neck. She looked at Beatrix.

For a moment, Beatrix thought she saw the shadow of a smile on her lips, but then it was gone, and she was back talking to Eli and Cleo.

She'd been thinking about Cincesse a lot lately. She found her intriguing.

Lucrecia cocked her head and watched Beatrix. "You should speak to her".

"What?" Beatrix snapped to, as if she'd been daydreaming.

"Cincesse".

"Why would I do that?" Beatrix said defensively.

"You like her", Lucrecia said matter-of-factly.

"No, I don't!"

Beatrix's tone shocked Gwinni and Edni out of their bickering.

"What's that?" Edni said curiously.

"Nothing, keep your beak out!" Beatrix warned.

"Oh, now I'm really interested". Edni leaned forward on her hands attentively.

Beatrix sighed angrily.

Edni looked at Lucrecia. "Spill".

"Don't-" Beatrix started.

"We were talking-" Lucrecia continued speaking.

"You-"

"About-"

"Dare!"

"Lucrecia".

They finished at the same time.

"Oooh, I knew it!" Edni seemed particularly pleased at this divulgence.

Gwinni looked at Edni strangely.

"Knew what?" Beatrix said in a high voice.

"You and Queen Cin", Edni said.

"Queen Cin?" Beatrix looked as if she wanted to be sick.

Edni nodded. "Been saying it for weeks".

"You have not", Gwinni said.

"Alright, days", Edni said.

Gwinni cocked her head side to side, but said nothing, accepting this revised claim.

Beatrix scowled at Lucrecia.

"Sorry", Lucrecia said politely. "But I thought it would be helpful".

"And how's that?" Beatrix demanded.

"Well, you might actually talk to her now, instead of just gazing longingly at her every time we eat". Lucrecia smiled apologetically.

Edni burst out laughing, her loud, brash cackle echoing around the hall. "Bahahaha. Oh. My. Goodness". She slapped Lucrecia on the back.

Lucrecia jolted forward, rather startled.

"You are the gift that keeps giving", Edni said. She pulled Lucrecia toward her and placed a kiss smack on her cheeks.

Lucrecia blushed.

"I do **not** gaze at her...longingly". Beatrix looked as if this cost her.

She glanced at Cincesse, who quickly turned away. She'd clearly been looking, intrigued by the bawling and guffawing of Beatrix's new 'friend'. It was hard not to be intrigued. Edni had a laugh that sounded like the world's happiest donkey.

"I'm sorry, but you do", Lucrecia corrected her.

"The brass neck on you!" Edni exclaimed.

Beatrix scowled and looked as if she was about to get up and leave, when Madame Tempest stood up.

The room went quiet.

"Ahem". She liked to clear her throat, even though the room was already quiet. Beatrix looked as though she might vomit.

"Thank you. As you know, it has been sometime since our last trip to the village".

Immediately the girls started muttering excitedly.

"What? What is it?" Beatrix turned to Gwinni and pulled at her arm. Gwinni wasn't paying attention though. She was watching Madame excitedly.

"This was for your own safety".

Some of the girls muttered as if they disagreed.

Beatrix frowned.

"It has now..."

The girls were now muttering rather loudly, and Madame stopped.

The muttering died down immediately. No-one wanted to incur the wrath of Madame or lose their village privileges.

When she was satisfied with the silence, Madame continued. "It has now been deemed safe. As such, we have planned a trip for this weekend".

Madame paused to allow the girls to react, as if she knew even her fearsome presence would not stop them reacting to this news.

"Woohoo!" Edni jumped out of her chair and punched the sky.

Beatrix caught Cincesse giggling at Edni. Their eyes met and Beatrix smiled.

"Habits will be handed out after final period on Friday. I expect you all to be on your best behaviour. Do not make me regret this decision". Madame stared at them all a moment, then took her seat.

The room broke out into excited chatter.

"We're going to the village?" Beatrix asked immediately. "But how? Aren't we...witches?"

Edni whooped again. "Yes, but that doesn't matter".

"Why not? Wait". Beatrix looked thoughtful.

Edni threw her arm out to stop Gwinni spoiling her fun. "Let her figure it out", she muttered to Gwinni.

Beatrix didn't hear, deep in thought as she was.

"Habits?" Beatrix looked up.

The girls were all looking at her expectantly. Edni looked mischievous as anything. Gwinni looked like she was bursting to explain. Lucrecia looked polite as always.

Suddenly, they all burst out laughing.

"Whaaat?" Beatrix wailed.

*

Later that night, she lay in bed with Felix, reliving the discussion in the great hall. Everyone else was asleep.

"And they expect me to wear a **habit**".

Even though she spoke with her mind, Felix could sense her disgust. He grinned, as much as a cat could.

"I don't know why you think it's so funny!" She thought.

"It is, rather".

"Will you come?"

"To the pub?"

"Yes".

"Of course".

"What about **Katy?**" Beatrix teased.

"What about her?"

"Will you bring her?"

"Perhaps"

"Perhaps...pfft".

Felix's tail started wagging playfully.

"I'm excited, Fe".

"I'd noticed".

"Maybe I can get a job at the bar, as a barmaid".

"That might be difficult".

"Why's that?" Beatrix thought defiantly.

"You are supposed to be **Sacred Sisters**, are you not?"

"Oh, that". Beatrix felt deflated. "**Text Keepers**, actually, not quite as important".

"That's not to say you couldn't in the future…"

Beatrix brightened. "You're right. I won't be here forever!"

"No. Not very long at this rate".

"What's that supposed to mean?"

"Well, if you keep destroying the castle at the rate you are, they shall have to remove you. Hazardous thing you are".

"Oi!" Beatrix turned haughtily to face Felix, who was lounging, stretched lengthways across her second pillow.

"Sorry. I'm sure you had a perfectly valid reason for destroying the castle".

"I didn't destroy the castle!"

"You didn't?"

"Just a few…bricks".

"Ah".

"Don't ah me".

"Just did".

Beatrix tutted again. "Honestly cat, I don't know why I keep you around".

"Because you love me".

"There's that, I guess".

They lay silently for a while.

"Cincesse is going", Beatrix said.

"Oh, is she?"

"Yes…"

"Well, do speak to her this time".

"You too?"

"Lucrecia finally nudged you?"

"What do you mean? You knew about that? Are the two of you in cahoots?"

"I don't know what you mean", Felix thought aloofly.

"Is this entire school in cahoots against me?"

"They still wouldn't stand a chance".

Beatrix blushed.

"I miss ma and pa", she thought.

"Me too...me too".

They fell asleep thinking of Winterweld.

The Text Keepers

"I still don't understand why I have to wear this horrible thing", Beatrix wailed, pinching the habit as if it was made of sewage.

"Because you're a **witch!**" Gwinni said.

"I know. But why can't I just wear something else. Something nice. Something **stylish**. This is gross. I look like an old woman in a young woman's body". Beatrix sniffed like there was a foul smell under her nose.

"I would have thought, you of all people, would understand the need for secrecy". It was Madame Tempest. Beatrix gave her a foul look.

They were all assembled in the main entrance, waiting to go.

"Now", Madame Tempest said. "Follow me in single file. No speaking. And absolutely no giggling".

"Are we going to walk all the way there?" Beatrix looked aghast at the thought. They were underwater for starters. The pub definitely wasn't close!

"No", Gwinni whispered. "Just watch".

They filed out of the castle into the sea.

There were lots of them. Beatrix had never really thought about it before, but now, seeing everyone lined up single file, it did seem like rather a lot of witches.

"How many of us are there?" Beatrix whispered.

"Oh, about a hundred or so", Gwinni replied.

"A hundred! A hundred girls won't fit in one pub!" Beatrix said.

Gwinni giggled silently into her hand. "We're not all going, stupid".

"Oh". Beatrix seemed embarrassed. "Course". She started counting the girls in her head. Ten. Twenty. Thirty. Thirty girls. Beatrix noticed that most of the girls were older than her. "Where's Lucrecia?" She spun around.

"Lucrecia is ten years old, Beatrix. She has no place being in a pub", Gwinni said sternly.

Beatrix looked sheepish. Gwinni was right.

"In fact". Gwinni looked up and down the line of girls. "I think you are the youngest".

"I'm fourteen soon!" Beatrix exclaimed.

"Keep your voice down", Gwinni hissed.

"Sorry".

Gwinni signalled that Beatrix should remain silent and turned back to the front.

They walked for what seemed like ages. Beatrix was beginning to get bored. She started whistling quietly and Gwinni shot her a warning look. She sighed and stopped.

Not even the novelty of being in the sea could distract her. It soon wore thin against the monotony of their silent march.

She started counting the fish that swam past. Strangely, none of them came too close. Maybe they couldn't see them. Maybe they were scared of them. She'd probably be scared too, if she were a little fish, and a bunch of big humans came traipsing about in habits.

"Ow!" She'd bumped into the back of Gwinni.

Gwinni kicked her in the shin with the back of her heel.

Beatrix opened her mouth to tell her off, then realised the line had stopped.

It was eerie, standing there in the darkness of the sea, waiting.

She didn't know what they'd do next.

Was there another lift?

Like at Gregor's?

A pub lift?

She smirked to herself.

She was funny.

Suddenly, a chanting reached her.

She frowned and concentrated hard on the sound.

She couldn't make out the words.

She didn't have long to ponder them, for there was a blinding flash of light, and then she was on land.

Gwinni looked back at her and smiled. "The pub!"

And there it was.

They'd emerged from the sea onto a hillside, hidden behind a treeline.

And there, below them, was a pub.

It was a big thing, with a thatched roof, and a big chimney, honking smoke happily into the sky.

There were men and women drinking outside on the grass and sitting at little tables.

A barmaid emerged balancing a tray precariously loaded with about six glasses. She skilfully swerved a drunk patron and placed the tray down on a table without spilling a drop.

A group of men thanked her gruffly then immediately began sucking down beer from the glasses.

Beatrix grimaced as one of them sploshed a huge sip of beer down his shirt and grinned at his friend. "Somethings never change..."

"The pub!" Gwinni squealed excitedly, squeezing Beatrix's shoulder.

Beatrix had never seen Gwinni like this and smiled. It was nice to see.

"Now remember, not a word", Madame Tempest warned.

"What's that about?" Beatrix asked Gwinni.

"She means about your old life", Gwinni said.

"My old life?" Beatrix hadn't thought of it like that before. It sounded rather final.

Gwinni nodded. "We're not allowed to talk about our old lives. In case we're found out. And, because it makes us sad".

Beatrix nodded. She could see the logic in it.

"One girl did once...and, well...it wasn't pretty", Gwinni said.

"Oh yeah?" Beatrix asked.

Gwinni started to reply, but something from below caught her eye. "Oh, he's here! He's here!"

Cincesse watched Gwinni with interest, then looked down at the pub.

A particularly handsome young man was setting up outside the pub. It looked like he was getting ready to play a harp.

"Ugh", Beatrix said. She hated the harp. There was always a man with a harp. And he always expected her to swoon. Why? Because he strummed a few strings? Gross. Get a trade. That's what her father used to say.

"Isn't he dreamy?" Gwinni swooned.

"Not particularly", Beatrix replied.

Gwinni looked taken aback. "Oh, well. I like him".

Beatrix smiled. She didn't want to kill Gwinni's enthusiasm for this outing. She rolled her eyes once Gwinni had turned away.

She heard giggling to her left and turned to see Cincesse smiling at her. She smiled back and blushed.

"Well then, shall we go?" Madame Tempest turned to the girl next to her and took her hand. That girl took the hand of the girl next to her, and so on, until they'd all joined hands. Beatrix found this weird but didn't say anything.

Madame led the first girl out from behind the treeline, and they began a slow descent down the hill.

After a few minutes, there was a cry from the pub. And then a whoop. And then a cheer.

"Hey, they're here! The Text Keepers!"

They were obviously popular with the villagers, which Beatrix found strange. She'd never been particularly popular.

Her mouth had always seen to that. But the villagers sounded genuinely excited to see them.

She found it kind of sickening. They hadn't wanted her when she'd been plain old Beatrix. But now she was a Text Keeper, preserving ancient texts that had led to the burnings of hundreds of witches, and countless more innocents, she was loved, apparently. It was wretched. It was wrong.

She pushed her loathing to the back of her mind. She hadn't been out of the castle in a long time. She intended to try and enjoy herself. And besides, she wasn't **really** a Text Keeper. She took some small solace in the fact.

"Hey, it's Gwinni!" A man shouted as Gwinni came into sight.

Beatrix blushed. She didn't like attention, and Gwinni was just in front of her.

Gwinni broke hand contact with the girl in front of her for a second and waved animatedly at a man next to the harpist.

"Ey, Gavin, it's Gwinni!" The man said to the harpist. The harpist looked up and saw Gwinni on the hill. He waved from his chair, and gave what Beatrix imagined he fancied was a 'winning smile'.

Gwinni swooned.

"Gwinni!" Madame hissed.

This was clearly a regular occurrence, because Gwinni quickly gripped the hand of the girl in front of her again.

Beatrix snorted.

Gwinni's neck had turned red.

Cincesse was a few girls in front of Gwinni, and she turned back to grin at Beatrix. Beatrix went a little red herself.

A young boy and a pompous looking fat man came hurrying into sight from the side of the pub.

The boy pointed at the girls on the hillside, and the fat man squinted up at them.

"Oh!" The fat man boomed.

Beatrix was surprised. He had such a deep voice. She hadn't expected much from him. He had a weak chin that wobbled when he walked, and thin shoulder length grey hair.

"Madame!" The fat man waddled forward. He had to stop to pull his trousers up. They'd fallen down his hips rather quickly, exposing some of his ample stomach.

He paused to retie his belt tie as some of the young men sniggered. It seemed to bother him not at all.

"Madame! Madame!" He ran out to greet Madame Tempest. He sunk into a courteous bow, extending his arm low in front of him.

His hat fell from his head to the grass, and he quickly swept it up as he exited his bow. Somehow, he managed to pull it off.

Beatrix was impressed. This man was seemingly immune to embarrassment. He did have a certain charm to him, she had to admit. Now that she was closer, she could see that he had dazzlingly blue eyes and rosy, red cheeks.

Madame broke contact with the girl behind her and extended her lead hand.

The fat man promptly kissed it. He let his lips linger, then looked up at Madame. "It is a pleasure to see you again".

Madame bobbed her head courteously. "It is a pleasure to be here".

"I did not know when I would see you again, after you left so...precipitously, the last time".

Beatrix wondered at this.

"Yes...well...I am sorry about that, my dear".

"My dear?" Beatrix mouthed. She couldn't believe it. Madame was usually as dry as a prune.

"Not at all, not all", the man replied silkily.

"Are you able to receive us?"

"Of course, of course Madame! Of course!" The fat man seemed only too happy to have Madame grace his door. "You are always welcome in my village".

Madame smiled prettily.

"As are your keepers", he addressed the girls behind.

"Most gracious of you", Madame said.

The fat man blushed. "Come, come", he extended his arm, which Madame took. "Let me find you a drink..."

With that, Madame walked off without so much as a backward glance. Beatrix couldn't believe it.

The harpist approached Gwinni and held out his hand. "Madame?"

Beatrix's mouth dropped open.

Gwinni took the harpist's hand and followed him back to his chair. Before long, she was sat in his lap, playing with his hair.

Cincesse approached Beatrix. "Shall we go?"

Beatrix suddenly felt nervous. "Why not?"

They walked slowly toward the pub together.

"It's crazy, isn't it?" Cincesse said, breaking the awkward silence.

"What is?" Beatrix said quickly.

Cincesse nodded toward the revellers.

Men and women had quickly approached the girls and made them feel welcome, drawing them into their midst.

"Oh, yeah", Beatrix said.

"And Madame…"

"And MADAME!" Beatrix exclaimed. "Right?"

Cincesse giggled. "I know".

"What is that?"

"I don't know", Cincesse said. "But it's rather amusing".

"I know!" Beatrix relaxed a little.

"Shall we get a drink?" Cincesse asked.

"Why not?"

"What do you like?"

"Sherry".

"Ooh, fancy".

"Not really".

Cincesse smiled and disappeared into the pub.

Beatrix found a quiet table and sat down to wait.

Before long, a young lad approached her. "Care to dance?"

"There's no musi-" She stopped, and grinned.

The harpist had just started playing.

"Very good", Beatrix said. She had to give it to him, it was a skilfully executed approach.

The lad grinned and held out his hand, waggling his fingers.

"Sorry, but I'm waiting for someone", Beatrix said.

The lad clutched at his heart, as if someone had shot an arrow into it.

"Sorry", Beatrix repeated. She really was a little sorry. He seemed like a nice lad. But he wasn't...

She glanced up.

Cincesse was walking back out of the pub with two glasses. They both looked like sherry.

"Thanks!" Beatrix said, as Cincesse set them down on the table. "You like sherry too?"

"I thought I'd try it", Cincesse said.

"You've never tried sherry?" Beatrix replied animatedly.

"No, should I have?" Cincesse asked.

"Oh, it's the best!" Beatrix exclaimed. "I can't believe you've never tried sherry!"

Cincesse blushed. "I feel rather foolish now".

"Don't! Try it!" Beatrix watched Cincesse intently.

She raised a glass to her lips and sipped it. A few drops of red slid down her lips to her neck.

Beatrix swallowed.

"Mmm, it is rather nice. I can see how one could develop a taste for it". Cincesse rolled the sherry around her mouth, like she was tasting a fine wine. "It is rather different to what I'm used to".

"And what is that?" Beatrix said, looking up from Cincesse's neck.

"Oh, you know. Just, different", Cincesse said lamely.

"Oh", Beatrix said.

They sat in silence as the harpist harped.

A man and woman rose from their seats and started dancing in the grass a few feet away.

After a few moments, another couple joined them.

Before long, there were lots of people dancing in the grass.

First the older villagers, and then young lads and lasses.

Beatrix and Cincesse sipped their sherry, watching the villagers, snatching glances at one another every now and then.

"Where are your friends?" Beatrix asked after a while.

"Oh, they didn't want to come", Cincesse said lightly.

"Oh". For some reason Beatrix didn't think this was the real reason.

"It's nice to be on my own for a change, you know?" Cincesse said.

Beatrix nodded.

"They're always with me...I love them, but..." She blushed.

"I'm glad they're not here", Beatrix said suddenly. She turned red as her sherry, after she realised the implications of what she'd said.

But Cincesse didn't seem to mind. "Me too", she said happily.

"Come and dance, Bea!" It was Gwinni. She was red in the face and hand in hand with the harpist, a rather good-looking lad with a cheeky smile.

"Oh, maybe in a bit", Beatrix said.

Gwinni glanced knowingly at Cincesse, then winked at Beatrix. "See you later!" She danced away with the harpist.

Cincesse giggled. "She is rather funny, isn't she?"

"Who Gwinny? Yeah, she's great. I've never seen her like this, to be honest".

"No, me neither".

"How long have you been in the castle?" Beatrix asked, searching for a way to keep the conversation going.

"Oh, a while". Cincesse's mood seemed to shift.

"Do you miss home?"

Cincesse nodded. "A lot".

"Was it hard...coming here?"

"Yes...but not in the way that you might think".

Beatrix opened her mouth, then closed it. Of course. They all knew Beatrix's story. The story of the 'dark one'. The first dark one in two hundred years.

"I'm sorry". Cincesse put her hand on Beatrix's.

Beatrix's mouth went dry. "It's ok".

"It's really not". Cincesse looked guilty. "I heard of the terrible way those villagers treated you...your friends, your family".

Beatrix looked away. She focused on a young couple dancing rather energetically a few paces away.

"Most of us...most of us are lucky".

"How's that?" Beatrix turned back to look at Cincesse. Her eyes were dull and guarded.

"Well, most of us, Gregor found us...before".

Beatrix waited.

"Before we showed signs...of who we were". Cincesse leant forward slowly. "The mark". She ran her fingers through Beatrix's hair, fondling the white patch by her temple.

She was close now, and Beatrix studied her face from the corner of her eye. Her skin was flawless. She had a patch of freckles on the tip of her nose that Beatrix thought was very cute, and her cheeks looked terribly soft. Her eyes were brown like her hair, and ever so inviting. They seemed to sing to her.

Beatrix turned to face her properly. Cincesse looked uncertain now, scared even. Beatrix ran her hand through Cincesse's hair. "And is this...your mark?" It was a question, but Beatrix already knew the answer.

Cincesse nodded softly, gently, so as not to break the spell.

"Goodwill to all", a booming voice roared suddenly.

The unwelcome distraction came from the fat man.

He was standing arm in arm with Madame at the front of the pub. He had a huge glass of beer in his hand. He raised it to his mouth and drained it, slopping large quantities down his finely made shirt and pants.

Madame affected not to notice. She seemed to be enjoying herself. She was a little red in the face and had a glass of wine in her hand.

The revellers all raised their glasses and cheered.

The harpist stopped his harping and cheered too. He was back at his chair now, Gwinny on his lap. She fed him a sip of beer from a large glass, and he smiled at her.

"I have to go", Cincesse said suddenly, getting to her feet.

"Wait, don't!" Beatrix's hand shot out to stop her.

Cincesse looked upset. "I need some air". She wouldn't meet Beatrix's eyes.

"But we're outside!"

"I'm sorry, I have to go". Her voice broke and she ran off around the side of the pub.

"Hey, wait!"

Beatrix ran after her, But Cincesse was already off running into the distance, and Beatrix was a glass of sherry deep. It had gone to her head, and she stopped around the side of the pub to steady herself. "Woah".

She wasn't usually allowed sherry and always had to sneak it. She certainly wouldn't be allowed a big glass like that, in broad daylight. Her mother always told her it was too strong for a girl her age. Beatrix guessed she'd been right. She took a deep breath and set off after Cincesse.

In the distance was a barn. She saw Cincesse run into it and breathed a sigh of relief. If she had to do much more running at this pace she might puke.

She walked into the barn, which was dark, the only light coming from the fading sun outside.

"Cinesse!" Beatrix called.

She couldn't see her.

"Cincesse! You in here?"

She heard sobbing from above and looked up. There was an upper level. Finding a ladder, she climbed it. The upper level had a hay floor and was rather cosy. The roof was still high above her head. It was a big barn.

"Cincesse", Beatrix called softly. She could see her now. Lying in the hay at the back. She had her head in her hands. She was in front of a little window that looked out onto the fields surrounding the barn.

The roof got lower the closer she got to Cincesse, and eventually, she had to approach her on hands and knees. "What's the matter?" she said, as she crawled forward and lay down next to her.

Cincesse didn't say anything.

"Is it something I said?"

Cincesse sniffed.

"If it is, I'm sorry. I know I got a big mouth, and sometimes I don't know when to shut it. My ma says-"

Suddenly, Cincesse rolled to her knees and kissed her.

Beatrix closed her eyes, as Cincesse's lips covered her own.

Cincesse placed her hands tenderly on Beatrix's cheeks as the kiss lingered.

Beatrix felt giddy. She never wanted to this end.

As soon as it had started, it was over.

Cincesse sat back and looked at her, shock in her eyes. "I'm sorry", she said immediately.

Beatrix wanted to say something. Anything. A million things ran through her mind. In the end, the thing that made the most sense, was to just kiss her.

She pulled Cincesse back to her and kissed her deeply. This time, it was Beatrix's turn to break the kiss, and Cincesse looked disappointed when she did.

Cincesse hiccoughed and giggled. She wiped the tears from her face.

Beatrix licked her lips. She could taste Cincesse's tears on her tongue.

"Sorry", Cincesse said quietly.

"Don't be", Beatrix said intensely.

Cincesse blushed.

"Do you know how long I've wanted to do that?" Cincesse asked.

Beatrix shook her head.

"From the moment I first set eyes on you".

"Really?"

Cincesse nodded.

"Why didn't you?" Beatrix said huskily.

Cincesse cackled. It was a rather lascivious thing, quite unlike her girlish giggles. "That wouldn't have been proper".

"To hell with proper". Beatrix felt emboldened.

"And what if you had spurned me?" Cincesse asked. "I don't think I could bear it". She turned away and looked out the window.

Beatrix turned her head back. "I'd never spurn you".

"No?"

Beatrix shook her head, and they kissed again.

Below they heard a drunk couple stumble into the barn.

They broke their kiss, and Beatrix raised a finger to her lips. Her eyes were wide and tense.

Cincesse went quiet.

The sound of kissing drifted up to them, and they stifled giggles. It sounded sloppy and wet.

Beatrix stuck her tongue out at Cincesse, who snorted.

Beatrix started to crawl away and Cincesse gestured frantically that she should stop.

Beatrix shook her head and beckoned Cincesse out of the little nook they had been lying in.

Cincesse reluctantly obliged.

They reached the edge of the upper level, and both peered over the edge. Below them a young lad and lass were slobbering over each other in the hay toward the back of the barn. They seemed totally oblivious to their surroundings.

Beatrix signalled silence again and swung her legs over the edge of the platform.

Cincesse looked petrified. She watched as Beatrix nimbly climbed down the ladder. Beatrix looked up and beckoned her down.

Cincesse breathed deeply, then climbed down. Halfway down, the lass started to moan. "Oh, Greggie". Beatrix snorted and covered her mouth with her hand. Thankfully, the lass hadn't heard.

Cincesse hot tailed it down the ladder and Beatrix took her hand. They ran out of the barn and around the corner. They didn't stop until they were behind the barn, then they let out an explosion of laughter.

"Oh, my goodness", Cincesse panted.

"Oh, Greggie", Beatrix breathed, using the same high-pitched voice the girl had.

"Stop!" Cincesse wheezed, breaking down into hysterics.

"Hey, look", Beatrix said after they'd finished laughing. "The moon is out".

"How odd", Cincesse said.

It was still light out, but there it was.

A full moon, in all its glory.

Cincesse gripped her arm excitedly. "Hey!"

"What?" Beatrix replied.

"Shall we visit?"

"What?" Beatrix frowned. "Visit what?"

Cincesse grinned excitedly. "The moon!"

A Witch, Her Cat, And The Moon

"What?" Beatrix looked at Cincesse in disbelief.

Cincesse's face dropped. "What? What is it? Have you already been?" She turned away stormily. Her back was to Beatrix now. "I knew it. I bet it was that Gwinny", she mumbled moodily.

Beatrix put her hand on Cincesse's arm and turned her back to face her. "Hey. What is it? I can't hear you when you mumble like that".

Cincesse looked away petulantly. "Forget it".

"Forget it? You said you wanna go to the frickin moon!" Beatrix blurted, her excitement getting the best of her.

Cincesse snorted. "WHAT!"

Beatrix stared blankly. "WHAT?"

Suddenly, they both started laughing.

"So, you do want to go, then?" Cincesse asked tentatively.

"Do I want to go..." Beatrix looked at Cincesse like she didn't know what to do with her. "Of course I do!"

"Oh". Cincesse sniffed. "Right. Well".

"Well, what! How do we go? Another lift?" Beatrix looked sceptical. But then again, they had been teasing about her climbing a rope to visit the boys school.

Cincesse giggled. "Oh, goodness no. Don't be silly".

"What then?" Beatrix looked around excitedly.

Cincesse frowned. "You really don't know?"

"NO!" Beatrix yelled. "In case you forgot, I'm new here!"

Cincesse seemed to be rather enjoying herself now. "Yes, I suppose you are".

Beatrix scowled. "Tell me, or I'm gonna drag you back in the barn and make you listen to Greggie".

"You wouldn't!"

"Would".

Cincesse looked like she couldn't tell if Beatrix was being serious or not. She placed her fingers between her lips and gave a high-pitched whistle. It was slightly odd in that it was different to a regular whistle. Beatrix noticed there was a slight glow to Cincesse while she whistled.

There was a pop of white smoke, and a cat appeared. It was a grumpy looking white Persian cat, with grey blue eyes. Cincesse picked the cat up and nuzzled it. "Hello, gorgeous".

Beatrix raised an eyebrow.

"Isn't she gorgeous?" Cincesse asked.

"Uhh, yeah". Beatrix didn't think so. She thought the cat looked squashed and grumpy. But she wasn't missing a trip to the moon. "Why'd you call your cat? I didn't know you could do that". She looked around. "Was that magic?"

"Sort of", Cincesse said.

"Sort of?"

"Well, yes, but not really. It's easy to channel your cat".

"Channel my...cat?"

"Right. Every witch has a bond with her cat. It's a simple bit of magic to call your cat. It's very basic channelling. There are no elements involved though". Cincesse looked cautiously at Beatrix.

"Then how's it channelling if there's no elements?"

"You can channel more than just the elements, you know".

"You can?" Beatrix was baffled. Gwinny had told her being a witch was all about channelling elements.

Cincesse nodded. "Cats are magic. You can channel anything magic".

"They are?" Beatrix looked thoughtful. "Is that why you can hear their thoughts?"

"You can hear **your** cat's thoughts". Cincesse looked like Gwinny for a moment and Beatrix grinned.

"What?" Cincesse looked self-conscious.

"Nothing. So, how's it work?"

"Well...you need to find The Place".

Beatrix nodded eagerly and closed her eyes.

"And then, you need to **will** your cat to you".

"How do I do that?" Beatrix mumbled with her eyes closed.

"Think of your cat. Their essence. Hold to it. Will it to you. Pull it close".

Beatrix frowned and breathed out deeply.

Cincesse watched her quietly. "You're rather beautiful, you know".

Beatrix's eyes flew open. "Stop it". She blushed. "I'll never get Felix here if you go on like that".

"Sorry", Cincesse said playfully.

Beatrix closed her eyes again and found The Place. She thought of Felix, and willed him to her. "Oh, it's no use", she said after a moment.

Cincesse placed her hands on Beatrix's shoulders, and she tensed. "Relax. Your mind is on...other things".

Beatrix blushed again.

"Think of when you first met Felix...your favourite times together. Your favourite memories. What reminds you of Felix? Picture it. Hold to it".

Beatrix slowed her beathing, and Cincesse felt her shoulders relax. "Good", she whispered. She began rubbing Beatrix's arms, gently up and down.

Beatrix smiled.

In her mind, she saw Felix in the kitchen, darting between Cath's legs, a large fish in his mouth. Cath was shrieking at him to come back, chasing him with a rolling pin.

The big window by the front door was open, and Felix hopped up onto the window ledge.

"Don't you dare!" Cath warned, waggling her rolling pin menacingly.

There was a standoff.

Felix gazed tantalisingly at Cath.

Cath glared back.

Cath made a dash for the window. Felix hopped nimbly out of the window, landing gracefully in the dirt outside.

"Ohhh, you!" Cath went for the door, ripping it open, but Felix was off, bolting down the side of the house.

Beatrix giggled from her room, where she was watching with the door ajar.

Graeme turned around from his chair before the fire. "S'matter?" he grumbled.

"That bloody cat has stolen my fish!" Cath yelled, stomping back into the house.

"Has he? Can't have". Graeme looked around dumbly. "In the kitchen in't it?"

"Yes Graeme, that's exactly where it is, in the bloody kitchen!" Cath yelled at Graeme. "Honestly, I don't know why I bother".

Beatrix clicked her door shut and opened the latch on her window. Felix jumped into the room and dropped the fish at her feet. Beatrix giggled silently into her hands. "Oh...my...goodness", she breathed. She bent down to pet Felix. He closed his eyes and purred magnanimously. "Shall we enjoy it a while, before I take it back to her". Felix's purring intensified, as if to say, I suppose so.

Beatrix would wait an hour, then take the fish back to her ma. It was too funny listening to her wail at Graeme for the time being, as if it were somehow his fault.

"Oh, yes, that's it!" Cincesse's excited voice distracted Beatrix from her daydreaming.

Pop.

Felix appeared in the air, falling nimbly to his feet. He looked rather confused. He sat down and stared at Beatrix as if to say, what the heck?

"Umm, yes?" Felix thought.

Beatrix opened her eyes. "Felix!" She dropped to her knees and scooped him up. He closed his eyes as she petted him.

"Can I help?" Felix thought.

"I channelled you, Felix!" Beatrix thought excitedly.

"Excuse me? I am not a spell". Felix seemed offended.

"Aren't you impressed?" Beatrix thought.

"Not particularly. I had just caught Katy".

"Eugh. Gross".

Felix waved his tail playfully.

"Says you", he thought.

"What's that supposed to mean?"

"Looks like you caught something yourself".

"Oh".

"Oh, indeed".

Cincesse was watching them curiously. "What's he saying?"

"Oh, nothing", Beatrix said quickly.

Felix opened his eyes lazily and flicked his tail at Cincesse.

"Hello, Felix", Cincesse said brightly, as she knelt to pet him. Felix closed his eyes again, enjoying the attention.

"She's rather good at this", Felix thought.

Beatrix felt a pang of jealousy.

Cincesse's cat meowed angrily.

"Oh, sorry Risk", Cincesse said.

"Risk?"

"Yes, that's her name", Cincesse said.

"Why?"

"It's a funny story..." Cincesse looked embarrassed.

"Tell me".

"No". Cincesse blushed.

Beatrix rolled her eyes. She didn't care that much. She was more interested in the moon. "So, what now? We've got our cats".

Cincesse looked a little flustered. "Aren't you excited; you just channelled your cat for the first time?"

"Oh, yeah, I was".

"You were?" Cincesse looked taken aback. "You did it rather quickly".

"I should have done it slower?"

"Do you have to take everything so literally?" Cincesse snapped. Truthfully, she was a little jealous. It had taken her several hours of practice to channel Risk for the first time. Beatrix made it look so easy.

"Sorry", Beatrix said, unsure what she had done to annoy Cincesse.

Cincesse sighed. "Well, perhaps the moon holds some mysteries that may yet excite you".

Beatrix grinned like a cheshire cat. "Yahoo!" She jumped up and punched the air like a kid.

Cincesse seemed to find this rather endearing. She placed her hand on Beatrix's arm and stepped in close. It was a soft touch, and their eyes met. "Are you ready?"

"Yes", Beatrix said breathlessly. Her heart had started beating fast again. She didn't know if it was the closeness of Cincesse, or the prospect of her imminent trip to the moon.

"Risk", Cincesse called her cat. Risk jumped up into her arms and wrapped himself around her neck. "Now you".

Beatrix looked bemused, but she called Felix, who did the same.

"Now take my hand".

Beatrix needed no further encouragement. She took Cincesse's hand. "What do I do?"

"Nothing".

Beatrix had butterflies in her stomach.

Cincesse started to glow softly. It was a soft thing. It reminded Beatrix of lavender, and doves. It wasn't gold like Gregor's glow, and it wasn't quite white like the aura she'd produced herself. It was like vanilla, or warm milk.

"Hold on tight", Cincesse whispered.

Beatrix opened her mouth, but there was no time to speak. "Woah, oh!"

They'd started levitating slowly. They were only a few feet off the floor, but Beatrix was exuberant. "Wooh, ooh! I'm flying!"

"Not yet you're not", Felix thought drily. "And I'm the one doing the flying".

"Shut it you!" Beatrix thought back.

"Charming", Felix thought.

Cincesse giggled. Beatrix's excitement was infectious.

"Woah!" Beatrix slid to the side, off-balance. In that moment, a spark shot from her hand, sizzling the grass beneath their feet.

"Wow" Cincesse said softly.

"Sorry", Beatrix said softly.

"So, it is true…"

"What?"

"You don't have to channel at all, do you?"

"I don't…I don't know". And that was the truth of the matter. Beatrix didn't know how she kept doing these apparently incredible feats of magic. They just happened.

Cincesse stared into her eyes, as if she thought Beatrix a wonderful thing. "Are you ready?"

Beatrix nodded.

"Then to the moon, we go".

Beatrix swallowed.

Cincesse looked up, and then they were flying upward, cats wrapped comfortably around their shoulders. Felix seemed to be rather enjoying the wind rushing past his face. He had his eyes closed and looked relaxed. Risk looked grumpy as ever.

"Woohoo!" Beatrix yelled, then closed her mouth as a bug flew into it. "Eugh, yuck".

Cincesse laughed. "Yes, it's best to keep your mouth shut".

Beatrix scowled.

She looked down. The pub and the barn were little specks in the distance now. They were travelling at quite some speed.

"Oh", she said with surprise, as they cleared the clouds. She smiled and ran her hand through the fluffy sky pillows.

Risk hissed loudly and lashed out with her paw, as a seagull swooped past them honking loudly.

Beatrix found this funny, but Cincesse looked nervous. "There, there, Risk".

They were climbing slowly now, above the clouds. The air was getting thinner. Suddenly, they came to a stop.

"Close your eyes", Cincesse instructed.

"Why?"

"It's just better if you do, trust me".

Beatrix obliged, then gasped as a bubble appeared over her face. "I can't breathe!" she gasped.

She heard a pop and opened her eyes.

A translucent bubble was now over Cincesse's face. "Yes, you can, calm down".

Beatrix looked like she was panicking and Cincesse gripped her face. "Breathe". Cincesse breathed slowly in and out through her nose, showing Beatrix what to do.

Beatrix copied her. After a while, her chest stopped heaving. "Thanks", she said sheepishly.

"So, you're not completely fearless", Cincesse mused.

Beatrix looked upset, at what she viewed as her cowardice. "Who says", she said defiantly.

"Me", Cincesse said challengingly.

Felix yawned.

"Are you ok?" Cincesse asked, breaking the rather charged silence that followed.

Beatrix nodded.

"Are you sure?"

"Yes, yes".

Cincesse nodded. Beatrix's bluster had returned. "It is rather uncomfortable, isn't it?" Cincesse tapped the bubble with her fingernail.

"Yeah, it's horrible, but I don't care if it gets me to the moon".

"That's the spirit". Cincesse looked upward again.

Beatrix knew what was coming next and braced herself.

"To the moon", Cincesse whispered.

The Moonlings

Beatrix held on grimly as they rocketed out of the atmosphere. She closed her eyes as the sky went dark around her.

Her ears popped, and she opened her eyes. "My god..."

"Incredible, isn't it?"

They were floating in orbit above the earth, in a sea of stars. They sparkled everywhere she looked, like luminescent little beacons, waypoints, in an uncharted ocean of adventure.

In front of them, sat the moon. It looked pensive. Or perhaps, apprehensive. Perhaps it sensed their approach.

Beatrix was crying. "It's the most beautiful thing I've ever seen...truly".

Cincesse was touched. She could feel the emotion coming from Beatrix. She knew what she was going through. She had felt the same.

She rubbed a tear from Beatrix's face.

Beatrix gasped as Cincesse's hand pierced the bubble around her.

"Don't worry", Cincesse said. "They're rather resilient".

Beatrix lowered her hand from her chest, then rocked backwards as a shooting star blistered past them. "Holy cow-"

"It's ok!" Cincesse assured her. "It's farther than it looks. Space is...big".

Beatrix felt foolish. She had been full of bravado when Cincesse first mentioned the moon. Now she was scared as a girl faced with her first hiding.

"Come on", Cincesse moved forward slowly.

They drifted toward the moon, hand in hand.

Beatrix looked back over her shoulder. "Wow", she mouthed silently.

The Earth looked divine. It was bathed in a soft white glow, that made Beatrix think of magic. Down there somewhere was the castle. Way down...

She looked forward. They were approaching fast, but it didn't feel like it. She frowned. Cincesse caught it. "It doesn't feel the same up here, does it?"

Beatrix shook her head.

"There's no wind, I think that's why".

Beatrix saw the sense in this.

"That looks as good a place as any". Cincesse was pointing to a patch of rocky ground marred by craters and hills.

"There we are". Cincesse touched down gracefully. Beatrix wobbled a little.

Cincesse closed her eyes again and squeezed Beatrix's hand. Beatrix felt a chill go through her.

"You can let go now", Cincesse said.

"What did you do?"

"Grounded you".

"Grounded me..."

"You won't fly off. Promise".

Beatrix looked down at the ground, then up at the endlessly black sky. It didn't feel very safe. It didn't feel very substantial up here. She felt like the slightest gust could blow her off her feet and send her spiralling into the abyss.

"You sure?"

"I promise".

Beatrix gently released Cincesse's fingers, watching her tensely, as if ready to snatch back Cincesse's hand at the smallest sign of danger.

"Told you", Cincesse said.

"Phew". Beatrix wiped her forehead, which was slick with sweat. She hadn't realised how worried she'd been.

"Oh, are we here?" Felix thought.

Beatrix spluttered. "Did you sleep through the **whole thing?**" She thought.

"Yes. Rather boring, wasn't it?"

"How would you know? You were **sleeping!**"

"And? You act like it's the first time I've been to the moon", Felix thought lazily.

"It isn't?" Beatrix was flabbergasted.

"Where do you think I go at night".

"I dunno...chasing cats...eating rats?"

"God, no. They taste something foul".

"Then why are you always bringing them into the house?"

"It's rather amusing".

"Amusing?"

Felix looked away haughtily and flicked his tail. "She doesn't like it".

"She..." Realisation dawned and Beatrix grinned. "You are a menace".

"Takes one to know one".

"True".

Cincesse frowned. "What is it?"

"Oh, nothing. Felix was just telling me about the moon".

"He's been before?" Cincesse looked surprised.

"Yeah. Why? Is that not normal?"

Cincesse didn't know what to say. "Not really..."

"Oh...well, Felix is a bit of a maverick".

Cincesse smiled weakly. "If you say so".

"So, this is the moon". Beatrix looked around expectantly. "Not much to do, is there?" She placed her hands on her hips.

Cincesse's mouth fell open.

"Are there any pubs?"

"Pubs?" Cincesse seemed at a loss.

"Yeah. This place could do with a pub. Liven it up a little".

"I am **SO** sorry that it doesn't live up to your expectations", a scratchy voice replied.

"AGHH!" Beatrix jumped backwards and tripped over her feet, falling to the floor with a thud. "What was that!"

There was a sound like a burrowing gopher, and a cloud of dust and rocks exploded out of the ground in front of Beatrix. Out of the cloud, popped a person.

The 'person' looked a bit like a human man, but there were some rather noticeable differences. The first being, their skin was completely white. Not white like snow, but milky white, like the surface of the moon. It was also slightly translucent and totally hairless. It looked a little like a suit made of velvet, rather than actual skin.

The second thing Beatrix noticed was the person had no ears, so Beatrix wasn't sure how it had heard her.

"What?" The person put its hand on its hips. "Are you just gonna stand there and gawk, or are ya gonna apologise for waking my chillun?"

In the distance Beatrix heard a wail. "Your...chillun?" She looked bemused.

"My chillun!" The person repeated angrily, pointing behind them to a small hill.

"I-" Beatrix didn't know what to say.

Cincesse started giggling into her hand.

Beatrix turned to her. "What? What did I-?"

Cincesse stepped forward, placing herself between Beatrix and the person. "Sorry, Tony. She's new".

Tony gave Beatrix an appraising look. He still looked a little agitated. "Yeah, well, just tell her to keep it down. I just got them down, and if Shelley comes back and hears em screamin I'm for it!" He drew his finger across his throat and Beatrix gasped. He only had three fingers!"

"Oh, what, you never seen a moonling before neither I guess?" Tony asked. "You people..."

He stood still for a moment, then started spinning in circles, like a drill. It was bizarre. His hands were by his sides, and he didn't seem to be producing any motion, yet somehow, he was spinning, like a translucent, spinning moon top. After a couple of seconds, he disappeared.

"He vanished!" Beatrix said.

"Well, he's got to get back to his children..."

"Oh, **children**". Beatrix hadn't understood him through the thick accent. "Who...**what** was that?"

"A moonling", Cincesse said simply.

"Am I supposed to know what that is?"

"They live on the moon".

"I gathered", Beatrix said drily.

"Shall we go?" Cincesse said brightly.

"Go where?"

"To the village".

"There's a village on the moon?"

"Oh, yes". Cincesse happily trotted off into the distance. They passed Tony's hill and another one soon came into sight.

"How far is it?"

"Oh, not far".

Beatrix rolled her eyes. Why was it no one in the magical community could ever provide accurate travel timelines? She'd even settle for an estimate.

To Cincesse's credit, not far actually turned out to be not far. After walking for five minutes or so, a huge, grey, rocky hill came into sight. It seemed to span as far as the eye could see. Beatrix couldn't see a way around it.

"What now?"

Cincesse hopped up to the hill and paused. She leant forward gingerly, knocked twice, then hopped back.

The hill moved, and a huge, grumpy face appeared. "Who is it?" The face grumbled.

"It's just me, Barry".

Barry scrunched his face up and his shoulders appeared, then an arm, then a hand. He pulled himself forward out of the hill slightly to get a better look. "Oh, it's you!" He smiled happily. Barry sunk back into the hill and turned his face out of sight. "Ere, Terry, it's pr-" It sounded like he was talking to someone next to him.

"Uh, Barry!" Cincesse shouted suddenly.

Barry paused, and his face appeared in the hill again. "What is it?"

"We're in something a hurry, today".

"Oh, alright. Sorry. Come in". Barry seemed a little disappointed. He disappeared, and the hill shimmered, then faded.

Beatrix gasped.

Behind the hill, was a carnival of activity. There were moonlings everywhere. Big ones, she assumed adults. And little ones, she assumed 'chillun', were cavorting all over the place. A young moonling skidded to a halt in front of her, kicking up dust as it slowed itself.

"Watch it, Eddie!" A shrill voice shrieked.

The moonling looked back over its shoulder, at what Beatrix assumed was its mother. She was leaning out the window of a thatched cottage with a disgruntled look on her face.

Smoke was lazily drifting from the chimney of the cottage, and another small youngling was playing in the dirt beneath the window.

The mother looked down at the wee one and smiled. She leant forward and rubbed the wee moonlings head.

The moonling pawed its mother's hand away distractedly and continued playing in the dirt. He was butting two sticks together into the dust, which was puffing up then hanging limply in the air.

"Got ya!" Another moonling child ran up and slapped Eddie on the back.

"OUW!" Eddie cried.

"No hitting!" The mother yelled.

The hitter smirked and ran off.

Eddie chased after.

Felix jumped down from her shoulder, and she gasped. She'd forgotten he was up there, with all the excitement. Risk joined him, and they padded away together into the village.

"Are they?" Beatrix started worriedly.

"They'll be fine", Cincesse assured her, watching the cats amble away.

Beatrix turned her attention back to the village. It was small. Much the same size as her own. There was a well in the centre, lined by houses and buildings on both sides. At the far end was what looked like a town hall. She guessed the bit they were in around the well was the 'town square'.

Just before the hall, she spotted a familiar looking building. She leant forward and squinted at it, shading her eyes against the glare from the stars above. "Is that?"

At that moment, the door to the building thundered open, and raucous laughter exploded out into the town.

"Har, har, har", a gruff voice roared. "And I'd like to see yer try, yeh pipsqueak". The gruff man slammed the door shut, then hawked and spat. He was rather stocky compared to the moonlings she'd seen so far. And he had a scar on his face, running from his right eye to his chin. He reminded Beatrix of a pirate.

A woman walked past the man, and he stuck his hand out, grabbing her arm. "Spare us a smoke, Maeve?"

Maeve shook his hand off. She looked disgusted. "Get off Buck, you pig!"

"Am I really that awful?" Buck closed his eyes and puckered his lips, like he expected Maeve to kiss him.

"Ugh!" She slapped him and walked off.

He rubbed his cheek and sat down in a rickety chair by the door. He pulled a small, grey pipe out of his pocket.

"Come on", Cincesse muttered, dragging Beatrix forward.

"But-"

"Come, **on**". Cincesse pulled her more insistently to the right, toward more cottages and shops.

"Aw, c'mon! He looks like a moon pirate!"

"He **is** a moon pirate!"

"What! Then we gotta go back! I bet he's got sherry!"

"Cmon!" Cincesse yanked her away. Beatrix looked past her, and Buck looked up. He smiled at her menacingly. He only had three teeth, and they were yellow.

Beatrix grimaced. "Aw, did you see? His teeth were yuck!" She found it rather excellent.

"No, I did not", Cincesse said primly.

"You're no fun", Beatrix said grumpily. "I thought you were fun".

Beatrix's last look was of a grim looking moonling stepping out of the building and standing over Buck. Buck looked rather serious. Then, they were out of sight.

"There's nothing cool about moon pirates", Cincesse said seriously.

"I'll be the judge of that", Beatrix said sassily.

This seemed to make Cincesse a little moody, and they walked in silence for a while.

The village was larger than it had initially seemed, but the cottages soon thinned, and so did the shops.

Cincesse took her hand. "This is not a nice part of town".

Beatrix frowned. It didn't look so bad to her.

"Moonrock, pretty missy?" A pungent smell hit her nostrils, like stinky, unwashed socks, and then a face assailed her senses. It was grinning, and there was not a single tooth in its mouth. "Best quality. I promise ya. You'll not fine' better".

It was a moonling, and it had a large, pitted rock clenched in its fist. Parts of it were shining like the stars, reflecting light this way and that.

Cincesse nimbly stepped to the side, pulling Beatrix with her. "No thank you", she said primly.

"What's a moonrock?" Beatrix asked.

"Don't ask".

Beatrix made a mental note to ask later, at the earliest possible convenience.

They'd reached the edge of the village now.

Cincesse paused and sighed longingly. "Isn't it wonderful?" She was looking down a long, sloping hill.

At the bottom, was a waterfall, spilling off a sharp rocky incline. The water was pooling into a bowl that was large enough to swim in. Around the bowl was what looked like sand.

It was the water that made Beatrix gasp, though. It was spilling slowly into the bowl below, like it was suspended in mid-air, like gravity didn't apply to it. Drip, drip, splash. As it joined the body of water in the bowl, little waves crept sneakily away in every direction. "Is that?"

Something about the water seemed familiar to Beatrix.

"Sea water? Yes".

The water wasn't quite aquamarine, but it wasn't quite milky white either, like most things on the moon. It was like…liquid crystal. Like little droplets of crystal, with sneaky stone-blue streaks running through them.

"Wow", Beatrix said.

"I know…"

"How did it get here?"

"Gregor", Cincesse said automatically. "Come on". She led Beatrix down the slope toward the bowl.

As they got closer, Beatrix heard a faint rushing. She smiled happily. The closer they got, the louder the rushing noise. But it was delayed. Slower. Sporadic. No, not sporadic, melodic. She'd been to a waterfall once before, and it was louder, and quicker. This was like music.

"Ooh". Cincesse skidded on the bottom of the verge.

Beatrix steadied her. "Careful".

Cincesse smiled, then walked to the edge of the bowl. She knelt and ran her fingers through the water, where they created little ripples. "Bea, come here".

Beatrix, who'd been standing watching her enjoy herself, walked over.

"Here". Cincesse pulled at her arm. Beatrix knelt. "Put your hand on mine". Cincesse held her hand in the water and spread her fingers.

Beatrix placed her hand on Cincesse's, and spread her fingers too, so they interlocked with Cincesse's.

Cincesse moved her hand side to side in the water. She had a childish wonder in her eyes. Beatrix watched her, and her heart swelled.

"Hey…" Beatrix softly turned her face.

Their eyes met.

Cincesse flushed and closed her eyes.

Beatrix placed her hand under Cincesse's chin, then kissed her, tenderly.

Cincesse opened her eyes.

Beatrix saw them widen.

"I really like you", Cincesse said quietly.

"Me too", Beatrix said.

Cincesse frowned.

"I mean I like you too!"

Cincesse giggled. "I hope so!"

Beatrix cursed inwardly. She'd ruined the moment. Cincesse was still staring fondly at her though, so maybe not.

"YAHOOO!" A hearty scream peeled out from the top of the waterfall.

"What the-!" Beatrix leapt backwards, as a figure came flying out of the sky.

"CAPN BUCKS'S BRAZEN BRAWS!"

The figure bombed into the centre of the bowl, splashing up a huge crescent of water.

"Back, back, back!" Beatrix quickly pulled Cincesse away from the bowl. The water fell on them in slower motion than it usually would, and they side stepped and dodged and danced and screamed, trying to avoid as much as possible. Enough landed on them that they were sufficiently peeved off.

"ARGHHH!" Beatrix shook herself off like a wet cat. An angry wet cat. "What the heck was that!" she yelled, storming into the centre of the bowl, where a moonling had just popped up in the centre of the pool.

"Oi! I said what the heck was that!" Beatrix approached the moonling and pushed it hard in the chest.

The moonling stumbled backward. It looked frightened.

"Well!" Sparks cracked in Beatrix's hair.

"Sorry!" The moonling held its hands up in surrender. "I was just bombin!"

"Just bombin? You got me soaked!" Beatrix turned round. "And Cincesse!" She gestured at Cincesse.

"Cincesse", the moonling muttered and snorted.

"Don't you laugh at me!" Beatrix pushed the moonling again. At that moment, a spark flew down her arm and connected with the moonling. It ran down the length of his body and then hit the water.

"UHHH" The moonling shook and juddered as the water electrified him.

"Oh, no!" Beatrix grabbed for the moonling, catching him as he stumbled backward. "I'm so sorry!"

The moonling looked dazed, but otherwise alright. "I'm fine", it mumbled. It looked a bit tired, but otherwise ok.

"I didn't mean to do that! Honestly!" Beatrix was flustered. "I mean, you peeved me off, and I wanted to whack you one...but the shocking... I didn't..."

Cincesse surged forward into the water. "I'm so sorry". She reached the moonling. "She really didn't. She's new, you know".

The moonling nodded. "Figured". He was giving Beatrix an appraising look. A speculative look. Beatrix wasn't sure what to make of it.

The moonling straightened itself and patted itself down. "I'm Tiger". It began preening a tiny black mustache above its top lip, then extended its hand to Beatrix.

Beatrix took it. "Nice to meet you…Tiger".

"Pleasure's all mine". Tiger sketched a courtly bow.

Beatrix snorted. "If you say so".

"And your lady friend?" Tiger asked.

"This is Cincesse". Beatrix introduced Cincesse, who was unusually quiet.

"Pleased to meet you". Tiger shook her hand too. "What are you two nightriders doin out here?"

Beatrix frowned and looked at Cincesse.

"It's what we call witches. Well, one of the things".

"There's more?" Beatrix seemed dubious.

Tiger grinned. "Plenty. Why don't you come down to the tavern and I'll-"

"Uh, we will be doing nothing of the sort, thank you **Tiger**". Cincesse gave him a warning look, as if to say, hands off.

"Come on, Bea, we should be getting back. We've been gone rather a long time already", Cincesse said.

"Oh, shoot, yeah!" Beatrix smiled pleasantly at Tiger. "See ya later, Tiger. Maybe I'll come visit sometime".

Cincesse gave Tiger a dark look and drew Beatrix away.

Tiger watched them cautiously start climbing the hill back to the village. "Some woman", he said wistfully, watching Beatrix pick her way up the hill.

A Reckoning

Beatrix could tell something was seriously wrong as soon as they landed. Her stomach felt queasy and unsettled.

They'd landed on the other side of the barn, a short walk from the pub, in a wooded area far from prying eyes.

As they emerged from the shade of the trees, a scream came from the pub.

"The pub!" Beatrix yelled.

They glanced at each other, then started running toward the pub as fast as they could.

"Ahyah, ya bassard!" A gruff, coarse voice yelled.

The sound of steel on steel rang out, and Beatrix paused. She turned white as a sheet.

"Jimmy, no!" It was a woman's voice, wailing piteously. "Get off him!"

She heard a grunt, then a sound like the ripping of wet cloth. "JIMMY NOOO!"

Beatrix ran around the side of the pub, and staggered, as she took in what was going on.

It was pandemonium.

There were knights everywhere. Blood everywhere. Panic everywhere. Everywhere she looked there were frightened faces and frightened eyes.

She watched a knight kick a man to the floor. The man hit hard and tried to get up, but the knight plunged his sword deep into the man's chest.

Beatrix watched as blood sprayed from the man's mouth, as he coughed red to his chest.

She stood, transfixed, paralysed, unable to move, as the slaughter went on around her.

Cincesse stood rigidly beside her, hand clasped over her mouth.

A group of men ran into sight from around the other corner. They were villagers, and they were armed with pitchforks, axes, and hammers. They charged into the knights and fell upon them, stabbing, hacking, and bludgeoning.

The knight who'd murdered the villager went down under a flurry of blows.

A hunting horn rang out from the roof of the pub.

It was the young lad from earlier, the friend of the harpist. He was issuing a call on the horn so that the surrounding hamlets might hear and come to their aid.

A knight, in golden armour at the centre of the fighting, looked up at the sound. He was fighting a villager and looked irritated that he couldn't deal with the lad on the roof.

The villager aimed a clumsy blow at the knight with a hatchet. The knight lazily stepped in and blocked the villager's arm, then threw him over his hip. He raised his boot, then stepped down hard on the villager's neck.

Beatrix turned away as a horrible crack rang out.

The horn rang out again.

The knight knelt and prised the hatchet out of the villager's hand. He hefted it once for weight, then drew his arm back and threw it fiercely at the lad on the roof. It flew true and caught him straight in the chest. The lad stumbled forward and fell from the roof.

Beatrix turned back at the sound of the lad falling.

The knight sniffed, then turned to assess the battlefield, using the moments peace wisely to judge the ebb and flow of the battle.

Beatrix stumbled forward from the side of the pub. Her eyes were glued to the lad, who was now lying on his back, staring sightlessly into the sky.

The knight stared at Beatrix and frowned. Then he smiled as realisation hit him, and stepped forward. "Beatrix...Bellafonte".

Beatrix hadn't heard.

Cincesse looked terrified. She ran forward and tugged at Beatrix's arm. "Bea, we must leave, it isn't safe".

The knight strode toward Beatrix. A villager ran at him screaming, and he sidestepped and chopped the villager's neck.

The knight continued talking as he walked. "You've caused me a lot of hassle, you know".

Another villager lunged at him with a crude sword, and he stepped backwards. The villager stumbled forward, off balance, and the knight brought his elbow crashing down on the back of the villager's head.

"A lot of hassle indeed...and I don't like hassle".

Beatrix was transfixed. She was walking slowly closer to the young lad on the floor, as if in a dream.

"Beatrix, please!" Cincesse wailed, pulling at her arm.

"Your friend is right, you know", the knight said, as he came closer to the girls.

Cincesse looked up and her eyes widened in terror.

"You really shouldn't have come here", the knight said grimly.

Beatrix seemingly didn't, or couldn't, hear him. She'd reached the villager now and knelt beside him. "So still", she said quietly.

"What do you want", Cincesse asked shakily.

"A good question", the knight said amicably. He unsheathed his sword and turned it, admiring it in the light. "But I don't think you'll like the answer". He grinned darkly and advanced on Cincesse.

"Wh-what do you want!" Cincesse said more forcefully. "We have done nothing wrong!"

The knight seemed amused at this. "Oh, is that right?" He turned and looked as though he were looking for someone. "Oh, sister!" He called as though he were in a pantomime, and this was all just fanfare.

He beckoned at a woman stood in front of the pub with her arms crossed serenely behind her back. She was ringed by three knights.

The woman looked curiously across at the knight.

The knight beckoned to her. "I think you'll like this!" he called.

The woman sighed, and walked toward the knight, flanked by her guards.

"We're just Text Keepers!" Cincesse said quickly. "I don't know what you think you are doing, but I assure you, you are mistaken!"

"Is that right?" The knight took another step toward Cincesse and began twirling his sword like a baton. He lunged toward her, and she stumbled back, losing her footing.

The knight laughed and continued twirling his sword. He threw it into the air, spun in a circle, and caught it on his forehead, butt first.

"You see, I have another theory", he said, eyes on his sword, as he balanced it on his forehead.

"And what...what is that?" Cincesse stammered, climbing to her feet and stepping back toward the pub. She jumped as she felt her back hit the wall.

Beatrix ran her hand softly over the lad's forehead, brushing his hair back out of his eyes. "So still..."

The knight sunk to his haunches, and sprung upright, doing a smaller twirl and catching the sword again. "You see, I think, you're **lying**".

"Is this what death is?" Beatrix asked. "This stillness...this nothing".

The woman approached the knight. "What is it?" She looked irritated.

The knight smiled. "I've a present for you".

The woman narrowed her eyes. She didn't think much of the knights' antics, clearly.

The knight let his sword slide forward off his head. He caught the blade between his hands.

"Oh, come now. Not even a smile?"

"What is it?" The woman said coldly.

The knight sighed. "Not a theatrical bone in your dried-up old body", he muttered.

"What was that?" The woman hissed.

"Nothing, nothing. Fine, there". The knight pointed at Beatrix.

"Goodnight", Beatrix said softly. "You can sleep now..." She gently closed the lad's eyes.

The woman's mouth fell open. "The dark one!"

"BEATRIX!" Cincesse shrieked.

Cincesse's cry pierced Beatrix's fugue, and she looked up quickly. "You". Her voice filled with venom as she took in the woman.

"Me". The woman replied, equally venomously.

It was Mistress Madele, The Sacred Sister from Beatrix's village.

"Well, isn't this wonderful?" The knight was looking jovially back and forth between Beatrix and Madele. "You two back together".

"SEIZE HER!" Madele screamed.

Her knights moved forward, but at that moment, a huge shockwave exploded from the pub, and everyone was thrown from their feet.

Beatrix moaned. Her ears were ringing, and she couldn't see properly. There was a haze in the air. Like when it's really hot and the air ripples.

She heard a scream then, and then more joined it.

She blinked hard to clear her eyes, trying to see what was going on.

Cincesse moaned softly a few feet away from her.

"Cincesse!" Beatrix crawled over to her. She was face down with her eyes closed. Beatrix pulled her close. "Cincesse! Are you ok?"

"Mmm", Cincesse moaned weakly.

A sound rang out like thunder.

A woman was…floating in front of the pub. Her hair was floating too, around her face. It was eerie. She floated forward a few paces, then her hand shot out. A gust of wind lanced from it toward a knight. It was like an arrow of wind, and it shot through his armour like it were made of paper. The knight crumpled instantly to the floor.

"Is that…" Beatrix couldn't look away from the woman. "It's Madame Tempest!"

Her hand shot out again, and another knight crumpled.

A group of knights came running from the side of the pub and locked shields. They advanced cautiously on Madame, shields in front of their faces.

"Fools!" Madame hissed. She clapped her hands together and a small wind began spinning at her feet.

The knights grinned at one another and advanced on her with less caution. If this was all she had, what worry was there?

Madame moved her hands in circles, and the wind began spinning faster and faster, until it resembled a baby hurricane.

The knights paused.

Madame screamed, and in seconds, the wind was a tempest. It flew forward and erupted with a howling bang. The knights disappeared as the tempest consumed them.

"Well, I better deal with the wench". The cocky knight, who'd been twirling his sword, got to his feet and brushed himself down.

Beatrix saw then that it was Gladius. Hate rushed through her. She wanted nothing more than to rip him to pieces.

Cincesse gripped her arm. "Beatrix!"

Gladius strolled toward Madame.

Her hand shot out and another wind arrow flew from it.

Gladius sword moved, seemingly of its own volition, to block the arrow. He staggered slightly as it hit his sword but kept advancing forward.

Madame's hand shot forward again, and again.

Each time Gladius blocked it with his sword. He was close now, and grinned.

"Rather attractive for a witch, aren't you?" Gladius said smugly.

Madame snarled, and both hands shot forward firing gales of wind at him.

Gladius grunted and staggered. He couldn't move forward under the weight of the wind buffeting his sword.

Madame screamed, and Gladius fell to his knees as the force of the wind intensified. It was blowing all around him now. His sword started to crack.

Madame tensed, as if preparing to finish him, but a rushing noise made her suddenly fly backward.

A brutal wind rushed outwards from where Madame had been standing, and Beatrix fell backwards, banging her head against the pub wall.

"This one's mine". A woman had landed in front of Madame. She was tall, haughty looking, and wearing a fur coat that came down to her knees.

"In your dreams", Madame hissed.

"Oh, I dream of many things darling. You are not one of them".

Madame fired a wind arrow at the woman. It hit her, and she didn't even flinch.

"Is that all you have for me?"

Madame fired more arrows. Again, and again, and again. Each time it hit the woman, she didn't flinch or show any reaction. In fact, she had started to glow. White. Like the first snow of winter. Pure, blinding, cold, white. It felt dangerous. It felt different.

"Well, if that will be all". The woman shrieked and soundwaves exploded from her mouth.

Beatrix clapped her hands to her ears. It was an awful, otherworldly sound. She saw Madame go flying. She landed with a thud in the middle of the grass and moaned weakly.

The woman walked over to Madame. "Call yourself a witch?" She sounded disgusted and shook her head. "What are they teaching you at that **school?**" She seemed to mutter this last to herself.

Madame had blood on her mouth. She glared up at the newcomer. "More than you'll **ever** know, **old one**", she hissed.

This seemed to incense the woman. "How dare you..." She stepped forward as if she might finish Madame, then stopped, seemingly bringing her temper under control. "Very clever. But there'll no swift death for you, Miri. Yours shall be a painful passing, with lots of delightful screaming". She brightened at this. "Delightful, delightful screaming".

"I don't think so".

A fireball flew from the door to the pub.

It hit the woman and engulfed her in an inferno.

At that moment, Madame rolled forward and encased her in wind.

The wind burned, and the woman staggered under the combined force of their spells.

A group of villagers came into sight, led by the harpist. "Get her!"

They ran toward the woman.

"There'll be another day". She spoke quietly, sibilantly, but all heard it. And then she was gone, flying upward like a rocket into the sky.

A shockwave rippled out from where she'd launched, and the villagers fell to their knees.

Gregor clapped his hands, and the villagers fell asleep. "Are you alright?" He ran to Madame and helped her to her feet.

She was limping and he helped her to a seat at one of the remaining tables. "I'll be fine. Go", she said.

Gregor disappeared. He popped back a moment later leading two girls. He disappeared, then reappeared several more times, each time with more girls.

It looked like everyone had managed to find somewhere to hide, because all the girls were accounted for.

Eventually just Beatrix and Cincesse remained.

Gregor approached them and knelt by Cincesse. He ran his hand over her face. She awoke. She looked sleepy, but otherwise alright. "Come on, we need to go".

Beatrix looked down at Mistress Madele. "What about her", she hissed viciously, lunging toward the mistress.

"Later", Gregor said warily, pulling her back. "There'll be time for a reckoning yet".

Beatrix looked like she might argue, but she heard more popping behind Gregor. There was more than just her vengeance at stake here.

She helped Cincesse to her feet. They both took Gregor's hand and found themselves on the hillside in the trees.

Madame and the girls were already there.

"Link hands", Madame called weakly.

The hillside glowed, and the girls disappeared.

Betrayed

Beatrix and her friends were in their beds. Madame and Gregor had hurried them upstairs and bade them goodnight.

Beatrix was quietly thoughtful, as her friends discussed the events of the night.

Lucrecia was upset she'd missed out.

"Yeah, it was wicked!" Edni exclaimed. "You should have seen Madame. Wow. She really kicked the heck out of that other woman".

"Where were you?" Beatrix frowned. She hadn't seen Edni at all the entire evening.

"Yes, where?" Gwinni frowned too.

"What do you mean where?" Edni blustered. She seemed a little off-balance. "I was there, same as you!"

"But we didn't see you". Beatrix and Gwinni looked at each other.

"So? Doesn't mean I wasn't there. Maybe I didn't want you to see me", Edni said haughtily.

"And why is that?" Beatrix asked.

Edni crossed her arms. "None of your business".

Gwinni blinked. She seemed surprised. "Is that so?"

"And what's it to you", Edni said defensively. "Sounds like you had a good time".

Gwinni blushed. "And what if I did?"

Edni shrugged. "You can do what you want. Just like me".

"And what's that supposed to mean?" Gwinni looked concerned.

Edni shrugged again and rolled over so that she wasn't facing Gwinni anymore.

Gwinni watched her.

Beatrix sighed. "You didn't miss much, Luce".

"Oh, rubbish. It sounds like you had a wonderful time", Lucrecia said.

Beatrix smiled knowingly. "It was alright, I suppose".

Gwinni snorted.

"What?" Beatrix said.

"Nothing", Gwinni said.

Lucrecia's eyes bounced between the two older girls.

"You can come next time", Beatrix said.

"Really?" Lucrecia's eyes lit up and she lay forward over the end of her bed, head in her hands, eyes fixed on Beatrix.

"Of course", Beatrix said cockily. "I'll sneak you out!"

Edni rolled back over. "And how are you going to do that?" She gave Beatrix a piercing stare.

"Just will", Beatrix said airily.

Lucrecia smiled happily. "Thanks, Bea".

"Don't worry about it", Beatrix waved her hand magnanimously. She felt a little uncomfortable. Edni was creeping her out. She wasn't usually so serious.

"What do you care?" Gwinni cut in to Edni. "You don't spend any time with us anyway".

Edni rolled her eyes and turned her back on Gwinni again. "You could spend time with **me**, you know", she mumbled quietly.

Gwinni heard, but didn't say anything.

Lucrecia frowned. "One thing I don't understand...is how The Sacred Sisters found you in the first place".

Beatrix thought she had a good point.

"Yes, I've been thinking about that too", Gwinni said.

"You have?" Lucrecia blinked.

Gwinni nodded. "And there's really only one explanation".

"What's that?" Beatrix asked.

"Someone must have betrayed us", Gwinni said.

There was a foreboding silence as this sunk in.

"Someone from the village", Gwinni said.

"Or someone from the school", Lucrecia said quietly.

It didn't bear thinking about, and they all looked at each other uncomfortably.

"No, I don't believe it. I refuse to believe another witch would...do that. And why? For what reason?" Beatrix looked shaken.

Lucrecia shrugged. "It's happened before".

"It has?" Gwinni sounded surprised.

Lucrecia nodded. "Some witches used to give up other witches to throw the sisters off the scent".

"That's ghastly!" Gwinni said.

"I know", Lucrecia said quietly. "They'd do it when they were worried about being exposed".

"There's no justification for…that". Gwinni looked horrified.

Beatrix shook her head sadly. "Just people being people".

"That's very cynical", Lucrecia said astutely.

"It's hard not to be". Beatrix seemed a little different after the events at the pub. A little sadder. A little greyer.

After a while, Gwinny said, "And who was that woman?"

Beatrix frowned, then she remembered. "Oh, her".

Gwinny nodded.

"I don't know", Beatrix said.

"Me either". Gwinny shrugged. "But she did some rather peculiar magic".

"She did?" Beatrix looked interested.

Gwinny nodded. "Not like any I've seen before. And she made Madame looked like a Novi".

Beatrix nodded. She hadn't thought about the finer details much yet, but Gwinni was right.

"And Madame seemed so powerful before the woman landed", Gwinni continued.

"Landed?" Lucrecia said.

Gwinni nodded. "She just dropped, out of the sky, like a comet. There was a massive…force…when she landed. It knocked everyone to the floor".

"Wow", Lucrecia said.

"She was very powerful...Madame hit her with everything she had, but it did nothing", Gwinni said.

Lucrecia looked like she couldn't believe it. It was well known Madame was the most powerful witch in the school.

"It took her **and** Gregor to drive her back...and to be honest, I'm not even sure it was that. I think she just didn't want to be exposed", Gwinni said.

"What makes you say that?" Beatrix asked.

"Well, as soon as the villagers arrived, she left", Gwinni said.

Beatrix hadn't thought of it like that, but it made sense.

"Perhaps she didn't want to be identified by any villagers", Gwinni said.

"And why is that?" Beatrix asked.

"Well...she's an incredibly powerful witch, that no one has ever seen before. Where did she come from? Where does she live? Who is he?" Gwinni asked.

They were valid questions.

"You think she's a villager, that she lives in a village somewhere?" Beatrix asked.

"Well, no. I don't think she is a commoner. But she doesn't come from here. And she must come from somewhere", Gwinni said. "Perhaps Brightcastle. A woman of her power, of her...magnetism".

"I can see her as a lady", Beatrix said.

Gwinni nodded. "A lady would be fitting. A position of power. High station".

"So, you're telling me that somewhere out there". Beatrix stood and gestured out the window. "Is the most powerful witch in the land. A witch so powerful she can make Madame look like a child. A witch so powerful, that no one even knows what spells she cast...or what type of magic she uses. And to top it all off, she's leading a double life, and is probably a lady or a noble in the city".

Gwinni nodded.

"Well, that stinks". Beatrix screwed her face up.

"Rather", Gwinni agreed.

Edni had remained rather quiet throughout all this.

"Nothing to say?" Gwinni asked Edni, trying to engage her in discussion.

Edni shrugged. "Sounds like a bit of a cow".

Beatrix snorted.

"And why is that?" Gwinni asked.

Edni faced her. "Well, if what you say is true, she's in league with The Sacred Sisters. And she's hunting her own kind, whilst pretending to be normal herself".

Beatrix nodded.

"I take it back", Edni said suddenly. "She's not a cow. She's vile. And evil. And I hope Madame burns her alive". She rolled back over and lay down, as if to go to sleep.

"Well", Gwinni said. "We've all had a long day".

Lucrecia huffed.

"Most of us", Gwinni corrected. "We should probably go to sleep.

Beatrix agreed. "Felix", she thought.

Felix hopped into bed with her, and she drew her drapes.

"Gnight", Beatrix mumbled.

"Goodnight", Lucrecia said. She sounded rather disappointed the theorising was over.

"When can we go back to the moon?" Felix thought.

Beatrix snorted quietly into her pillow and closed her eyes.

A Sidequest

Beatrix tossed and turned.

Beside her, Felix fidgeted too.

"No", she moaned. "I can't do it".

Lucrecia's eyes opened.

It was dark, but the dawn was close. It was hard to tell under the sea, but it did get lighter the closer it got.

"You can do it!" The woman hissed through Beatrix's mind.

"I can't", Beatrix wailed.

"You can!"

"AHHH!" Beatrix screamed suddenly, and jolted upright, wideawake. Her hair was drenched in sweat, and it was coursing down her face. She was breathing heavily.

Lucrecia padded across the room and got into bed with her. "What is it?"

"I don't-" Beatrix's eyes were wild and panicked.

"Shh", Lucrecia said. "Lie back". She pulled Beatrix back down into the bed. "It was a bad dream".

Beatrix lay back and her eyes closed. "Mmm". She fell back asleep quickly.

Lucrecia rubbed her hand delicately across Beatrix's face. She smiled contentedly and snuggled down deeper under the blanket, closing her eyes.

When they awoke, it was morning, and there was movement in the room.

Edni was stomping about. "Where is my pinafore! Grrr!" She swung on Gwinni. "Did you move it? You're always moving it!"

"I haven't touched your pinafore! Why would I!" Gwinni snapped back.

"Because you're always interfering with my stuff! You can't help yourself! Bloody clean freak!" Edni yelled.

"You could do with being a little cleaner! I'm always finding your socks everywhere!" Gwinni replied.

"Well stop touching them! I like them where I like them!" Edni said.

"Which is in **my bed!**" Gwinni snapped.

"No, it isn't!" Edni snapped back.

Beatrix groaned. "Ohhh". She stretched her hands stiffly into the air. "Will you two shut up!" She snapped, eyes still closed. "It's too early for this!"

Edni narrowed her eyes at Beatrix and stomped out of the room. Gwinni watched her go, then returned to folding her clothes.

Lucrecia smacked her lips and rolled over. It looked like she didn't want to get up and was enjoying the body heat provided by Beatrix and Felix immensely.

Across the room, Katy the cat was enjoying the bed to herself. She looked very regal, tucked half under the covers, eyes closed, head elevated slightly on the pillow.

"Grrr", Beatrix growled. "I'm tired".

Lucrecia opened her eyes. "Good morning", she said dreamily, before closing her eyes again.

"I dunno about good..." Beatrix grumbled.

"I slept brilliantly. Did you?" Lucrecia seemed to not want to discuss Beatrix's nightmare. Or perhaps she thought it best not to.

"Not really", Beatrix said. "Hey, why are you in my bed?"

"Oh, sorry", Lucrecia said dreamily. "Sometimes I sleepwalk".

"Oh. Well, we better get up".

"I suppose".

When they arrived in the great hall, Edni and Gwinni were sitting opposite each other in a frosty silence.

Beatrix sunk into her chair with a grunt and pulled a tureen of potatoes toward her.

Edni's lip curled in disgust.

Beatrix flashed her a warning glare, that said, don't even start.

She poured gravy over a large helping of potatoes, then sat eating them like she'd just got out of prison; head down, eyes glancing shiftily side to side, elbows stuck out protectively, lest someone try to nick a potato.

"Good morning", Gwinni looked up, chancing some conversation.

"Morning", Beatrix grunted.

"Did you sleep well?" Gwinni asked.

"Not really", Beatrix said.

"Oh". A look passed between Gwinni and Lucrecia. Beatrix didn't see.

"Well, we have lots to do today, I hope you'll be ok", Gwinni said.

Beatrix groaned. "Let me have it".

"Well, Gregor asked me-"

"Gregor?" Beatrix seemed more attentive at this.

"Yes...Gregor asked me if we'd help Dimitri with a little problem of his-"

"Not the bloody swordfish". Beatrix groaned.

"Oh, yes, err-". Gwinni seemed taken aback.

"Sorry". Beatrix shook her head. "Go on".

"Yes, it's about the swordfish...apparently Dimitri has been having problems with them, and Gregor, well he asked if you and I might help him".

"You and I? What do I know about swordfish?"

Gwinni shrugged apologetically. "I thought we might come up with some sort of solution. Perhaps an electrified fence of sorts".

"An electrified fence?" Beatrix snorted. "What a stupid idea".

Gwinni looked crestfallen.

Beatrix sighed heavily. "Fine. What else?"

"Well, this morning we have Scrying".

"Scrying? What's that?" Beatrix had gravy dripping down her chin. She'd just swallowed a huge mouthful of potato. Gwinni affected not to notice.

"Finding things".

"Things?" Beatrix said through a mouthful of potato.

Edni smirked.

"Yes". Gwinni nodded cautiously. "Things. People. Scrying".

Beatrix put her fork down and swallowed. **"People?"**

Gwinni nodded.

"Is it a little circle?"

Gwinni frowned. She looked like she was thinking. "Circle-"

"Gregor did a little circle and showed me my parents".

Gwinni blinked in surprise. "Yes, I suppose that's one way to do it. That might be a bit advanced for us though".

Beatrix looked like she didn't think much of this. "Then what?"

"Well, I expect we'll start with other students. Try and find them. Horace has us hide, and then we try to scry them out".

"How do we do that?"

"We find The Place, then think of them".

"Doesn't sound very **magical**", Beatrix scoffed.

"Well, there's a bit more to it..."

Beatrix waved her hand airily. "Fine, let's scry". She got up suddenly from her seat and brushed herself down. "Where is it?"

"Uhh".

Beatrix stared expectantly at her.

"Horace's classroom is in the castle...near the big window that looks onto the sea".

Beatrix nodded. "I know where it is". She pushed her chair in. "I'll see you there".

Lucrecia sat down quietly next to Gwinni as Beatrix left.

"Is she alright?" Gwinni asked Lucrecia.

Lucrecia nodded quietly. "Just tired".

"Oh", Gwinni said, watching Beatrix leave the hall. She wasn't the only one with her eyes on Beatrix. "Well, I hope she's alright. Scrying requires rather a lot of patience".

Beatrix stomped her way through the castle until she came to the window. The window from her dreams. She looked to her right. There was the wall she'd blown a hole through. There was a corner to the right. She guessed the door to the classroom was just around it.

She leant forward on the stone sill and gazed out the window. The sea was hypnotic, and she felt her eyes drooping shut. Before long she was dozing.

*"No, no, no!" The voice snapped like a whip. "How many times do I have to tell you? You don't have to **channel!**"*

"I don't get it!" The little girl's voice cried.

*"You are not a **witch!**" The woman replied coldly.*

"Why not?" The little girl asked defiantly.

"Witches channel, we do not".

The little girl crossed her arms petulantly. "Don't care".

The woman's face turned icy cold, and the little girl paled. "You'll learn", the woman said quietly, with infinite menace in her voice.

"Beatrix". Beatrix felt a hand on her arm and her eyes snapped open.

"Oh! Careful!" A girl's voice cried.

Beatrix fell sideways as her arm slipped off the sill.

The girl caught her. "Are you ok?" It was Cincesse. She looked concerned.

"Sorry", Beatrix said. "I'm fine".

"You look tired". Cincesse was looking at her like a mother.

Beatrix sighed and shrugged.

"I've missed you", Cincesse said quietly.

Beatrix had missed her too, truth be told, but she was too tired for much in the way of affection. "Missed you too". She was looking past Cincesse as she said this, at the approaching students.

"It doesn't sound like it", Cincesse said haughtily.

Beatrix sighed. "What do you want from me? I'm tired!"

Cincesse pursed her lips. "Nothing at all". She spun away and walked over to her minions, who accepted her graciously back into their midst immediately. The minions began to mutter quietly, casting accusing looks at Beatrix all the while, while rubbing Cincesse's back consolingly.

"Ah, to hell with it", Beatrix grumbled. "I can't be bothered with this". She turned the corner and walked into the classroom.

Horace turned around from a black chalkboard, a look of surprise on his face. "Oh, Miss Bellafonte". He looked at a strange device on his wrist. "I wasn't expecting you yet".

Beatrix sighed deeply and opened her mouth, but Horace hastily cut her off. "But it's fine. Why don't you take a seat there?" He gestured at a table and chair at the front of the room near the chalkboard.

Beatrix slouched over and threw herself into the seat. She sat, head in hand, eyes drooping closed and snapping open every now and then.

After a while, students began filing into the classroom. The room filled around her.

Gwinni took the seat to her left and gave her a reassuring smile.

Beatrix smiled back tiredly.

Horace cleared his throat. "Good morning, ladies".

"Good morning, professor", the girls chimed back.

Beatrix pursed her lips and said nothing. She crossed her arms grumpily and stared at Horace as if to say, "I dare you".

Horace affected not to notice. "Now then, shall we begin?" He turned to the chalkboard and wrote a single word on it. Scrying.

He turned back to face the class. "Scrying". He nodded. "What do we know about it?"

A hand raised excitedly, Gwinny's.

Horace nodded at her.

"It's finding things, professor", Gwinny said.

Horace nodded again. "That's right". He wrote 'finding things' on the chalkboard. "What else?"

Gwinny frowned. Was this not it?

Horace looked expectantly around the room. "No?"

Silence.

Horace wrote something else on the chalkboard. They couldn't see it until he turned back to face them. It said, 'finding that which cannot be found'.

It was Beatrix's turn to frown. She uncrossed her arms and sat straighter in her seat.

Horace nodded as the girls began to mutter. "That's right. Scrying is not just finding things, or people. It's finding things that cannot be found. That do not **wish** to be found".

Beatrix licked her lips.

"The power of Scrying is really down to the witch. Or wizard".

The girls sniggered at this.

"That's right, even wizards can scry".

The girls booed.

"I know, I know", Horace said amiably. He seemed to find this amusing too. But then, he wasn't a 'wizard' in the traditional sense. He was a goblin. They were different.

"How hard you can scry, depends on how hard you can feel. How hard you can search. How hard you can **pull**". He wrote these three words on the chalkboard. Feel. Search. Pull.

"Scrying isn't about finding a pair of socks, or a lost pinafore under the bed".

Gwinni clapped her hand to her head, as if she'd just remembered something.

"It's about **finding something**. Truly finding something. Something once **found**, can never be truly lost".

The class had gone quiet.

"To truly **scry**, you must truly know".

The girls were hanging on his every word.

"Now, stand up then, and let's give it a try".

The girls seemed surprised. This was rather anticlimactic. They thought they were on the verge of a profound revelation.

There was a lot of scraping as they pushed back their chairs and got to their feet.

"Now, turn around, and look at the girl behind you".

Beatrix obliged. There was no girl directly behind her, the seat was empty. In the seat behind that, was Cincesse, who looked away.

"Picture her in your mind. Now, turn back to the front. I want you to hold that picture in your mind".

Some of the girls closed their eyes.

Beatrix sighed wearily and did the same.

"Hold it. And now, find The Place. Relax your minds. Let them drift. But do not forget the picture. Keep it present, floating, in the back of your mind. Once you find The Place, let the picture move forward".

Beatrix frowned. She was struggling to find the place. She sighed. This was stupid. She just wanted to draw the bloody circle.

"There, there, that's fine".

Clio had opened her eyes and stomped down on the floor. "I can't do it!" She wailed. "Everytime I picture Eli, I lose The Place!"

"It's quite alright", Horace said. "I don't expect you to be able to do it the first time".

Horace droned on then, talking about the importance of relaxing the mind.

Behind Beatrix, Cincesse and her minions were whispering. Beatrix became agitated. What were they talking about? She looked back over her shoulder. Cincesse was whispering animatedly to Eli and Clio, and they were giggling. What was so funny? Were they talking about her?

"Miss Bellafonte, if you please". Horace tapped a pointer on her desk.

Beatrix gritted her teeth and turned her attention forward as Cincesse started giggling too. She closed her eyes and took a deep breath. "Find The Place", she muttered. She began to relax.

"Good", Horace said, eyes on Beatrix.

He turned back to the chalkboard and began scratching something down.

Beatrix frowned. She felt weird. Her mind was like a maze. It felt like she was turning down dead ends and empty tunnels.

More giggling from behind.

She scrunched her face up.

"You don't need to channel!" The voice surged through her mind like a bolt of lightning.

At that moment, a piece of parchment soared through the air, shaped like an eagle. It had a sharp end, and it struck Beatrix on the back of the neck.

Beatrix's eyes burst open, and a flash of light escaped them. She jerked in her seat and sprung to her feet, like she'd just had a particularly violent twitch. "No!" She screamed.

"Woahhh!" Another voice cried.

There was a crash and a wobble.

"Uff". Beatrix fell backwards over her chair.

"Agh!" A girl screamed.

"What is going-" Horace paused.

Beatrix was on the floor, and Cincesse was on top of her.

"What is...what have..." Horace looked at a loss for words.

Cincesse pushed herself quickly to her feet. "What happened?" She asked breathlessly. She looked panicked.

Beatrix sat up, but remained on the floor, hands pressed out behind her, like she was too tired to get up.

"What did you do!" Cincesse cried.

"Nothing", Beatrix said tiredly. "I didn't do anything..."

Cincesse scampered away from Beatrix to hide behind Horace. "Yes, you did! We all saw you!"

Beatrix sighed and pushed herself to her feet. "I didn't do anything...one minute you were there...then you were here. Maybe the spell worked. I don't know". She spread her hands.

Cincesse moved toward Beatrix, as if to tell her off, but Horace stuck his arm out, blocking her. "Yes, thank you, that will be enough for now". He looked confused, and a little worried.

"But she-" Cincesse began.

"I said **enough**, Miss Loiyaté".

"Loiyaté?" Beatrix mouthed. So that's Cincesse's family name. It was odd.

Cincesse narrowed her eyes petulantly. She crossed her arms and stormed back to her chair. She sat down with a huff, and her minions immediately leant in close and started whispering.

Horace walked over to Beatrix and helped her right her desk and chair. "Are you alright, Miss Bellafonte?"

Beatrix nodded. She wasn't. But she didn't want any more attention. Truthfully, she didn't have a clue what happened, or what she'd done.

Horace nodded and returned to his chalkboard. "Well then, I think for the rest of the lesson, we will focus on this".

He wrote a series on instructions on the whiteboard that were basically just alternating between finding The Place and holding an image in the mind. It seemed like he didn't want them actually trying to scry anything again. At least not with Beatrix around.

At the end of the lesson, Beatrix hurried toward the door as fast as she could.

"Bea! Wait!"

It was Gwinny. She ran over to Beatrix and grabbed her arm. "Did you forget?"

Beatrix looked blankly at her. She just wanted to go upstairs and lie down.

"The swordfish!"

Beatrix sighed. It was just one of those days. "Come on then".

Gwinny led her toward the Sea Lift.

"Are we allowed to use this?" Beatrix asked.

Gwinny nodded. "Gregor said we could, just this once".

"So, we're not usually?" Beatrix asked.

"No".

As they approached the lift, Beatrix paused, and looked to the right.

"What is it?" Gwinny asked.

There it was. The misty door from her dreams. Calling to her. Perhaps she was just tired, but the call seemed to be getting stronger.

"We're not allowed down there", Gwinny said, looking forebodingly down the corridor.

"Why not?" Beatrix asked dreamily.

"We're just not", Gwinny said tightly. She gripped Beatrix under the arm. "Come on".

Beatrix scowled but let Gwinny lead her into the lift.

Once they got out of the lift, Gwinny set off immediately.

Beatrix slouched after her.

She saw the gnome peek his head inquisitively out of the ground. Beatrix glared at him, and he disappeared with a 'pop'.

They walked past Gregor's cottage and kept going.

After a while, Beatrix saw a vegetable patch in the distance. It was ringed by a low wooden fence and there was some sort of netting floating over it.

As they got closer, Beatrix saw there were several large holes in the netting. There was a gate in the fence and Dimitri was waiting in front of it.

He was floating nervously, staring in their direction. "Hello, ladies", he said pleasantly.

"Hello, professor", Gwinni said.

Beatrix grunted.

Dimitri didn't know what to make of this. "Err, shall we get started?" He had some netting in his hands.

"What are we doing?" Beatrix asked.

"Well, I don't know if Professor Firewind told you-" Dimitri started.

"He did", Beatrix interrupted him curtly.

"Ah, well, excellent, so, yes, we'll be-" Dimitri began again.

"You want us to patch the holes?" Beatrix asked in disbelief. "Won't they just chew back through?"

Gwinni shifted uncomfortably.

"Well, yes, er, no, rather..." Dimitri seemed rather nervous.

Beatrix sighed. "Give it here then". She grabbed the netting from Dimitri and walked away.

"Beatrix!" Gwinni hissed, running after her. She smiled back apologetically at Dimitri, as if to say, sorry for her.

"Beatrix!" Gwinni hissed again, catching up. "You can't talk to a professor like that!"

"Why not", Beatrix said bluntly. "It's bloody stupid".

"Beatrix!" Gwinni sounded like a broken record at this point.

"What. It is stupid. They're just gonna bloody chew back through the minute we're gone". Beatrix had started tearing patches of netting and threading it through the holes, tying little knots at the end.

In the distance, a school of swordfish had appeared and were swimming back and forth.

"Look, see". Beatrix stopped and pointed. "Stupid bloody things". She stomped toward them.

"Bugger off! Stupidy bloody fish". She kicked out at them and slipped a little on the reedy floor. "Bloody reeds".

Gwinni was at a loss. "Give it here". She took the netting from Beatrix and began patching the holes with rather more care. "They're just going to swim right through these", she said disapprovingly, as she untangled some of Beatrix's rather rushed handiwork.

"You do it then", Beatrix said grumpily.

Dimitri was standing guard in front of the gate, trident crossed against his chest, as if he were watching for trouble.

"What's he bloody doing", Beatrix grumbled, watching Dimitri.

"Shut up, you're going to get us in trouble!" All this insolence seemed to be rather bad for Gwinni's blood pressure. She was sweating a little bit.

Beatrix scoffed. "What are they gonna do. Send me to bed with no dessert".

"Don't", Gwinni warned.

"Why can't he do it?" Beatrix asked.

"Dimitri is standing guard, so we aren't-"

"Guard from what?"

"Oh, will you stop!" Gwinni snapped suddenly. "Please stop. You're giving me a headache".

"You're giving me a headache", Beatrix shot back.

"I am not. I'm just trying to help you".

"I don't need your help".

"Really? Because it doesn't seem like it".

"Give it here", Beatrix said shirtily. She snatched the netting back and threw it on the floor, then stomped on it. "This is a waste of time". She was feeling reckless. She felt something bubbling up in her.

"Beatrix!" Gwinni wailed. "What are you doing!"

"Shut up", Beatrix said.

"No, I won't!"

"You're getting on my nerves", Beatrix warned. "You and this stupid net". She stomped on the netting again.

"I said stop!"

"Make me". Beatrix had a challenging look in her eyes.

Gwinni closed her mouth. "I don't know what has gotten into you, but I want no part of it". She looked a bit tearful, and walked off.

Dimitri watched Gwinni go. He didn't know what to do, from the looks of it.

Beatrix felt bad, but she was in such a foul mood, that she didn't care much right there and then.

Dimitri turned to watch her.

"Don't even start", she warned.

Behind her, the swordfish advanced.

They looked rather menacing, and their eyes were red. Was that normal for swordfish?

"What do you want?" Beatrix asked challengingly.

They came closer, until they were maybe twenty feet away.

"I said what do you want? Little punks". Beatrix kicked up some dust at them.

Suddenly, one of them lunged forward and nipped at her.

"Hey!" Beatrix jumped back.

Dimitri swam toward her. "Perhaps it is best if-"

"Stay back you, I can handle this".

"Now really, I am a professor at this-" Dimitri seemed a little irritated at this.

"Back!" Beatrix hissed. Her hair stood up straight for a second, and the swordfish paused.

Then, another lunged forward and jabbed Beatrix's leg with the sharp end of its bill.

"Ah! Ow!" Beatrix's hand flew to her leg. It was bleeding. "What are you-"

Before she could finish, another flew forward and jabbed her. She managed to avoid it.

"Back!" Dimitri cried, lunging forward with his trident. Another school of swordfish appeared to his right and began circling just out of reach. "We should go", he said, white faced.

Beatrix's face darkened. "Like hell". Her hair was floating a little more rigidly around her face now.

"You don't need to channel!" The woman from her dream screamed through her mind.

A swordfish lunged forward. This time, she was ready. She snarled, and a crack of lightning exploded from her finger through the water. It hit the swordfish and charred its face. It swam away rapidly.

This seemed to agitate the other swordfish, and they began circling aggressively. The two schools merged. There were now more than twenty swordfish in the school.

"A flotilla", Dimitri said softly.

"What?" Beatrix asked.

"A school of swordfish like this...it's called a flotilla". Dimitri looked scared.

"I don't care what it's called", Beatrix seethed. "If it gets much closer I'm gonna toast it". Her fingers crackled menacingly.

Dimitri's eyes widened. "We should go back and get Gregor-"

"Why? So he can tell me I'm no good?" Beatrix asked.

"No, Professor Firewind-"

"Professor Schmessor". Beatrix waved her hand. She was angry. Frustrated and angry. All the stresses of the past month were boiling up inside her. And the voices in her head were starting to wear on her. It wasn't the first time she'd had bad dreams. But last night was by the far worst. They were getting more persistent, the dreams. The lack of sleep was getting to her.

"Really, we must-" Dimitri gripped Beatrix's hand and yelped. "Ouch!" He rubbed his hand.

Beatrix looked apologetic. She opened her mouth to say sorry, but the flotilla moved aggressively in her direction. "Back!" she hissed.

The flotilla lunged forward, and she fell backwards onto a rocky patch of ground. "Ugh". She'd cut her hand. "Ow".

Dimitri stepped in front of her with his trident. "Go back up to the school".

"I'm not leaving", Beatrix said suddenly.

"I'll be right behind you", he said.

A swordfish broke from the flotilla and flew straight at his face. His trident flew up and blocked it. He stepped forward and twirled his trident. A gust of wind blew from it toward the flotilla, scattering them, but only for a moment, they regrouped quickly.

Dimitri took another quick step forward and slipped on the reeds. He wasn't floating, Beatrix noticed. She didn't know why.

As he slipped, the flotilla surged forward and swarmed Dimitri, lunging, nipping, biting.

She saw red flecks flying from Dimitri.

"No!" She cried, surging to her feet. "Get off him!" She ran to Dimitri waving her hands wildly.

"Ow! Oh!" The swordfish started biting and cutting her arms as she held them over her head. She stood protectively over Dimitri.

"Get back!" Dimitri cried from the floor.

As the swordfish nipped and scratched at her, she felt something snap inside her.

"GET BACK!" She shrieked. Her hands flew forward, as if pulled by a strong current, and a torrent of lightning gushed from them.

As far as the eye could see, the water flashed white, it was blinding.

She closed her eyes against the blinding light. When she opened them, she winced, and wrinkled her nose.

On the floor, were twenty dead swordfish, particularly charred and blackened. A strong, acrid smell filled her nostrils.

"What did..." She looked down at her hands. "What did I do".

Dimitri stood up. "You killed them", he said grimly.

"I guess I did", Beatrix said numbly.

"Come with me". Dimitri pulled her by the arm. This time it didn't hurt him.

She sighed. She'd done it now. Goodbye witches school. She assumed he was taking her to Gregor, or that horrible Madame Tempest woman. She hoped it was the former. At least Gregor would dismiss her nicely, with a cup of tea.

Dimitri led her to Gregor's cottage and opened the door. He waited politely for her to enter. "Please wait here". He gestured to the table, then left and closed the door. She watched him walk back toward the lift until he disappeared from sight.

"Bugger", she said quietly to herself.

Consequences

The wait for Gregor was tense. When she finally saw him coming, she scrambled back to the chair by the fire and sat with her back to the door.

She heard the door open and tensed.

The door closed.

Still Gregor hadn't said anything.

She turned to look at him, he looked impassive and wasn't giving anything away.

He stared at her silently for a long moment.

Beatrix stared defiantly back.

"Tea?" Gregor said finally.

"Wh-what?" Beatrix was taken aback. This isn't what she had expected.

Gregor walked toward the kitchen. "Tea?" he repeated, putting a pot to boil.

"Y-yes", Beatrix said. "Thanks", she added as an afterthought. What was going on? Why was he making her tea? Was this his dismissal ritual? Perhaps he made tea for every student he dismissed.

There was silence as Gregor brewed the tea. When he'd finished, he walked over to the armchairs by the fire.

Gregor sat the tea down and sighed. "What am I to do with you?"

"Dismiss me?" Beatrix said moodily.

"Dismiss you?" Gregor seemed surprise. "Oh no, no, no".

Beatrix felt a flicker of hope. "No?"

"No", Gregor said more definitively. "I think that would do more harm than good".

Beatrix frowned.

"And quite honestly, I wouldn't want to inflict it on the people of Brightcastle. I'm not sure they'd manage".

"Hey!" Beatrix exclaimed. "I'm not even from Brightcastle!"

"But you do want to work as a barmaid there, correct?" Gregor had a knowing glimmer in his eye.

"How do you..." Beatrix narrowed her eyes.

"I listen, Miss Bellafonte, which is more than can be said for you". He looked stern.

Beatrix longed to lash out and tell him to stick it, but she contended herself with a scowl. She'd done more than enough already.

"Be thankful it is me you're sitting in front of, and not Madame".

Beatrix opened her mouth to retort, then shut it tightly.

Gregor nodded. "Wise. The wisest thing you've done all day".

She swallowed his barbs. They tasted of bile and ashes in her mouth, but she kept her mouth shut.

"Ah, Beatrix", Gregor mused.

She wanted to retort, but she said nothing.

"You must learn to control yourself". He looked pleadingly at her. "Not just for your own safety, but the safety of those around you. You are powerful, perhaps more powerful than you realise", Gregor said.

She looked at him blankly.

"Surely you've realised by now, you are not the same as your friends...the other...witches?" Gregor asked.

She shook her head. She hadn't realised anything.

Gregor shook his head as if he was disappointed. "I expected more of you".

Beatrix sighed. Another barb. But she deserved it, she realised. She'd been reckless and put Dimitri at risk.

Beatrix shook her head desolately and stared into her tea.

Gregor said nothing and drank his tea. They sat quietly a while. Gregor shot his finger at the grate and flames sprang up.

Beatrix smiled weakly. She liked how he did that. "Wish I could do that", she mumbled.

Gregor smiled. "But you can".

Beatrix shook her head in disagreement. "Can't do anything but blow things up", she mumbled. "Or kill them", she added.

Gregor snorted. "Quite".

She scowled.

"You do seem rather adept at destroying things...and fish", Gregor ventured.

She looked at him. He was teasing her. She grinned sheepishly.

"What did those poor fish ever do to you?" Gregor asked.

"Poor fish!" She lunged forward, and almost spilled her tea, but caught herself this time. "Those bloody things are feral! They're dangerous! Vicious!"

Gregor didn't say anything. He was watching her, an amused glint in his eye. He was clearly baiting her again, and she'd taken the bait.

"Brr", Beatrix growled.

Gregor chuckled. "See what I mean? Rather a hothead, aren't you?" He looked pensive. "You rather remind me of someone". He looked down and began twiddling his thumbs.

"Oh yeah?" Beatrix asked.

Gregor sniffed. "She was also very powerful. And in possession of a temper to match".

Beatrix frowned. This woman sounded interesting. "Who was she?"

"Someone I once knew", Gregor said mysteriously.

"Helpful", Beatrix said.

Gregor cocked his head and laughed.

Beatrix couldn't help but smile. Gregor's laugh was infectious, and it broke the tension.

"She'd like you...well, she might have, once upon a time", Gregor said.

"What happened to her?" Beatrix asked.

Gregor looked sad. "She changed", he said simply.

Beatrix sensed a change in his mood and decided to drop it. "So, what about me? Am I in trouble? You know, for the...fish?"

"Oh yes", Gregor said suddenly. "Though I haven't figured out what yet...for your punishment". He scratched his chin. "But I will, don't you worry".

Beatrix scowled.

"For now, though, we have rather a lot of fish", Gregor said.

Beatrix didn't know what he meant.

"Oh, it's just the outer layer you scorched to smithereens. They're rather fine to eat, still", Gregor said.

"We're going to eat them?" Beatrix looked horrified.

"Oh, yes!" Gregor enthused.

Beatrix didn't know what to make of this.

"They'll know just what to do with them in the kitchen. Frankly, I hope they stew them or make that glorious swordfish soup..." Gregor faded off thoughtfully.

"Swordfish soup?" Beatrix thought this sounded disgusting. She just wanted some potatoes. Maybe some roasted chicken and gravy. She liked eating the same thing and wasn't much for variety when it came to food.

"Oh yes. Delicious". Gregor smacked his lips.

"But...what about my punishment?" Beatrix asked.

"What about it?" Gregor stood up. "I just told you; I haven't decided yet".

Beatrix stood up too. "When will you know?" She felt weird, enquiring after her fate.

"Oh, sooner or later. I'm sure some swordfish soup will help me decide". He smacked his stomach again. It appeared he'd decided what the kitchen were to cook for dinner. "Now off with you, back to the castle. I'll deal with Dimitri".

Beatrix stared at him in disbelief. "But I-"

Gregor raised his hand like he didn't want to hear it. "We all have bad days. Go back to the castle. Eat some dinner. Get a good night's sleep. We'll talk later".

This sounded very reasonable, even to the overtired Beatrix. Suddenly she yawned loudly, as if now she didn't have to worry, she could relax. She felt a wave of tiredness wash over. "I am pretty tired".

Gregor nodded. "I can tell".

She smiled wanly. "Bye then".

She walked out of the cottage and glanced back from the path.

Gregor was making himself another cup of tea in the kitchen and whistling happily to himself.

She shook her head.

He was a strange man.

*

"So? What'd he say?" Beatrix was back in the great hall now. Edni had started interrogating her the moment she sat down. Gwinni was studiously avoiding eye contact.

Beatrix shrugged. "It's between me and him".

"What?" Edni wailed. "That's rubbish!"

"It is rather", Lucrecia chimed in.

Beatrix looked at her, and she smiled meekly.

"Well it is rather interesting..." Lucrecia trailed off.

Beatrix shook her head. She didn't have energy to gossip. It seemed like the other girls realised this, for they dropped it. Edni rolled her eyes and made a face of disgust, then turned away to talk to a girl on her left, seeing as Gwinni wasn't saying anything.

Beatrix watched Gwinni. She was staring down at her food, not making eye contact with anyone. Beatrix figured she was still upset from earlier.

"Gwinni", Beatrix muttered.

Gwinni looked up. Her face was set and impassive.

"Sorry", Beatrix mumbled.

Gwinni frowned. She looked like she had something to say, but she simply nodded. She seemed to lighten up a bit after that.

Beatrix ate her food quietly and without her usual gusto. She chanced a look down the table. Cincesse was still ignoring her. "Great", she muttered.

Lucrecia frowned. "Trouble in paradise?"

Beatrix ran her tongue inside her cheek. "Something like that".

Lucrecia brightened. "All clouds pass eventually".

Beatrix raised her eyebrows. "I suppose you're right". She ate with a little more gusto.

Lucrecia was right. Cincesse would be ok, once she apologised to her. She just needed to say sorry for being such a grumpy toad.

Cincesse put her knife and fork down and got up. Her minions reached out to her, but she shook her head and walked out of the hall.

Beatrix swallowed, put her utensils down and got up. "See you later", she muttered. She hurried after Cincesse.

"Cincesse!" She called.

Cincesse ignored her.

"Cin! Hey!" Beatrix caught up with Cincesse. "Will you stop!" She pulled her by the arm.

"What is it?" Cincesse said coldly. "I wouldn't want to delay you".

"What do you-" Beatrix started. "Hey, stop!"

Cincesse had turned to leave again.

"I'm sorry alright! I was tired! I've had a thumpin bad day, please just, stop". Beatrix pleaded.

Cincesse stopped and turned reluctantly. She crossed her arms.

"I've missed you", Beatrix said.

Cincesse looked like she wanted to milk it some more, but also like she was desperate to speak to Beatrix. She uncrossed her arms. "Really?"

"Yeah…" Beatrix said. "It's been one of those days".

"What happened?" Cincesse touched Beatrix's arm.

"Where do I begin?" Beatrix looked wan and tired.

"Come on", Cincesse led Beatrix away, up to the Witches Den.

"Hey, I never asked, where do you live? It's obviously not with us in the den", Beatrix asked.

"There are multiple living quarters, you know", Cincesse said in a voice like Gwinny's.

"Oh". Beatrix accepted this without comment. She was still grouchy but wasn't going to blow it with another outburst.

"Mine's up there", Cincesse pointed to a staircase to the right of where Beatrix lived.

Cincesse looked mischievous then. "Come on". She dragged Beatrix up the staircase.

"Wait! Won't I get in trouble?" Beatrix exclaimed.

"Do you care?" Cincesse asked daringly.

"I mean..." Beatrix wondered what would one more infraction matter. She really shouldn't put another foot out of line, but she felt she owed Cincesse for her earlier attitude. She reluctantly agreed.

They tip-toed up the staircase, glancing down behind them now and then.

Cincesse's living quarters was much the same as the Witches Den. "Come on", Cincesse mumbled, leading Beatrix straight through to the bedroom. There were a couple of girls who watched them suspiciously as they went.

"Is that another bedroom?" It looked like there were two more bedrooms off Cincesse's.

Cincesse nodded. "There's four, actually. It's one of the largest living quarters in the castle".

"Wow". Beatrix wondered at this. That's a lot of girls to juggle. And a lot of personality. She wondered how four Edni's would get on with each other.

"Come on, no one will say dare anything. Eli and Clio sleep here too", Cincesse said. "Here, you can wear these". Cincesse handed her a pair of pyjamas. "You can get changed there". She pointed to a bed opposite her own. When they were changed, they got into bed. It felt nice to be cuddled up to Cincesse.

They lay quietly in the bed, Cincesse playing softly with Beatrix's hair. She seemed fascinated with Beatrix's mark. "I've never seen one like it".

"What?" Beatrix whispered.

"Why are you whispering". Cincesse giggled. "There's no one here yet".

"Oh, sorry. What haven't you seen?" Beatrix was insistent.

"Your mark", Cincesse said quietly.

"Oh". Beatrix didn't know what to say. "Is it not normal?"

"Well, no", Cincesse admitted. "Usually, it's a strip of white hair, like mine". She pulled at her hair, running her fingers through the white, that ran from temple to tip. "Yours is like...a splash of snow".

"A splash of snow?" Beatrix didn't know what to make of this.

"Mhm...like someone decided halfway through making you a witch, you know what? No". Cincesse giggled.

Beatrix snorted. "What are you talking about". She rolled over and faced Cincesse.

"I don't know", Cincesse said softly. Her eyes were sparkling.

"Then maybe you shouldn't", Beatrix said huskily.

"What?" Cincesse whispered.

"Talk". Beatrix kissed her and ran the back of her hand tenderly across her cheek.

"Maybe I shouldn't", Cincesse agreed.

Beatrix smiled lazily.

"Cinny?" A high-pitched voice called from outside the bedroom.

Cincesse rolled her eyes. "Here we go", she mumbled.

"Are you in here?" Another voice.

"I'm in here", Cincesse called back.

"Oh!" The door burst open, and Eli and Clio strode in.

"Oh". It was a different oh, this time. Eli and Clio stood by the door watching Cincesse and Beatrix in the bed. "I didn't know you had...company".

"Oh, stop". Cincesse blushed. "I'm fine. Thank you for thinking of me, though".

Eli brightened a little at this. "Anytime".

"Go to bed", Cincesse instructed. "I'm tired".

"Alright". Clio seemed slightly less enthused, but she obeyed. So did Eli.

Beatrix and Cincesse lay quietly, waiting for the minions to stop their twittering. Once Clio and Eli had gotten into bed and drawn the drapes, they smiled at one another.

"Tomorrow is a new day", Cincesse said softly.

"Mmm".

"Did he punish you?"

"Who?"

"Gregor".

"No. We just drank tea".

"Strange".

"He's a strange man".

"Very".

"But I like him", Beatrix admitted.

"Me too", Cincesse decided. "What about Madame?"

"What about her?"

"Did she punish you?"

"I don't know, I didn't see her".

"Oh".

"What?" Beatrix sat up suddenly. She felt a chill of premonition.

"Nothing". Cincesse didn't want to scare her before bed.

"No, what?"

"Well, it's probably nothing, but sometimes, when Gregor is...lax...she...steps in".

"**Steps in?**". Beatrix didn't like the sound of this.

"Yes, nothing serious, but yes. She is rather strict. Believes in consequences". Cincesse trailed off.

"Consequences?"

"Actions have consequences", Cincesse mimed.

Beatrix frowned.

"But I'm sure you'll be alright", Cincesse assured her. "It'll probably just be cleaning duty, if anything".

Beatrix wasn't so sure. She felt that Madame really hated her. She felt the same about Madame.

"Don't worry". Cincesse petted her face softly and pulled her back down into the bed. "I'll protect you", she said lovingly.

"You will?" Beatrix asked.

Cincesse nodded. "Yes", she replied huskily.

"How noble", Beatrix said.

"Quite".

Cincesse kissed her.

"Thank you", Beatrix whispered sleepily.

"For what?"

She didn't hear what.

Beatrix had fallen asleep.

Cincesse smiled happily and went to sleep too.

A Magical History

"Oh, god", Cincesse moaned.

"What?" Beatrix straightened her pinafore.

"Magical History". Cincesse grimaced. "Gross".

"What's that?"

"A bunch of boring dates and facts, mostly".

"About what?"

"The history of **magic**. Witches, mostly".

Beatrix brightened. "That sounds rather interesting".

Cincesse looked at her as if she was crazy. "Have you hit your head?"

"No". Beatrix smirked mischievously. She felt better after a good sleep.

Cincesse grinned. "I see you are feeling better". She was happy to see Beatrix back to herself.

"But, I would like to know more about witches and their...history", Beatrix admitted.

Cincesse studied her. "I suppose you've never done any, have you?"

"What?"

"Magical history".

"No, not yet".

"Then, I understand", Cincesse admitted magnanimously.

"Good of you", Beatrix quipped.

Cincesse arched her eyebrows.

Beatrix winked. "Come on, I don't want to be late".

"Oh, really? Who are you, and what have you done with Beatrix Bellafonte", Cincesse asked.

Beatrix giggled. "She's right here!" She'd forgotten all about Cincesse's warning, and a vengeful Madame waiting in the wings.

"Let's go eat". Cincesse led Beatrix out of the room. Eli and Clio followed a few paces behind, unsure of how to act.

Beatrix glanced back at them and giggled.

"They are rather funny, aren't they?" Cincesse murmured so the girls wouldn't hear.

"Rather", Beatrix admitted. "Do they just not say anything?"

"I don't think they will now, no", Cincesse admitted.

"Why?"

"I think you scare them".

"I do?"

Cincesse nodded. "And they're used to having me to themselves. I think they're a little jealous".

"Understandable". Beatrix nodded.

Cincesse seemed to like this. She took Beatrix's hand.

Behind, the girls gasped.

They didn't care, and walked hand in hand into the great hall, to much muttering and staring.

At the professor's table, Madame Tempest looked up and stared fixedly at Beatrix as she took her seat. Beatrix didn't see.

Cincesse and Beatrix joined Gwinny, Edi and Lucrecia who were already at the table.

Beatrix sat next to Gwinny.

Cincesse took the seat next to Beatrix, with Clio and Eli next to her. It was a rather odd and awkward looking arrangement.

Gwinny still seemed a little uncomfortable.

Beatrix squeezed Gwinny's hand. "Sorry, Gwin", she said.

Gwinny looked up and smiled. "It's quite alright, you were having a bad day. Me too, to be honest".

Beatrix felt better. She felt like they hadn't made up properly yesterday.

"Finally". Edni rolled her eyes. "She's been intolerable since you bickered".

"You're one to talk!" Gwinni's eyes flashed, and she flicked her hair back from her neck.

It looked like Edni mouthed 'yap, yap, yap', but her eyes were down, and she did it completely silently, so she didn't rile Gwinni further.

"How are you feeling?" Gwinni placed her hand on Beatrix's.

Cincesse stiffened. It seemed like she was jealous.

Gwinny quickly removed her hand. "Are you ok?"

Beatrix found this rather amusing. "I'm fine, thanks, Gwin".

"Good. I was worried about you. After the...shenanigans...with Dimitri". Gwinni did look rather worried.

"Shenanigans?" Beatrix grinned.

"She means when you toasted those fish", Edni said bluntly through a mouthful of toast.

"She didn't toast-" Gwinni steadied herself.

"Sorry, burnt the bajeezus out of them". Edni cackled her wicked cackle.

Beatrix snorted.

"It's not-" Gwinni didn't know what to say. Eventually she smiled too. "I suppose you did rather fry them".

Cincesse looked on curiously. "Were they rather cooked?" She took Beatrix's hand possessively and looked pointedly at Gwinni, who looked away.

"Yeah", Beatrix admitted sheepishly. "Just a little".

"Oh, that must be why there was so much fish last night. And tonight I'd imagine", Cincesse said.

"Oh yeah, Gregor said about that, I didn't even realise", Beatrix said.

"You were tired", Cincesse said.

"True", Beatrix said.

"But you can try it tonight!" Cincesse said brightly. "Swordfish soup is rather delicious".

Beatrix looked dubious. "Maybe".

"I like it", Lucrecia said happily.

Beatrix hadn't seen her and smiled. "Hey, Luce".

"Hello Beatrix". Lucrecia looked happy to see her friend.

"You alright?" Beatrix asked.

"Mhm", Lucrecia said. "Just fine thank you".

"Are you looking forward to Magical History?" Beatrix asked.

"Oh yes". Lucrecia nodded.

Cincesse rolled her eyes.

"Me too. I want to know more about witches", Beatrix said.

Edni narrowed her eyes at this.

Gwinny looked surprised.

"What? Don't look so surprised", Beatrix said.

"No, it's just, I didn't take you for a historian", Gwinny said.

"I'm not", Beatrix admitted. "But I want to know about where I come from". She blushed as if this was embarrassing.

"Quite understandable", Gwinni said.

"Yes, it makes perfect sense", Cincesse added, perhaps to one-up Gwinni.

Gwinni looked uncomfortable.

Beatrix looked between Gwinni and Cincesse. "I hope I like it".

"I'm sure you will", Cincesse said quickly, taking Beatrix's hand again.

Beatrix smiled awkwardly and took her hand back to eat.

Cincesse looked slightly miffed at this but said nothing.

"Has she whacked you yet?" Edni said bluntly.

"What?" Beatrix looked up quickly.

Edni gestured with her head to the professor's table. "Madame Misery".

"Edni!" Gwinni hissed.

"What?" Edni said.

"Shut up!" Gwinni said.

Beatrix's stomach dropped. She'd forgotten all about the warning.

"She's not 'whacking' anyone", Gwinni insisted.

"Whacking?" Beatrix frowned. She pictured Madame hitting with her a stick.

"Ignore her", Gwinni said.

"Ignore me if you want, won't stop her whacking you", Edni said matter-of-factly, eyes on her desert, a lemon tart.

Beatrix looked disbelieving. "She wouldn't actually whack me, would she?"

"No". Gwinni rubbed her arm reassuringly. "Don't mind her".

Edni smirked into her tart.

"I've never heard of anything like that", Cincesse said pompously. She glared at Edni.

Edni shrugged.

"So, what will I learn in Magical History?" Beatrix asked, seeking to change the subject.

Lucrecia perked up. "Oh, lots of stuff".

Gwinni nodded.

"When witches were first discovered, what their powers used to be, how they were hunted". Lucrecia trailed off sadly. "What happened when they were caught".

Beatrix swallowed.

"But also, other fun stuff, like the origin of spells, how they were invented, how witches learned to channel, who taught them". Lucrecia paused, thinking.

"Taught them?" Beatrix asked.

"Mhm, before the schools", Lucrecia said.

"The schools haven't always been here?" Beatrix asked.

Lucrecia shook her head seriously. "Oh, no. They used to be underground".

"Underground? Like secret?" Beatrix asked.

"No. Underground". Lucrecia smiled.

"Like **actually** underground?" Beatrix was fascinated.

"Mhm". Lucrecia nodded. "Oh yes".

"Wow". Beatrix was amazed. It was certainly an intriguing thought. She shifted her feet gingerly and looked down at the floor.

"Not under the sea". Lucrecia giggled.

"Oh, right", Beatrix said.

"Under Brightcastle, in fact", Lucrecia said.

"Really?" Beatrix asked.

"Yes. There used to be a lot of witches living under Brightcastle at one point. There still are some, I expect".

"What!" Beatrix leaned forward excitedly. "Really?"

Gwinni nodded, eyes on Lucrecia. "She's right".

"Holy heck", Beatrix said. "All this time and I didn't know".

"They don't come out much, obviously", Gwinni said. "Rather secretive".

"And they're still there?" Beatrix asked.

"Yes", Gwinni agreed.

"How do they not get caught?" Beatrix asked.

"Well, they're very good at it", Gwinni said.

"At what?" Beatrix asked.

"Not getting caught", Gwinni replied. "They've been doing it for hundreds of years".

"Of course..." Beatrix looked pensive. "But it must be horrible down there...under the city".

"I rather think not", Gwinni said.

"You don't?" Beatrix replied.

"They are witches, after all. Accomplished ones", Gwinni said.

"I suppose you're right", Beatrix conceded. "But where do they live?" Beatrix couldn't picture it. Living underground like rats. Gross.

"Well, there's caves, and tunnels, and other places..." Gwinni trailed.

"Other places?" Beatrix asked.

"It's something of a mystery, actually", Gwinni said.

Lucrecia was listening intently now. It seemed as though Gwinni knew more Magical History than her, which made sense, as Gwinni was older.

"What do you mean?" Beatrix asked.

"Well, no one knows, entirely. Only The Fledgelings".

"The Fledgelings?"

"That's what they're called, the witches who live underground".

"Oh".

Edni looked up from her tart as curt footsteps sounded on the stone floor. "Uhoh", she mumbled.

"Miss Bellafonte". It was Madame Tempest. She was standing behind Edni staring at Beatrix.

Beatrix looked up. Her stomach dropped. "Oh".

"If you would come with me, please". Miss Bellafonte swept her arm out, gesturing that Beatrix should follow her out of the hall.

"What's it about, Madame?" Beatrix asked.

Madame said nothing, she simply stood with her arm outstretched.

Beatrix got up slowly. "Bye then", she said to the girls.

"Bye", Gwinni said weakly.

Edni had a look on her face that said, I told you so.

"Bye Beatrix", Lucrecia said politely.

"This way please". Madame strode off with Beatrix in tow.

"Where are we going?"

Madame didn't reply.

They walked through the castle taking passages Beatrix didn't know. Up and up, they went, until they were on the top floor of the castle. They walked toward the end of a corridor. It was cold and dark and dusty. At the end, was a foreboding wooden door. The door was dark, as was the handle.

Madame opened the door and waited for Beatrix to enter, then she closed the door behind them. It thudded heavily into the frame and Beatrix jumped.

In the room was a stern wooden desk and two chairs either side. Madame had a great view of the sea through a big window to the right of her desk, which faced the door.

Behind the desk with a stone fireplace. The grate was empty and looked like it hadn't been used in a while.

There was a picture above the fireplace. It showed a beautiful woman with a dazzling smile and her hand on her hip. Was it Madame? Beatrix studied the picture, then Madame's face, trying to make the connection.

"Do I pass muster?" Madame said coldly.

"Sorry", Beatrix said quickly.

"Sit down". Madame sat herself behind the desk. Beatrix took the seat in front of it.

"I understand you do not know how to follow instructions", Madame began without preamble, fixing Beatrix with a piercing stare.

"I-" Beatrix began.

"It wasn't a question", Madame curtly cut her off.

Beatrix sighed.

"Do not sigh", Madame instructed.

"What?" Beatrix asked.

"Did I stutter?" Madame asked.

"No, but-" Beatrix began.

Madame raised a hand for silence.

Beatrix gritted her jaw and narrowed her eyes.

"How like your mother you are", Madame said, rather poisonously. It looked like Madame hated her in that moment.

Beatrix was taken aback. "You don't know my mother".

Madame rose suddenly. "Stand up".

Beatrix was getting sick of this. "I thought you wanted me to sit down?"

"Stand up!" Madame ordered.

Beatrix stood up and glared at Madame across the desk.

"I am going to teach you to follow instructions", Madame said tersely.

"How are you going to do that?" Beatrix asked warily.

"Trial and error", Madame said.

"What?" Beatrix was worried now.

"I am going to take control of your mind. In a sense, I will channel you. If you attempt to repel me, or disobey me, you will experience pain. Do I make myself clear?" Madame asked.

"What, no", Beatrix stuttered.

Madame tensed and Beatrix raised a hand.

"No, wait!" Beatrix yelled.

Beatrix grunted and her head fell forward. Her eyes were closed. Her mind was elsewhere now.

A cold, cruel voice rang through her mind.

"If I wanted you to channel the spell, I would have asked you to do that".

A woman was standing in front of her, bent low so that her face was almost touching Beatrix's.

"Did I ask you to channel the spell?" The woman asked.

Beatrix hung her head. "No", she said meekly.

"Then why did you do it?" The woman asked.

"I didn't", Beatrix replied.

"Yes, you did", the woman corrected her.

"I didn't", Beatrix insisted.

"Do not argue with me", the woman warned.

"But I don't know what you want!" Beatrix yelled suddenly, stomping her foot and clenching her fist. A spark flew up from the floor at her feet.

The woman grinned wickedly. "Better".

"I don't know what's better about it. It's stupid. So are you", Beatrix said.

The woman's face darkened. "We shall see about that". She straightened and stared ominously down at Beatrix.

Beatrix swallowed.

In Madame's office, Beatrix moaned.

Madame watched, a cruel look on her face, as if she were enjoying herself.

"No", Beatrix moaned. "I won't".

Madame narrowed her eyes and raised her hand, which had a soft red aura around it. She clenched it slowly whilst looking at Beatrix.

Beatrix tensed, like an invisible hand had gripped her.

"No", Beatrix moaned again.

Madame frowned and clenched her fist tighter.

"No!" Beatrix said. Her voice was strong and firm this time.

Madame's hand sizzled and she unclenched it, shaking it quickly to clear the smoke coming from it. She looked petrified and took a step back from Beatrix.

Beatrix opened her eyes. The pupils were huge and dilated, like giant black moons. "Don't touch me", she said dreamily.

Madame took another step back. "Awaken".

Beatrix continued to stare. Her unblinking moons bored pitilessly into Madame's frightened eyes.

"Awaken!" Madame cried, pointing at Beatrix.

"I've had enough of this. And I've had enough of you". Beatrix took a step toward Madame.

Madame frowned. Her mouth was hanging open in disbelief.

It looked as though Beatrix was not entirely aware of where she was, or who she was talking to.

"Awaken!" Madame cried again, pointing aggressively at Beatrix, as if she expected this to do something.

Beatrix didn't even flinch.

Madame licked her lips and looked around the room, as if for an escape route.

"You can't hurt me anymore". Beatrix took another step toward Madame. "I won't let you".

Madame backed away toward the fireplace.

Beatrix advanced slowly.

"Back!" Madame cried.

Step. Step. Step.

Beatrix's shoes echoed ominously on the stone floor as she inched closer to Madame. She was only feet away from her now.

"BACK!" Madame's hand flew forward and wind shot from it.

It whipped Beatrix across the face, to no effect.

Madame's hand flew forward, again, and again, wind gusting across the room. She was sweating and breathing heavily now.

Beatrix snarled and her hands began to sizzle.

"No!" Madame cried.

"Beatrix!" The door flew open, and Gregor appeared. He was ashen faced and panting.

Beatrix flinched and her head snapped back. She blinked and her eyes returned to normal.

"Beatrix!" Gregor cried again.

She turned at the sound. "What's going on?"

Gregor ran forward and took her in his arms. "Are you alright?" He pushed her hair back from her face.

"I'm fine..." Beatrix said dreamily.

Gregor tilted her head back and examined her eyes. He started lifting her eyelids open with his fingers and she brushed him off.

"Get off", she grumbled. "What the hell are you doing?"

Gregor breathed a sigh of relief. "Beatrix, go downstairs. I believe you have Magical History".

"I haven't missed it?" Beatrix asked.

"Only the beginning. I am sure Pietro will fill you in". Gregor wasn't looking at her. He was staring at Madame, who looked like she'd been caught in the act. He looked furious. He was speaking tersely in short, blunt sentences.

"Alright", Beatrix said. Truth be told she felt very tired and wanted to go and sit down somewhere.

She couldn't be bothered to argue right now. She walked through the door and gave Gregor and Madame one last look, before closing it behind her.

As she started walking down the corridor, she heard Gregor hiss, "What the hell do you think you are doing? Have you lost your mind, you horrible, bitter, little woman?"

"How dare you speak to me like that, foul man", Madame hissed back.

Beatrix sighed. She reached the end of the corridor and descended the spiral staircase. She shook her head and traipsed back to the great hall.

She didn't want to think about what happened in Madame's office right now. And it was blurry in her mind. She could remember going in, and arguing with Madame, but not much after that.

"Ah, Beatrix". It was Dimitri, floating along happily. "What are you doing here? Shouldn't you be in Magical History?"

"I don't know where it is", Beatrix said glumly.

"Ah, not to worry. Follow me". Dimitri led her along a hallway that was new to her. "Here we are. Magical History".

It was a hallway much like the rest of the castle, but the door to the classroom was low and arching. She frowned. It looked like it was made for a very small man, or a child.

"In you go", Dimitri said amiably.

She opened the door and bent her head. She had to stoop to get in.

"Bye then", Dimitri called as he floated away.

She stooped in and closed the door behind her. Inside, the room was normal size, as was the ceiling. Everyone was waiting quietly, eyes on her. They'd obviously gone silent as they heard her open the door.

There was a chalkboard and in front of it was a small red man. He had a furry red mane of hair and looked a bit like a lion. His eyes were yellow like a cat.

Beatrix's eyes widened.

His hair was smoking softly, like it was on fire!

"Who are...what are..." Beatrix was captivated.

"Pietro Salvatore". The red man bowed. "At your service".

"Pietro...nice to meet you", Beatrix stammered, catching her wits. "Professor".

Pietro grinned. "You, too. Now, take your seat if you please. I was just telling the other ladies about The Fledgelings".

"The Fledgelings?" Beatrix was instantly interested.

"Indeed. Young Gwinni here has been asking me about them". Pietro smiled warmly at Gwinni.

Beatrix quickly took the empty seat next to Gwinni. Lucrecia was the other side.

At the back of the room, Cincesse's face fell.

"That's right", Pietro continued. "And young Lucrecia also seems rather interested in them".

"Me too", Beatrix admitted.

"Well then, allow me to continue", Pietro said. He turned to the chalkboard and began speaking, jotting words down every now and then.

Gwinni immediately leaned in toward Beatrix and whispered, "Are you alright? You're white as a sheet".

"I'm alright", Beatrix lied. Truth was she was very far from alright, but she didn't want to think about it. Not right now.

"Are you sure?" Gwinni whispered.

Beatrix nodded.

Gwinni didn't look convinced but bit her lip.

Lucrecia smiled at Beatrix, as if to say, I'm here for you. Beatrix was grateful. She didn't want to speak right now, but it made her feel loved, that her friends cared for her, in their own way.

Beatrix stared at the chalkboard, but her mind was elsewhere. Her eyes were faraway. She wasn't really listening. She was mulling over what had happened in Madame's office.

Gwinni kept glancing at her, as if she might break.

Eli and Clio were whispering and sniggering at the back of the room again.

"That will be enough, thank you", Pietro turned to tell them off, then carried on.

Beatrix was grateful that Gwinni had asked Pietro about The Fledgelings. It was rather cute how she'd done that for her. But it went over her head. Her initial interest had quickly disappeared, and she was finding it hard to concentrate. She just wanted to go and lie down. Her eyes were drooping.

"Professor?" Beatrix raised her hand suddenly, after her head fell forward then snapped back.

Pietro turned. "What is it, my dear?"

"May I be excused? I don't feel well", Beatrix said wanly.

Pietro looked concerned. "Yes, of course, if you're not well".

Beatrix got up. "Thanks".

Cincesse stopped whispering to Eli and Clio and stared at Beatrix. She looked worried.

Beatrix glanced at Cincesse over her shoulder and smiled meekly.

Pietro watched her to the door. "Get well soon, my dear".

"Thanks", Beatrix said again.

She shut the door behind her and breathed a sigh of relief. She leant back against the wall for a moment, gathering her thoughts. A tear slid down her face.

She traipsed slowly up to her bedroom and threw herself face down on the bed, still fully clothed. She leant across and whipped the drapes closed around her.

She closed her eyes, and sleep took her quickly.

I Miss Them

"Hey, Bea". A soft voice whispered through her consciousness.

Beatrix moaned and moved gently on the bed.

"I brought you some food".

"Mmm". Beatrix moaned as the words got through. She smacked her lips and opened her eyes. She felt better after a nice nap.

Lucrecia was sitting on the edge of the bed beside her. In her hand was a small plate with a chicken sandwich on.

"Mmm, thanks". Beatrix sat up and blearily began eating the sandwich. She was rather hungry now she'd calmed down.

"That's alright". Lucrecia smiled happily. She seemed pleased that Beatrix appreciated her kindness.

"Thanks, Luce", Beatrix said. "I couldn't face dinner".

"I thought so", Lucrecia said. "You looked rather tired". Lucrecia studied Beatrix.

Beatrix shifted uncomfortably. Lucrecia's eyes were knowing. Very knowing for one so young.

"I was", Beatrix said.

"Oh, hello". It was Cincesse. She also had a sandwich on a plate. "I brought you a sandwich", she said lamely, sitting on the other side of Beatrix.

"Thanks", Beatrix grinned through a thick mouthful of sandwich.

Cincesse placed her plate down on the side-table by Beatrix's bed. "I was rather worried about you". She looked at Lucrecia. It seemed she felt a little uncomfortable speaking candidly in front of her. Perhaps she wanted to be more affectionate.

"Thanks". Beatrix reached out and took her hand. This seemed to cheer her.

"What happened?" Lucrecia asked.

Beatrix sighed. "I don't want to talk about it. Not yet".

Cincesse swallowed. She seemed disappointed, but let it lie. "Alright". She squeezed Beatrix's hand.

"We learned about Fledgelings", Lucrecia said happily to Cincesse.

"I know, I was there". Cincesse seemed bemused.

"Oh, yes", Lucrecia agreed.

Beatrix grinned.

"Hello", Gwinni said brightly, as she entered the room.

"Ello", Edni said, following Gwinni in. She skulked over to her bed and sat down. "How's the head?"

"Head?" Beatrix seemed confused.

"You looked like you had a headache", Edni said, throwing herself back on the bed and resting against the headboard. "I would, if I'd spent time alone with Madame Misery".

"Oh, right, that". Beatrix went quiet.

Gwinni flashed Edni a look that said, shut up you tactless idiot.

"What?" Edni shrugged. She'd also brought a sandwich up, but hers was ham. She ate it enthusiastically and stared around the room like a puppy just happy to be included.

"How was dinner?" Beatrix asked, seeking to change the subject.

"Oh, fine", Gwinni said airily.

Edni snorted.

"What?" Beatrix asked.

Edni shrugged. "I'm sayin nothin".

Gwinni shook her head.

"What is it?" Beatrix asked.

"Madame wasn't there. And Gregor was furious. He stormed in and broke the side door", Gwinni said.

"Side door?" Beatrix asked.

Gwinni nodded. "There are two little side doors. Postern doors. The professors use them sometimes to get into the great hall. They're at either end of the professor's table".

"Oh", Beatrix said.

"He slammed it so hard it came off its hinges", Gwinni said.

"Oh, wow", Beatrix said.

Edni sniggered. "Angry ol boy".

Gwinni gave her a disapproving look.

"Why was he so mad?" Beatrix asked.

"We were hoping you could tell us, actually", Gwinni replied.

"Oh". Beatrix reddened. Of course. It must have been about her. She'd forgotten the argument between Gregor and Madame.

They all stared at her expectantly.

"I don't know", she said lamely.

Edni tutted. "What a letdown".

"Sorry". Beatrix blushed.

She glanced at Gwinny, who looked as if she didn't believe that was all there was to it. She felt uncomfortable with all the eyes on her, so she picked up the second sandwich and shoved it into her mouth.

Lucrecia giggled. "That's rather a big bite".

"I know", Beatrix said thickly.

"Eugh, gross". Edni stuck her tongue out at Beatrix's mouthful of half-eaten sandwich.

Beatrix swallowed. "Delicious".

"I'd hope so", Edni said.

When Beatrix was finished eating, Gwinni said, "Well I'm tired, I'm going to turn in".

"But it's early", Edni wailed.

"An early night would probably benefit us all", Gwinni said pointedly.

Edni sighed dejectedly. "Whatever". She disappeared behind her drapes.

Lucrecia looked at Cincesse sitting awkwardly next to Beatrix. She smiled at Beatrix then waltzed over to her bed, so Beatrix and Cincesse could be alone.

They lay back against the headboard together.

Cincesse pulled the drapes closed.

Felix hopped through them just before they closed.

Katy followed.

"Oh, hello", Cincesse said, surprised. She petted Felix, who purred.

"Four's a crowd", Felix thought.

Beatrix smirked.

"What did he say?" Cincesse asked.

"Oh, nothing".

Cincesse frowned. "Were you being mischievous?" She gripped Felix's face in her hands.

Felix batted his eyelids lazily and waved his tail. He was sitting between the two girls.

Katy stood up, circled, then slouched down, resting her chin on Felix's back, looking out into the room through the drapes.

Beatrix grinned and petted Katy.

"She likes it", Felix thought.

"I'm glad", Beatrix thought back.

"Are you alright?" Felix thought.

"Yes".

Felix paused. "You don't seem it".

"And you can tell, can you?"

Another pause. "They might be your new best 'girls', but I've been your 'best cat' for a long time. I know you".

Beatrix blinked. She felt like crying for a moment.

"And I love you", Felix thought.

Beatrix swallowed. "I love you too", she thought back.

"Are you alright?" Cincesse rubbed Beatrix's arm.

Beatrix couldn't find the words, so she simply nodded.

Cincesse cuddled into her, resting her head on her shoulder. She closed her eyes and ran her fingers up and down Beatrix's arm. It was soft and soothing. Not too incessant.

"Did she hurt you?" Felix thought.

"Who?" Beatrix thought back.

Felix didn't say anything, but Beatrix could feel what he was thinking. He was thinking, don't try to fool me.

Beatrix swallowed again. "No. But she tried to, I think".

Felix hissed suddenly showing his teeth. Katy's head jolted up. She looked like she wasn't sure what had just happened.

"What is it?" Cincesse asked.

Felix closed his eyes and laid his head on Beatrix's leg. Katy lay back down on Felix.

Felix didn't say anything else, but Beatrix felt a wave of empathy, and anger, coming from him.

She blinked back more tears. "I miss them", she whispered.

Cincesse opened her eyes. "Who?"

Beatrix hadn't realised she'd spoken aloud. "My parents", she admitted.

"Oh". Cincesse looked at her sadly. "I expect you do after today".

Beatrix looked sadly down at Felix and Katy dozing together. "Sometimes, I don't want to be a witch. I just want to go home".

Cincesse was quiet for a moment. "Me too", she whispered.

"I wish I could just...run away sometimes. Run away and wake up in my bed. And my ma would be shouting from the kitchen at Felix. And he'd jump through my window, with a mouse in his mouth, and she'd come chase him". Beatrix smiled wistfully. "And my da would try calm her down. But he never would. Felix would always rile her. And she'd always chase him".

Cincesse smiled as she listened to the story, eyes still closed.

"Sometimes I think she didn't want to catch him. That she enjoyed it. The game of cat and mouse they played. It's funny that, isn't it?" Beatrix asked.

"What's that", Cincesse said dreamily.

"When it seems like people don't like each other, and they bicker and argue, but really, that's their way of showing affection, of showing love", Beatrix asked.

"I hadn't thought of it like that before", Cincesse admitted. It looked like she was thinking of something similar. "But now that I do, yes, it is funny".

"My ma and Felix would always bicker. She'd always fuss him and chase him. And he'd always rile her up, always tease her. But I think that's just how they showed each other they liked each other. How they played with each other, you know?" Beatrix said.

Felix waved his tail mischievously.

"Like they couldn't just come out and say it. She was no good with feelins. Ma". Beatrix trailed off. "Me neither, to be honest".

Cincesse bobbed her head gently.

"My pa would always try and say, why can't you just get along with her Bea? Why you gotta rile her up? Maybe it was the same thing".

"Mmm?" Cincesse said.

"Me and ma. Maybe Felix knew something I didn't. Maybe he knew my ma didn't know how to show her feelins. Maybe that was my ma tryna show her feelings". Beatrix looked thoughtful. "We always bickered, and I always riled her up, just like Felix. But now that she's gone, I miss her something awful. I'd give anything to see her come through that door. To bicker with her. To tease her about something. To have her tell me off for bein cheeky".

"Maybe", Cincesse said dreamily. "Maybe she just didn't know how to speak to you".

Beatrix sniffed. "Maybe. Maybe I didn't know how to speak to her neither. Maybe we were just...different. Maybe that scared her".

"It's hard when you don't understand the people you love", Cincesse admitted.

Beatrix looked at Cincesse. "You sound like you've experience of that yourself".

"Maybe", Cincesse breathed.

"Maybe". Beatrix shook her head. "Mysterious Cincesse. Always mysterious".

Cincesse smirked as if this pleased her. "That's me".

Beatrix could tell she was tired. She was tired too. An early night would be good, she supposed. She was having a lot of them lately. She wiggled down in the bed. Cincesse wiggled with her, as if her head was glued to Beatrix's shoulder.

"Scooch up", Beatrix whispered to Felix.

Felix obliged, but only a little.

Beatrix pushed him a little further and he whipped his tail at her.

"Little hecker", Beatrix whispered, slapping his rump.

Katy yawned.

"Gnight", Beatrix whispered to Cincesse.

She was already asleep.

Homesick

The next day at breakfast, Beatrix wasn't eating anything. She looked thoughtful.

"What is it?" Gwinni asked.

"Nothing".

"What?" Gwinni repeated.

Beatrix sighed. "I've been thinking".

"Oh, no", Edni said.

Lucrecia giggled.

Edni looked surprised.

Beatrix tutted at Lucrecia, but with a smile in her eye.

"About what?" Gwinni asked.

"Scrying", Beatrix said.

Cincesse stopped drinking her fruit juice.

"Oh". Gwinni looked uncomfortable. "Why is that?"

"Well, I was thinking...I might be able to do it to see my parents", Beatrix said.

"Oh". Gwinni looked thoughtful. "Well, I suppose..."

"Bad idea". Edni shook her head.

"Why's that?" Beatrix crossed her arms.

"Make you homesick", Edni said.

"I'm already homesick", Beatrix said.

"Make you more homesick", Edni said.

"That doesn't even make sense", Beatrix said.

"Doesn't now. Will if you scry them", Edni said.

Beatrix scowled, like this wasn't the answer she'd been looking for. She turned to Gwinni. "Can you help me?"

"Me?" Gwinni asked.

Beatrix nodded.

"With scrying?" Gwinni asked.

Beatrix nodded.

Gwinni looked at Cincesse, who was watching her closely. "Err...I suppose so".

Cincesse watched impassively.

"It's just..." Gwinni looked sheepish.

"Out with it", Beatrix said.

"It's just, last time, it didn't go so well, did it?" Gwinni asked.

Beatrix blushed. "No. But that's why I want your help. I want it to go well this time".

"Well, Edni is better than me at-" Gwinni began.

"I want your help", Beatrix said firmly.

"Suit yourself", Edni said. She looked truly unbothered and was applying liberal amounts of butter and jam to a slab of toast.

Gwinni swallowed. She seemed acutely aware Cincesse was still staring at her.

"It's fine", Cincesse said. "Don't let me stop you".

"Are you sure?" Gwinni replied.

Cincesse nodded. "I don't want Beatrix to be sad. Missing her parents makes her sad, so..." She focused her attention on her breakfast.

Beatrix smiled and turned back to Gwinni. "So, you'll help me?"

"I mean..." Gwinni started.

"What?" Beatrix asked.

"What if...what if..." Gwinni stopped.

"Out with it", Beatrix said impatiently. She was sick of everyone tiptoeing around her.

Gwinni breathed deeply. "What if you pull them to you, like you did with...Cincesse".

Cincesse pretended not to hear.

"I won't", Beatrix said firmly.

"And what if something goes wrong? What if they get hurt? What if they're not meant to be scryed?" Gwinni began.

"What if, what if, what if". Beatrix waved her hand. "What if".

"Gregor said that..." Gwinni stopped herself.

"What did Gregor say?" Beatrix's eyes were piercing.

Gwinni shook her head. "Forget it".

"No, tell me", Beatrix insisted.

Gwinni took a deep breath. "Gregor said, not to help you scry your parents".

Beatrix raised her eyebrows. "He did, did he?"

Gwinni seemed relieved. She'd expected a much worse reaction. "You're not mad?"

Beatrix shook her head and took a bite of toast. No", she said through a mouthful. "Nothing surprises me about this school anymore. Or Gregor. I'm sure he had a good reason".

"That's...very mature", Gwinni deduced. She seemed surprised.

Beatrix nodded. "Maybe I'm growing up".

Lucrecia raised an eyebrow, but Beatrix didn't see. It looked like she was surprised too at Beatrix's lack of reaction.

"So...that's why", Gwinni continued.

"That's why what?" Beatrix countered.

"Why I'm not sure I should do it", Gwinni said.

"When did Gregor tell you that?" Beatrix asked.

"When you first arrived", Gwinni confirmed.

"And since then, do you not think I've grown as a witch? As a person?" Beatrix asked.

Gwinni squirmed. Beatrix had put her on the spot, and she knew it.

"Well, yes", Gwinni admitted.

"So, do you not think I deserve this?" Beatrix asked. "That I've earned this? When I first got here, I couldn't control my powers, or my temper. I was blowing holes in the school. You've just told me Gregor has gone behind my back and kept secrets from me. And did I get mad at all?"

"Well, no, but I don't see the connection between that and-" Gwinni began.

Beatrix interrupted her. "If I can control my temper, I can control my power. I can control what I do. I can **listen**. To you".

Gwinni frowned. She felt as though Beatrix was trapping her in a web of logic. She didn't know if this proved Beatrix's point, or if she was just being manipulated. She was also mindful of the rough time Beatrix was having. In the end, her empathy won. "Fine".

Beatrix grinned happily.

"But on one condition". Gwinni raised a hand.

"Anything", Beatrix conceded.

"You do **exactly** as I say", Gwinni ordered.

"Fine", Beatrix said airily.

"And not until later", Gwinni said. "There's something I have to do first".

"What's that?" Beatrix said suspiciously.

"Never you mind", Gwinni scolded.

"Fine". Beatrix supposed she shouldn't pry any further and annoy Gwinni when she was already on thin ice.

"We don't have any lessons this afternoon, so we'll do it after lunch", Gwinni said. "I have to go".

"Wait, why?" You haven't finished your breakfast", Beatrix asked.

"I'll see you later". Gwinni ignored her and hurried out of the hall.

At the professor's table, Gregor watched her go.

"What's she up to?" Beatrix mused.

"I don't know. But you'll get to see your parents!" Cincesse leaned over and kissed Beatrix on the cheek.

"Euch", Edni said quietly.

Cincesse flashed her a dirty look.

Edni looked away quickly.

"Come on", Cincesse said, rising to her feet and reaching for Beatrix's hand.

Beatrix smiled apologetically at Edni and took Cincesse's hand, allowing herself to be led out of the hall.

"That was rather tactless", Lucrecia said seriously.

"Shut it you", Edni grunted. After a moment, she rolled her eyes apologetically at Lucrecia and carried on munching her toast.

They had Magical History again that morning, and it went quickly, the words flowing over Beatrix's head without registering.

She sat at the back with Cincesse this time. Cincesse took her hand and didn't let it go for the entire lesson.

Beatrix found it comforting, but also a little irritating. She was grateful of the contact, and grateful that Cincesse cared, but she felt a little smothered. A little overwhelmed. She wasn't used to this much "love". Her relationship with her parents was...different. This was all so new. She sighed and looked out of the window at the sea.

"Are you alright?" Cincesse murmured, squeezing Beatrix's hand.

Beatrix forced a smile and nodded. She turned her gaze back to the sea. She frowned and her mouth fell open.

In the distance was a small flotilla of swordfish. They were swirling aggressively and swishing their tails at her. It almost looked like they were gesturing rudely at her. But swordfish didn't "gesture", did they?

She nudged Cincesse and gestured with her head out of the window.

"Mmm? What is it?" Cincesse peered past Beatrix.

"Look, the swordfish", Beatrix whispered. "Little buggers". She looked back out of the window. The swordfish had gone. She narrowed her eyes angrily.

Cincesse smiled strangely at Beatrix and returned her attention to Pietro and his chalkboard.

Beatrix shook her head. Maybe she was imagining things. Her mind was running a hundred miles an hour. She kept thinking of her parents, and her stomach kept clenching and unclenching with excitement. Was it excitement? Or nerves? Why would she be nervous! They were her parents after all! And she hadn't seen them in ages. She didn't know what she felt. But she felt a sense of unease. A sense of foreboding.

Maybe Gwinny was right. Maybe she was rushing this scrying business. Every time she tried some magic things seemed to go wrong.

But she'd done it now. She'd opened her big fat gob and convinced Gwinny. She'd "made the sale" as Graeme used to say. She was always "making the sale" at home when she wanted something. At least, according to her father.

She smiled and her eyes took on a glazed look as she gazed happily out the window, head cupped in her hand.

"You'll no take no for an answer, child", Graeme said.

"Yes, I will", Beatrix argued.

"Never". Graeme shook his head. His mouth was a grim line.

"You don't know that", Beatrix corrected him.

Graeme sighed. "What I don't know could fill many a book. But I do know this".

Beatrix put her hands on her hips and arched an eyebrow at him. "And how's that?"

"Cause I know you, girl". Graeme nodded as he stared at his daughter.

Beatrix didn't know what to say.

"I know you", Graeme repeated. He smiled suddenly, and his heavily lined face suddenly didn't look so gruff.

In the classroom, Beatrix's eyes watered. She sniffed as she rubbed her nose with the back of her hand.

"Bea? What is it?" Cincesse asked.

Beatrix shook her head and ran out of the room.

"Bea!" Cincesse called, jumping to her feet and running after her.

"What is-" Pietro turned from the chalkboard to watch Cincesse whip out the door after Beatrix. "What is it?" He looked flabbergasted.

"I don't think Beatrix is well, professor", Gwinni called. She was sitting just in front of where Beatrix and Cincesse had been. "Shall I go and check on her?"

"Well, what about the other girl, isn't one enough-" Pietro wasn't sure about all this.

"Professor Firewind asked me to check on her", Gwinni said pointedly. She looked quite nervous.

"Ah". Pietro nodded suddenly. "Yes, go on then. Off you go".

Gwinni got up from her seat.

"Chop, chop". Pietro seemed rather nervous too now.

Gwinni nodded quickly and hurried from the room. She ran down the corridor, shoes tapping loudly as she went. "Where are they?" she breathed.

"What's the matter? Please". A pleading voice drifted to her.

Her prayers were answered.

She hurried off in the direction of the voice.

"I can't do it anymore!"

Gwinni heard Beatrix wail and increased her pace. She rounded the corner and saw Beatrix and Gwinni standing in front of the great hall. She slowed to a walk, then stopped just out of sight.

"Do what?" Cincesse looked distraught.

"This!" Beatrix was crying and her face was wet with tears. She threw her hands out to encompass the castle. "This place! This school! This...sea!"

Cincesse gasped and placed her hand over her mouth. "Bea". She reached for Beatrix.

Beatrix stepped back quickly, raising her hands to stop her.

Cincesse looked truly hurt.

"Beatrix", Gwinni called, walking forward so the girls could see her.

Beatrix licked her lips. "Gwinni. What are you doing here?"

"I came to see if you were alright", Gwinni said tentatively. She walked over to Beatrix and stopped alongside Cincesse. "Are you?" It was a silly question, but she didn't know what else to say.

"Not really", Beatrix said numbly. She couldn't even muster any sass. She'd had enough of it all. She just wanted to see her parents. Her home. She shook her head and turned away. No, not her home. Not now. Not anymore. She started crying and fell to her knees, head in her hands.

Cincesse didn't know what to do.

Gwinni stepped forward and sunk gently to her knees beside Beatrix. "What's the matter?" She began gently rubbing Beatrix's back. "If you don't tell me, I can't help".

Beatrix sniffed. "I've got nowhere to go. No home. No friends. No family. Nothing. I can't do anything. I can't go anywhere. I'm useless".

"No, you are not", Gwinni said certainly. "Where is this coming from?"

Beatrix sniffed again. "I can't do any spells. Anytime I try, I make something mad happen. I blew open the classroom. I almost hurt Cin. Madame was right to punish me".

"Punish you?" Gwinni looked seriously at Cincesse, as if to say, do you know what she's talking about? Cincesse shook her head slightly.

Beatrix shook her head. "I'm useless. I'm no good at this. I was never meant to be a witch. I'm meant to be a barmaid. A bloody good one".

Gwinni snorted.

"What?" Beatrix wailed. "I would be". She wiped her eyes with the back of her hand.

"I'm sure you would be", Gwinni agreed.

Beatrix took a deep breath, which seemed to calm her down a little. "I'm sorry for crying".

Gwinni looked puzzled. "Why are you apologising?"

"I don't know", Beatrix said lamely. "I've been feeling so weird lately...it's like I don't even know who I am anymore".

"What do you mean?" Cincesse knelt on the other side of Gwinni, and brushed Beatrix's hair out of her face. Beatrix smiled apologetically at her.

Beatrix shook her head again. "I've been having these...nightmares. Visions. Flashes of light. A woman. She's..."

"What?" Cincesse said softly.

"Hurting me", Beatrix said quietly.

"Hurting you?" Cincesse's eyes flashed.

Gwinni looked worried. She looked like she was mulling something over in her head and kept looking toward the great hall.

Beatrix sighed. "I dunno. Hurting me...torturing me".

"TORTURING you?" Cincesse gasped as if she found the very thought abhorrent. "What do you mean torturing you? Who would torture a child?"

"Maybe I deserved it", Beatrix said grimly.

"Beatrix!" Cincesse sounded aghast.

"Don't be stupid". Gwinni added her voice of reason to the mix.

Beatrix looked at her feet but raised her eyebrows slightly to show she was listening.

"Whoever this woman is, you should pay her no mind", Gwinni said seriously. "She is obviously unhinged".

"I quite agree", Cincesse said pompously.

For some reason, this cheered Beatrix up a little. She gave Cincesse a gooey smile, and Gwinni rolled her eyes.

They heard footsteps, and all turned at once, like cats being startled by a sudden noise.

Whistling followed the footsteps. A pair of feet came into sight, and then, a girl.

The girl stopped suddenly. She had a sandwich in her hand. "What are-"

Gwinni leapt to her feet. "What are **what?**" She looked dangerously angry.

"Err". The girl was Edni, and she looked like she had well and truly been caught out.

"What are you doing here?" Gwinni demanded, advancing on Edni and poking her in the chest. Her voice was shrill and accusing. "Why weren't you in Magical History?"

Edni looked very shifty and looked around left to right before responding. "What's it to you?"

"What's it to me?" Gwinni's voice was getting shriller by the moment. "I was worried about you! Can't you see what a stressful time I'm having!"

Edni licked her lips and looked quickly down at Beatrix and Cincesse on the floor, who were both watching her strangely. "I can see something alright", Edni mumbled.

Gwinni growled and Edni stepped backwards. "If you're not going to explain yourself, get out of my sight". Gwinni turned her back on Edni.

It looked like Edni muttered something to herself.

Beatrix frowned. It sounded like she had said "bloody hell".

Gwinni whipped back round to face Edni. "I'm sorry, what was that?"

"Nothing, nothing!" Edni said quickly, throwing her hands up and retreating a few paces from Gwinni.

Gwinni scowled and turned her back on Edni again. "I don't have time for this", she said.

Edni scurried forward. "What's wrong with Beatrix?" She took a bite of her sandwich.

"I am right here, you know", Beatrix said from the floor.

"Sorry", Edni said sheepishly, as Cincesse glared at her.

"Yes, do control yourself why don't you?" Gwinni said icily.

Edni licked her lips. "What's up, Bea?" She offered her sandwich to Beatrix. "Want some sandwich?"

Beatrix snorted. "Oh my..."

Edni licked her lips again. Her eyes were darting side to side to Gwinni and Cincesse who were both giving her daggers. "What? I thought she might be hungry".

"I hardly think a sandwich is the appropriate-"

"No, it's fine", Beatrix broke in. "I'll have some". She grabbed the sandwich out of Edni's hand and shoved it into her mouth.

Cincesse gaped.

Beatrix struggled to chew the sandwich. They sat in silence while she tried. When she was done, she swallowed it in one great gulping swallow. It looked rather painful going down. Beatrix grimaced and stuck her tongue out. "Why do you always have a bloody sandwich?"

Edni grinned.

Gwinni snorted.

Edni looked quickly at Gwinni, as if to check if she were out of the doghouse.

Gwinni narrowed her eyes dangerously, but her mouth was twitching.

"This is all rather unorthodox, you know", Cincesse said suddenly, in her prim and proper little way.

A peal of laughter escaped Beatrix's lips. Suddenly she was laughing. Then they were all laughing. And the frowns were smiles, and the tears were no more.

Edni breathed a sigh of relief and wiped her forehead with the back of her hand. "Phew, I thought I was for it then".

"You still are", Gwinni warned. "Once we get back upstairs".

Edni gulped.

Beatrix beamed. "You two are so funny".

Gwinni rolled her eyes. "That's one way of putting it".

"What other way would you put it?" Edni said silkily.

Beatrix interjected before Gwinni could reply. "Gwin". She stood up, helped Cincesse to her feet, then gripped Gwinni's arm quickly.

"Yes?" Gwinni refocused her attention on Beatrix. She looked serious again.

"Can you show me?" Beatrix asked.

Gwinni licked her lips. "Now?"

Beatrix nodded.

They stared at one another a moment, then Gwinni nodded too. "Alright. But not here".

"Show her what?" Edni asked curiously.

"Then where?" Beatrix asked, ignoring Edni.

"Come on", Gwinni instructed.

"Hellooo?" Edni asked.

"Where?" Beatrix repeated insistently.

"Somewhere safe", Gwinni replied.

"Let's go". Gwinni looked at Edni as if to say shut up, then walked off.

Beatrix grinned at Edni, then she took Cincesse's hand and led her after Gwinni.

"Fine", Edni grumbled. "Last time I bring you a sandwich".

*

"Somewhere safe" turned out be the garden in front of Gregor's cottage. Well, it wasn't much of a garden. But there were some small plants and shrubs. Beatrix hadn't really noticed them before.

"Why have you brought us here?" Beatrix asked, glancing around. "Is Gregor here? You said he didn't want me doing this".

"Gregor is teaching some of the older students", Gwinni said airily.

Beatrix had a feeling she was lying. "And how you do you know that?" She put her hands on her hips.

Cincesse looked like she wanted to know to.

"I just do, alright. Now do you want my help or not?" Gwinni replied.

"Oooh!" Edni cooed. "Someone's touchy".

"Shut up", Gwinni shot back.

Beatrix giggled. "It's fine, it's fine!" she interjected, raising her hands before Gwinni and Edni got into it. "I believe you".

"Why ask then", Gwinni muttered grumpily.

Edni sniggered quietly.

"So how are going to do this, exactly?" Cincesse asked.

"I've been wondering that myself", Gwinni replied. "But I think I have it figured out".

Gwinni beckoned Beatrix closer.

Beatrix obliged.

"Beatrix", Gwinni said formally. "I'm going to help you scry your parents".

Beatrix nodded.

"I want you to do **exactly** what I say, **when** I say it. Do I make myself clear?" Gwinni asked.

Edni raised her eyebrows, eyes wide with surprise.

Beatrix smiled but nodded. She found bossy Gwinni cute.

Cincesse frowned, like she wasn't sure what to make of this.

"Alright". Gwinni breathed out deeply. Take my hands. She turned her palms upward.

Beatrix placed her hands on Gwinni's, palms down.

"I'm going to help you **channel**", Gwinni said seriously. "Do you understand what that means?"

Beatrix shook her head.

"It means we'll be linked. I'll feel what you feel, and any...magic...you channel, will also flow through me", Gwinni said.

Beatrix swallowed nervously.

"I am going to help you **channel** the scrying spell. I want you to focus on your parents. Their faces. Their essence. What makes them **your parents**", Gwinni said.

Beatrix sighed. She was worried. Now it was actually here, she didn't know if she wanted to do it. "Gwinni, I-"

"I believe in you", Gwinni said firmly, squeezing Beatrix's hands.

Beatrix closed her mouth. After a moment, she nodded resolutely.

"Just do what I tell you, and everything will be fine", Gwinni instructed.

Beatrix nodded again. She looked very tense.

"I'm right here with you", Cincesse said quietly from beside her.

"And me", Edni grumbled.

Beatrix's mouth twitched.

It looked like Gwinni was trying not to smile too.

Beatrix hissed suddenly, as a little swordfish swam into sight around the side of the cottage.

The swordfish swam off like its tail was on fire. Which it may well have been, if it stayed much longer and got on the wrong side of Beatrix.

Gwinni pulled her lips back as if to say, uhoh not this again.

"Come on", Beatrix said. "Let's do this. I want to see my parents". She had a steely glint in her eye now. The same glint Gwinni had seen before. It reassured her that Beatrix seemed more herself again.

Gwinni nodded. "Let's begin".

Beatrix was deadly focused now. "I can do this".

"You can do this", Gwinni repeated. "Think of your parents. Find them. And hold them in your mind". She closed her eyes.

Beatrix closed her eyes and relaxed her shoulders, letting them slump down.

She thought of Graeme and Cath. She heard them playfully bickering. The fire was crackling. Felix was padding lazily back and forth across the windowsill, waving his tail in Cath's direction.

She grinned.

Gwinni tensed. "I see them". She smiled as she caught Beatrix's memory. "Now, pull them toward you, gently".

This was the part Gwinni was dreading.

Beatrix breathed out deeply through her mouth. She willed her parents toward her. Gently, ever so gently.

"Oh", Gwinni said suddenly. Her head jerked back as if stung.

"Are you alright?" Beatrix said suddenly, one eye shooting open.

"Fine", Gwinni said shortly. "Keep going. Slowly". She looked like she was struggling to contain something.

Beatrix closed her eyes and continued.

Gwinni took a deep breath.

Edni stepped forward and placed a hand on Gwinni's shoulder. This seemed to help Gwinni a little.

"That bloody cat!" Cath hissed, lunging forward suddenly toward Felix, who nimbly leapt down past her onto the living room floor. He jumped up onto the table and prowled to the end of it, where he sat down and stared at Cath as if to say, "Yes?"

"Grrr!" Cath waved her fist at Felix.

Beatrix smiled dreamily, lost in her memory.

Gwinni flinched, as Beatrix began to glow. Edni closed her eyes and placed her open palm firmly on Gwinni's back.

"I will get you! And when I do, I'm gonna feed ya to the dogs!" Cath warned.

Felix cocked his head to the side as if to say, "You are quite welcome to try".

"Oohhh!" Cath growled.

Graeme chuckled from his armchair before the fire.

"And what are you laughing at, you great lump!" Cath warned.

"Yeh never learn, do yeh?" Graeme replied loftily.

"Don't you start!" Cath replied.

"Just leave him. He's just rilin yeh up", Graeme replied.

"I know what he's doing! He's after my chicken!" Cath replied shrilly. "And he'll not have it!" She turned her glare back to Felix, who was watching her as if she were a particularly interesting mouse. A big mouse.

"Jus give him a bit and he'll leave yeh alone", Graeme said.

"Why should I!" Cath shrilled.

"He's hungry. I'm hungry", Graeme admitted.

Cath glared at Felix then put her hands on her hips. "If he apologises".

"Apologises?" Graeme said incredulously. "He's a cat, woman!"

Cath narrowed her eyes at her husband as if to say, you think I don't know that.

"Oh, fine!" Cath walked through into the kitchen and began aggressively cutting something on a wooden chopping board. When she returned, she had a large hunk of roasted chicken in her hand. It looked like she hadn't decided if she would throw it at Felix or give it to him.

"Y'know, he wouldn' try n steal it if you jus gave him some when it was done", Graeme said.

"Why should I!" Cath shrilled.

"I-" Graeme began.

"Just shut up!" Cath said. "I'm giving him some, aren't I? Not that he deserves it!"

Cath still hadn't forgiven Felix for stealing the apple pie she'd spent all morning making. She'd meant to give it to The Sacred Sisters who were passing through, but Felix had other ideas.

He had nimbly hopped up onto the kitchen counter and eaten a significant portion of pie when Cath's back was turned. She had *foolishly gone out onto the porch to gossip, and Felix had seized his opportunity. She'd returned to find his furry face covered in crumbs and apple. He even had some on his chest.*

She'd shrieked and almost hit the roof, running forward and batting at him with her rolling pin. But she didn't catch him. She never did.

"He's ony hungry", Graeme said.

"Only hungry?" Cath was aghast. "That cat is fed better than some of our neighbours!"

Graeme didn't have a retort to this. Felix was rather well fed. But Graeme had a soft spot for Felix. Something he and his daughter had in common.

Outside Gregor's cottage, Gwinni moaned. Sweat was coursing down her face now.

Beatrix was floating slightly above the floor. Cincesse was holding her tethered in case she rose any higher.

Beatrix grinned. The water around her feet started to hiss, like a hot spring, and Cincesse quickly moved her foot back.

Beatrix continued dreaming.

Cath walked over to Felix and dropped the chicken in front of him. She folded her arms and waited.

Felix watched Cath carefully. He leant forward and sniffed the chicken gingerly. This was too good to be true. Why was she giving him chicken? He was suspicious.

"Go on then! Eat it!" Cath unfolded her arms and waved her hand at the chicken.

Felix licked his lips and began nibbling on the chicken.

Cath gritted her jaw and walked back into the kitchen.

Graeme turned in his chair and winked at Felix.

"Ohh", Gwinni cried.

"Hold on", Edni muttered. She was sweating now too.

A crack at Beatrix's feet made Cincesse cry out. She rubbed her ankle with one hand, holding on to Beatrix with the other.

"Now!" Gwinni said suddenly. Her eyes flew open, and she drew a circle in the water. The circle grew, then opened, like a portal to another world.

But the portal was black, and they couldn't see anything.

"What? But I did everything correctly..." Gwinni frowned. She was shaking slightly as if it was costing her to hold the circle open.

"Don' know why we're keepin em" a gruff voice said suddenly, the noise flowing out of the portal clear as day.

A pair of armoured men walked into sight. One had long curly red hair. The other had no hair to speak of and was holding a lantern.

Gwinni blinked as bright yellow light filled the circle.

"Beats me", the bald man said.

"Then why're we doin it?" Curly Red said. "Why don't we just chuck em in the pit and be done with it".

"You wanna tell The Inquisitress you chucked her prisoners in the pit?" the bald man replied.

"The Inquisitress asked you to guard them?" Curly Red's face went white as a sheet.

"Mhm", the bald guard replied smugly.

"Then why didn't you say so man!" Curly Red hissed.

"You din' ask", the bald guard replied amicably.

"Shh man". Curly Red cut himself off before swearing. He looked around conspiratorially. "What's a bunch of peasants done to earn the ire of er?"

"Beats me", the bald guard said. "But bes' not let em rot in the pit ay?"

"Right". Curly Red breathed in deeply through his nose. "Right", he repeated for his own benefit.

The bald guard walked forward, and Gwinni gasped as the light from the lantern threw his surroundings into focus. They were in a dungeon lined with cells. Gwinni saw men and women, and even children, huddled behind rusty black metal bars.

"Oi, you". The bald guard stopped in front of a cell and rattled his nightstick on the bars of the cell.

A man stepped forward from the back of the cell, moving a woman protectively behind him. The woman squinted from behind the man's back, her eyes trying to adjust to the light.

The man raised a hand to his forehead, shielding his eyes from the harsh glare of the lantern. He looked like he hadn't seen light in a while. He was emaciated and thin, and his face was pale and grey. "What do you want?"

"She wants to see you", the bald guard replied.

"So?" The man replied.

"How dare you-" Curly Red stepped forward aggressively, one hand on a shining silver sword scabbarded at his waist.

The bald guard threw out his arm, holding Curly Red back.

"You want a repeat o last time?" The bald guard asked.

The man in the cell glanced at the woman behind him. "No", he said begrudgingly.

"Then come with me", the bald guard ordered.

"She stays here", the man in the cell said, gesturing with his head at the woman behind him.

"She comes too", the bald guard said.

"Graeme, no", the woman in the cell said weakly, gripping the arm of the man.

The bald guard raised his lantern to see better, and the light threw the woman's face into focus. It was Cath.

Graeme gave the guards a half snarl, then gently shrugged Cath's hand off his arm. He turned to her and pulled her close. "I love you", he whispered into her ear.

"And I love you too, great oaf", Cath whispered back.

"This is awful touching an all, but she's waitin", the bald guard said tiredly, as if he was rather bored of this.

"It's not good to keep The Inquisitress waiting", Curly Red said nervously.

Cath shook her head at Graeme.

Graeme sighed then turned to face the guards. "Let's be on with it then". He walked out of the cell hand in hand with Cath.

Suddenly, the ground started to shake, and dust fell from the ceiling.

"What was that!" Curly Red said nervously, glancing around like a frightened hen.

"I don' know do I!" The bald guard shot back. "Shut up will ya!"

The bald guard looked slowly around the cells, as if trying to find the source of the shaking and the noise.

The ground started shaking again and a loud rumble came from above.

"What was that!" Curly Red backed into the cell away from them.

"Shut up!" The bald guard hissed. Even he looked a little frightened this time.

"What's going on?" Graeme asked.

The bald guard raised a hand for silence.

There was an ominous groan, like a cellar door being opened far above, then the guard's lantern went out with a pop.

"Oh, no, oh no, oh no", Curly Red moaned.

"Will you be quiet man! You're an embarrassment to The Guard!" The bald guard hissed angrily. He walked quickly to the entrance of the dungeon and returned with the lantern relit. He turned to Graeme. "Sorry about this", he said apologetically. "Rich boy, you see. Bought is' way in. Probably never thought he'd see any action. You know ow it is".

Graeme nodded understandingly.

"Oh no, oh no", Curly Red mumbled quietly from the back of the cell, where he now had his back to the wall.

The bald guard shook his head. He was looking at Curly Red distastefully, as if he couldn't believe he was forced to work alongside him.

"What's going on?" one of the other prisoners asked. He was peering through the bars of his cell, his dirty face pressed up against them. He was trying to squeeze part of his face through the bars so he could look down the corridor, at the stairs that led out of the dungeon.

The bald guard turned to face the prisoner. "Nothin, now get back in your cell".

"I am in my cell", the prisoner corrected him.

"Back in your cell!" The bald guard whacked his nightstick against the bars of the cell, and the prisoner leapt backwards.

"Jeez, no need for that now is there?" The prisoner shook his head. "No manners you lot".

"I'll give you manners in a minute, now zip your mouth!" The bald guard ordered.

A loud howl rang out from above. It sounded like a wolf.

The bald guard tensed and put his hand on his sword.

"Howww". The prisoner with the dirty face echoed the howl.

"Shut it!" The bald guard roared.

The prisoner obliged, and the dungeon went completely silent.

Graeme took Cath's hand and backed away quietly from the bald guard.

The silence was tense, and the only thing that could be heard were the deep, nervous breaths of Graeme, Cath and the bald guard.

"You're mine". A sibilant whisper exploded in Gwinni's ears.

"Aghhh!" Gwinni screamed, as a hand reached through the circle and gripped her by the scruff of her pinafore.

Beatrix"s eyes flared open as Gwinni released her hands.

"Get off, get off!" Gwinni beat at the hand and pulled backwards, but she couldn't move more than a few inches. The hand had her pinned.

Cincesse ran forward and tried to beat at the hand, but she was thrown backwards as soon as she made contact with it.

"Cincesse!" Beatrix cried.

"Edni!" Gwinni wailed. "Help!" She looked terrified.

Edni clenched her jaw and grabbed the hand with a two-handed grip. She bucked, as if something had surged through her, but hung on. "Ahh!" She screamed as her hands started to blacken and smoke. After a few moments she had to let go, and sunk to her knees, cradling her burned hands uselessly against her chest.

The invading hand belonged to a woman. It was feminine, but strong. The fingernails were black. The hand began to glow a musky black, like dark, dirty smoke, and Gwinni screamed in terror. Her hair stood on end, and she began to glow the same black colour as the hand.

"Gwinni no!" Beatrix cried. Without hesitation she gripped the woman's hand with both of her own. Her cheeks twitched and she snarled as pain burst through her. Blackness quickly flowed from the woman's hand along her own and covered her completely. "Get off her", Beatrix growled, managing to hold onto the hand.

"Who...are...you?" The sibilant voice rang out. It was like a snake's whisper on the wind.

Beatrix closed her eyes. She was struggling to hold on to Gwinni. But she wasn't going to let go. She'd never let go!

She felt something probing her mind.

Something like...fingers.

The fingers probed and pressed and poked.

It was painful and Beatrix grimaced.

"You?" The voice sounded slightly less sibilant. "It can't be..."

"Oh, but it is", Beatrix replied angrily.

"Is it really you?" The voice asked longingly. It sounded almost human now.

"What? I don't know who you are, and I don't know what you want. I don't care", Beatrix said. "Just leave my friend alone!"

"GREGOR!" Gwinni screamed suddenly.

"Wench!" The sibilant voice hissed.

There was a pop and Gregor appeared on the path.

The hand and the circle disappeared.

The Great Lie

"You lied to me!" Beatrix hissed, advancing quickly on Gregor, sparks of misty black lightning cracking from her hair.

"Woah!" Gregor threw his hands up defensively as he stepped back. The sparks hit his hands and sizzled before disappearing.

"Explain yourself! Beatrix demanded, poking her finger into Gregor's chest.

"Beatrix!" Gwinni cried, running forward to restrain her friend. "Ow!" She stepped back rubbing her hand. She'd gotten a rather nasty shock when she'd grabbed Beatrix's arm.

"I...sorry". Beatrix stepped back uncertainly. Her hair fell tiredly to her shoulders.

Gwinni frowned as she peered into Beatrix's eyes, which seemed to dilate for a moment, then return to normal. "What's wrong with you?"

"He...he lied to me!" Beatrix pointed at Gregor, regaining some of her bluster. "He told me they were safe! He told me they were fine!"

"Who?" Gwinni asked, momentarily bemused. "Ah". She licked her lips guiltily.

"My parents..." Beatrix looked at Gwinni strangely. "Wait...you knew?"

Gwinni swallowed. "Well, I-"

Beatrix raised a hand. "I don't want to hear it!" She looked terribly fierce. "You lied to me, both of you!"

"Beatrix!" Gwinni looked crestfallen. "It's not like that at all!"

"Then what is it like?" Beatrix placed her hands on her hips. But there was none of her usual spiciness. Her expression was glacial.

"It's...I..." Gwinni looked to Gregor for support.

"Beatrix, this is entirely my fault", Gregor interjected.

"And why is that?" Beatrix spun to face him.

"I told Gwinni not to tell you about your...parents. I forbade her", Gregor said.

Gwinni looked down at her feet sheepishly.

"Why would you do that! And why would you lie to me! All this time I've been here, wasting time, prancing about playing witch! I could have been helping them! How could you do this to me?" She advanced on Gregor again. He stepped back to match her steps forward.

"It's not like that, I assure you", Gregor said.

"Rubbish!" Beatrix spat.

Gregor sighed and licked his lips. How was he going to unpickle this one? "Beatrix".

"Don't Beatrix me. Explain. Quickly", Beatrix demanded.

Gregor ran his tongue inside his cheeks. He looked like he wanted to tell Beatrix off, but realised he was in a situation of his own making. "Please, not here".

Beatrix looked quickly around at her friends. "I'll only tell them later".

"Maybe so. But not here. Not if you want the truth", Gregor said tiredly.

Beatrix looked strangely at Gregor. It looked like part of her wanted to rip his head off. The other part, the prevailing part, was desperate for answers. She gritted her teeth. "Fine". She jerked her head toward the sea lift. "Lead the way".

Gregor breathed out heavily and raised his eyebrows, but said nothing. He walked away toward the castle, Beatrix in tow.

The girls stood in silence for a while, watching Beatrix and Gregor disappear into the distance.

Finally, Edni broke the silence. "**Blooody hell**. What on earth was all **that** about?"

Gwinni looked at Edni like she was a perpetually misbehaving child.

Cincesse was unusually quiet.

"Are you alright?" Gwinni asked, watching her.

"Yes", Cincesse said dreamily, her eyes faraway. "I suppose so".

"She'll be alright", Gwinni said, rubbing Cincesse's back.

Edni nodded as if she didn't doubt it. "Come on. It's dinner time".

Gwinni gave Edni a look of disgust. "Do you ever think of anything but food?"

Edni looked thoughtful for a moment. "When it's not dinner time".

Gwinni shook her head despairingly. "Come on, they should have gone up by now".

*

"Sit". Gregor gestured to the chair on the other side of the desk. They were in Madame's office. Beatrix was tempted to ask if Madame would mind, but she was too angry and had too many other things on her mind.

She glared at Gregor from across the desk.

"Please", Gregor asked.

Beatrix begrudgingly obliged and took the seat opposite him. Her curiosity got the better of her in the end. "Won't Madame mind?"

Gregor shook his head. "I think not".

Beatrix wanted to ask more. But what she really wanted to know, was why the man opposite her had lied to her. She stared at him expectantly and crossed her arms.

Gregor sighed. "I didn't lie to you, Beatrix, at least, not at first".

"What's that supposed to mean?" Beatrix asked, uncrossing her arms and leaning forward in her chair.

"Your parents **were** safe. I saw to that myself. When I scryed them for you, that wasn't a lie…a mirage…a falsehood". Gregor waved a hand dismissively. "They were quite safe".

"Well, they aren't now!" Beatrix exclaimed. "I saw them myself!

Gregor nodded. "Quite".

"Quite". Beatrix tutted and shook her head disgustedly.

Gregor grimaced.

"What are we going to do about it!" Beatrix demanded.

"**We** are going to do nothing. **I**, am working on it", Gregor explained.

"No, you don't seriously expect me to just sit here and do nothing while my ma and da rot in a dungeon somewhere?" Beatrix was incredulous. "You got the wrong witch!" Her eyes flared and Gregor shifted nervously in his seat.

"There is nothing you can do. In fact, the worst thing you could do would be to go looking for them now", Gregor explained.

"And why is that?" Beatrix asked.

"I…cannot say. But please, I beg of you, you must trust me on this". It was Gregor's turn to lean forward. His eyes were pleading, and Beatrix had never heard him talk like this before. He was always so calm, collected, suave almost.

Beatrix frowned. She wasn't pacified though. "And why is that? Why shouldn't I rescue them? What sort of daughter would I be if I just did nothing!"

Gregor opened his mouth, but Beatrix stood up suddenly.

"You think I'll just let them hurt my parents!" Beatrix began to glow. But this time, it wasn't her usual white. It was black. Like the woman from the Scrying circle. Her eyes were dilated. She clenched her jaw, and her fists followed. "If they dare hurt them!"

Her chair began to float above the floor, and her hair was standing on end.

Gregor's eyes widened. "Beatrix, please!"

Something in his tone got through to Beatrix, and her eyes returned to normal.

The chair clattered to the floor behind her.

Beatrix looked back in surprise. She blinked, then righted the chair. "I'm just saying..." She took a deep breath and turned away from Gregor.

"I won't let anyone hurt them", Gregor said softly.

Beatrix sniffed and rubbed her eyes. She turned back to Gregor. "You better not. Or I'll never forgive you". She had her usual steely glint in her eyes. And thankfully, no black glow around her.

She looked at Gregor appraisingly. "So how are you going to save them?"

Gregor raised an eyebrow and gave Beatrix an appraisal of his own. "I have my ways".

"And they are?" Beatrix looked at Gregor as if he were stupid.

"I have...allies", Gregor said lamely. "Allies that I can call on in the event of...an emergency...like this".

"Allies", Beatrix said blankly.

"Allies", Gregor agreed.

"They must be powerful indeed", Beatrix teased.

Gregor nodded.

Beatrix narrowed her eyes. "Well, they can't be human".

Gregor's mouth fell open. "And why is that?"

"The only humans with the power to help my ma and da are in this room, and in this castle. And if it was one of them, you'da said", Beatrix said.

Gregor licked his lips. "Perhaps".

Beatrix shook her head. "Perhaps". She shook her head again. "Enough with the lies, Gregor".

Gregor looked affronted at being addressed like this by his student. But he sensed that Beatrix was not to be pacified so easily. Perhaps best to give her an inch, so she didn't take a mile. "You're right".

Beatrix nodded. "I know". There was no trace of arrogance, just cold certainty.

Gregor frowned. "And what else do you know?"

Beatrix looked like she was on the verge of a discovery. "Enough". She got up from her chair.

"Where are you going?" Gregor said suddenly.

"To eat", Beatrix said. "I take it that's allowed?" Her hands were back on her hips.

"I...yes". Gregor looked flustered. He also looked worried. How much did she know?

Beatrix turned to leave.

"Beatrix!" Gregor called.

"Yes?"

"Please promise me...you won't do anything reckless", Gregor pleaded.

"Me?" Beatrix paused. "Wouldn't dream of it".

Gregor looked like he'd swallowed a teaspoon of particularly foul-tasting medicine, and there was absolutely nothing he could do about it.

He nodded.

Beatrix nodded back, then left.

*

"Beatrix!" Gwinni said breathlessly, as Beatrix sank into the seat beside her.

Cincesse took her hand immediately. "Are you ok, Bea?"

Beatrix nodded. "I'm fine". She didn't look fine. But she didn't look angry or frightening anymore. She looked something else. Something certain.

Edni raised an eyebrow. "You didn't look fine. You were all...black".

Gwinni's eyes bulged as they screamed "shut-up" across the table.

"What?" Edni shrugged. "She did. It was spooky".

Beatrix didn't say anything. She pulled a tureen of roasted potatoes toward her and began ladling them calmly onto her plate.

Gwinni was looking at Beatrix like she was a bomb that might go off at any moment. "Beatrix, I-"

Beatrix cut her off. "It's fine". She smiled politely at Gwinni.

"It is?" Gwinni didn't seem so sure.

Beatrix nodded maturely. "Gregor explained, didn't he?"

"He did?" Gwinni asked, bemused.

"That's right. He forbade you. You were just following the rules". Beatrix seemed oddly distant and detached.

"I was?" Gwinni seemed uncertain.

Beatrix nodded again.

"Well…are you sure?" Gwinni looked worried she had upset her friend deeply.

Beatrix paused for a moment, then nodded.

"You look weird", Edni interjected.

"Thanks", Beatrix replied.

Edni's eyebrows arched.

"Are you alright?" A calm voice, a quiet voice. A caring voice. Lucrecia.

"Hello, Luce", Beatrix said, with a bit more warmth in her voice. "I'm alright, thanks". She forced a smile.

Lucrecia watched her quietly.

Beatrix wasn't sure Lucrecia bought her 'everything is alright' act, so she looked away quickly, back to her food.

"Enough potatoes?" Edni asked, as Beatrix absentmindedly scooped more onto her plate.

"Just about", Beatrix replied.

"What did Gregor say?" Cincesse was still being unusually quiet and subdued.

"This and that", Beatrix said airily.

"This and that?" Cincesse didn't know what to make of this.

Beatrix waved a hand. "He tried to weasel out of it. But I know the truth".

"The truth?" Cincesse looked slightly worried at this.

Beatrix nodded. "He lied to me, plain and simple".

Gwinni opened her mouth, then closed it with a pop. She felt she didn't have a right to interject, when she too had lied to her friend. "I agree".

Beatrix looked at her strangely. "You do?"

"Oh yes". Gwinni nodded fervently. "We should have told you. I'd have been most upset".

Beatrix looked slightly amused. Some of the ice seemed to melt around her. "Is that so?"

Gwinni nodded enthusiastically. "I felt awful about it. The whole darn thing".

Beatrix raised her eyebrows. "Then, why'd you do it?" Her eyes were cold.

"I..." Gwinni paused.

Beatrix continued to stare.

"I...don't know". Gwinni swallowed and looked down at her plate. "I just wanted to keep you safe". She was talking rather quietly now. "Gregor said it was the only way to keep you safe".

Beatrix frowned.

"He said you'd...run off and do something stupid. Said you'd get captured. Burned". Gwinni was mumbling now, but they all heard her.

Beatrix went white, but her jaw was clenching and unclenching angrily. "Is that right?"

Gwinni looked up. Her eyes were filled with tears. "I'm so sorry Beatrix!" she gushed suddenly. "I wanted to tell you, honestly, I did. I felt **awful** when he made me promise not to. I haven't slept in nights!"

"It's true", Edni said quietly.

Beatrix turned her angry gaze from Gwinni to Edni.

Edni stared back calmly.

"I'm so sorry!" Gwinni pulled Beatrix into a hug. "Please forgive me".

Beatrix sighed over the top of Gwinni's shoulder and looked up at the ceiling. "I forgive you".

"You do?" Gwinni broke their hug. Her eyes shone with hope.

Beatrix sighed again. "Yes. Just don't ever lie to me again", she warned.

"I won't, oh I won't!" Gwinni gushed. She hugged Beatrix again then beamed.

Beatrix smiled wearily.

"Oh! And besides! Now that the cats out of the bag, I can tell you!" Gwinni gushed.

"Cat? Bag? What are you talking about?" Beatrix frowned.

"Your parents. I've been thinking about how we can rescue them! Since Gregor told me", Gwinni said.

Beatrix looked surprised, impressed and touched in equal measure.

"And I think I've figured it out!" Gwinni said.

"You needn't", Beatrix said cooly.

"Oh?" Gwinni seemed dejected.

"I know exactly how we're going to rescue them", Beatrix said, a resolute gleam in her eyes.

"And how is that?" Gwinni asked uncertainly.

Edni was watching Beatrix carefully over her half-eaten plate of lemon tart.

Cincesse and Lucrecia gave each other a glance that said, do you know what she means?

"Tis a pirates life for me", Beatrix replied mysteriously, her eyes on the professor's table.

Tis A Beautiful Night For It

"You're not serious about this?" They were back in the Witches Den after dinner, and Cincesse was trying to talk Beatrix out of her plan.

"Deadly", Beatrix replied. "If you don't want to help me, fine".

Cincesse looked hurt. "It's not like that at all!"

"Then what is it like?" Beatrix asked.

"I just..." Cincesse trailed off and looked away.

Beatrix felt like Cincesse wasn't telling her something. But she didn't have time to dwell on it. She had to rescue her parents.

"Are you coming, or not?" Beatrix asked.

Cincesse grimaced. "Yes".

"Well alright then", Beatrix said awkwardly.

Cincesse looked like she might say something, but then she walked off to sit on Lucrecia's bed next to Lucrecia.

Beatrix sighed.

Felix wound himself about her legs. "You always were something of a rulebreaker", he thought.

"And you weren't?" Beatrix thought back.

"Not at all", Felix thought cheekily.

Beatrix smiled and bent to rub his head.

"And I suppose you'll need me for this trip?" Felix thought lazily.

"Yes", she thought back.

If a sigh could be thought, then that is what Felix did now. "Fine". He wagged his tail lazily and sauntered away to rub himself against Katy, who was sitting by Beatrix's bed.

Lucrecia smiled happily at Katy and Felix, then she looked up and beamed at Beatrix.

Edni was laid back on her bed snacking on a handful of nuts. **Cronch. Cronch. Cronch.**

Gwinni approached Beatrix. "When are we going to do it?"

The girls all listened for Beatrix's response.

"After lights out", Beatrix replied.

Gwinni nodded.

"I don't want any chance of being caught", Beatrix said.

"Smart", Edni said drily from her bed. She brushed a handful of crumbs from her chest.

Gwinni pursed her lips distastefully.

"I like to go dancing in the moonlight", Lucrecia volunteered suddenly. She was looking out the window into the deep blue sea.

Beatrix frowned. "You're not coming".

Lucrecia's eyes snapped back to Beatrix. "And why is that?" She sounded polite, but her eyes were blazing.

"It's not safe", Beatrix said.

"For you either", Lucrecia said.

There was silence for a moment, then Lucrecia continued, "You can't stop me, you know. If you try, I'll simply come **after you**, and then I really will be unsafe".

Edni's mouth fell open.

Gwinni and Cincesse both looked shocked.

Even Beatrix was taken aback. She approached Lucrecia on the bed and knelt, taking her hands. "I just want to keep you safe. I..."

Lucrecia was watching Beatrix strangely, as if not sure what to expect.

"You're like a little sister to me", Beatrix said quietly, looking down at the floor.

Lucrecia didn't know what to say. She leant forward and kissed Beatrix gently on the forehead.

Beatrix looked up, shocked.

"You're like a sister to me, too, Bea", Lucrecia said.

Beatrix was touched, and swallowed deeply.

"Which is why, I shan't let you go by yourself", Lucrecia said quickly.

"I won't be by myself-" Beatrix started.

"And as any little sister, it is my duty to follow you into mischief and mayhem", Lucrecia cut her off. "You can't stop me. So don't even try".

Beatrix smirked. She'd tried. "Can't argue with that".

Cincesse was gazing lovingly at Beatrix. Beatrix smiled, then looked away, a little uncomfortable at the intensity of feeling in Cincesse's eyes.

Gwinni strode over and hugged Beatrix from behind. "Oh, you!" She pulled Lucrecia into the hug. "Come here!" She pulled Cincesse in too. "All of you, come here!" She turned and looked expectantly at Edni over her shoulder.

Edni rolled her eyes and slouched over to them. She knelt down so Gwinni could pull her into the impromptu group hug.

"I love you all!" Gwinni exclaimed.

"You hardly know us!" Beatrix replied.

"Oh, I know...I just...do, alright?" Gwinni replied. "Is that alright?"

"I suppose", Beatrix said wrily.

Edni grumbled. It sounded like she was still chewing.

"Are you **still** eating!" Gwinni looked under her arm.

Edni grinned up at her, from where she'd been unceremoniously pulled into the group hug.

Gwinni smiled and shook her head. "Even you", she said, gazing lovingly at Edni.

Edni winked.

"Goodnight girls!"

They heard Madame Tempest's curt voice from outside the bedroom. Beatrix's eyes snapped toward the door. She looked like she was waiting for something.

Thunk.

The door to the Witches Den slammed shut. It was big and heavy and clunky, and its sound was unmistakable.

"It's time", Beatrix said.

"We're really going to do this?" Edni asked. She looked incredulous.

Beatrix nodded.

Edni looked thoughtfully out the window, then turned back and grinned. "Always wanted to be a pirate".

Cincesse stared forlornly out the window as the girls giggled at Edni.

*

The girls were huddled outside Gregor's cottage in the sea.

"Why are we going from here?" Lucrecia whispered.

"You don't need to whisper", Edni said matter-of-factly.

"Why not?" Lucrecia whispered.

"Gregor isn't here. He's drinking whisky up at the castle", Edni replied.

"How do you know?" Gwinni whispered, looking around conspiratorially.

"He always does when he's mad or stressed", Edni said.

Gwinni looked impressed at the astuteness of her friend.

"You're sure he's not here?" Gwinni asked.

Edni rolled her eyes. "Greeegs!" she yelled suddenly.

"What are you doing!" Gwinni hissed, pulling at Edni's arm aggressively.

"Ow, get orf!" Edni yelled.

They all went silent then and waited tensely to see if they were for it.

Edni grinned smugly. "See? Told you".

A burst of air escaped Gwinni's lungs as she sighed with relief. "There's no need to behave like that!" she hissed in a half whisper.

"Why are you still whispering". Edni chuckled.

"Just shut up, ok?" Gwinni said.

Beatrix turned to Cincesse. "Ready?"

Cincesse nodded quietly and smiled weakly. She took Beatrix's hand and gave it a little squeeze. Beatrix smiled back.

Gwinni licked her lips apprehensively and looked up.

"You're sure this will work?" Beatrix asked.

"Well...no", Gwinni admitted.

"No?" Beatrix's eyes widened.

"What do you want me to say!" Gwinni snapped. She looked tense.

"I want you to say this will work", Beatrix replied calmly.

"It will work. It should work". Gwinni bit her lip.

"Great". Edni snorted.

"I believe in you". Lucrecia smiled happily at Gwinni. "You're very smart".

Gwinni blushed. "Not that smart", she mumbled. She took a deep breath. "It **should** work. I see no reason why it won't".

Felix, who had his nose buried in a hole on the path, looked up at Gwinni.

Katy appeared out of the reeds lining the path and rubbed her nose against Felix's face.

"Come on," Beatrix said. "Gather round. But not too close", she warned. "Not like that", she corrected Edni. "In a line. Like when we went to the pub. **No not like that**". Beatrix pulled Edni to her left. "Cin". She held her hand out for Cincesse.

Cincesse took it and stood to the right of Beatrix.

"Felix". Beatrix called Felix over to her.

Felix padded over and leapt nimbly to her shoulder.

"Katy". Lucrecia kissed at Katy, who leapt to her shoulder.

"Risk!" Cincesse called a little louder. Risk came running and took a running jump to her shoulder. "Oof!" She staggered under the force of his jump. "Ow, silly cat".

Lucrecia giggled.

Edni's cat, Boris, a large grey shorthair, leapt into her arms. She dropped her hands and caught him, then heaved him onto her shoulders where he wrapped himself leisurely around her neck.

Beatrix waggled her fingers expectantly, and Edni took her hand again. Gwinni took Edni's other hand, and Lucrecia grabbed Cincesse's free hand on the end of the line.

Beatrix looked up and down the line. They were a funny sight, the five witches outside Gregor's cottage, cats wrapped around their necks. Beatrix grinned wickedly. She loved it. "Tonight, we fly!"

Gwinni whispered a prayer as they turned their eyes skyward.

*

They touched down on the moon with a **thump!**

"Oof", Edni said. She looked a little sick and was rubbing her stomach. "Didn't like that at all".

"Was that your first time flying?" Gwinni asked.

"No", Edni said defensively. "What do you think I am, a Novi?"

"What's wrong with being a Novi?" Gwinni shot back.

"You two", Beatrix moaned. She was rubbing her stomach too. "Give it a rest".

Gwinni looked apologetically at Beatrix. "Sorry. That was rather a bumpy ride".

Cincesse sighed. "Agreed".

"Witches don't usually fly in fives", Gwinni said.

"Oh, no?" Beatrix asked wrily.

"Well, not always. And I'm sure that if they do, they all know how to fly", Gwinni said.

"We do know how to fly", Beatrix corrected her.

"Two trips doesn't exactly make you an accomplished flyer", Cincesse said quietly.

"What was that?" Beatrix asked.

"Nothing", Cincesse said sweetly.

Beatrix gave Cincesse a look that said, you're for it if you keep it up.

"Come on, let's go", Cincesse said. "Where is this pirate you've dragged me up here for". She looked around impatiently.

Beatrix grinned. "Don't you remember?"

Cincesse frowned. "Oh, no, surely you don't mean that-"

Beatrix shushed her and raised a finger to her lips.

Cincesse tutted. "Don't you shush me".

Beatrix grinned. "Just did".

Cincesse scowled and huffed.

"What pirate?" Lucrecia said sweetly, looking around expectantly as if expecting to see one appear on the horizon.

Gwinni frowned and shielded her eyes with her hands, as the shine from a large star hit her.

"**That pirate**". Beatrix was grinning wickedly and staring into the distance.

Lucrecia frowned and looked where Beatrix was staring. "Oh, my". She covered her hand with her mouth.

"Thar she blows, boys". A coarse voice bellowed in the distance.

Gwinni's mouth dropped open. "Is that..."

"Yup". Beatrix was beaming from ear to ear.

Cincesse swallowed and took a step back. "Bea". She pulled at Beatrix's arm. "I'm not sure this is such a good idea..."

Beatrix gave her a resolved look, and Cincesse gave a small nod. There was no talking Beatrix out of this.

"Yahooo!" A large pirate jumped into the air and kicked his legs together out to the side.

"Ah, Buck! Watch yerself man!" A smaller pirate shook his hands out. They were drenched with some luminous, violently red liquid, that looked like it had been electrified.

"Mmm, ah". The large pirate raised a glass bottle full of the red stuff to his lips and took a mighty swig. His lips were shining red in the moonlight.

Beatrix crossed her arms and watched as the pirates approached. There were four of them. The man, Buck, that she'd first seen outside the tavern. The lad from the waterfall with the moustache, and two others she hadn't met. She was surprised to see that one of them was a girl.

"Chu lookin at?" The girl was staring challengingly at Beatrix.

"Nothing, sorry". Beatrix blushed. She had been staring after all.

The girl seemed taken aback, like this wasn't the sort of behaviour she expected from humans. She looked away.

"Bahahah". The big pirate laughed and slapped the girl on the back. She stumbled under the weight of his slap and scowled up at him. "See you've met Violet? Charmer, en't she?"

"Sod off". Violet shrugged Buck's hand off. "You're drunk".

"Am not!" Buck roared, sloshing a measure of the red liquid onto Violet's shoulder.

"Ahhh! Get off you lout!" Violet turned and pushed Buck away with both hands.

He stumbled a little then righted himself. "HEY NOW!" He looked down at his bottle. "You made me spill me Bucky!"

"Serves you right". Violet gave Buck a look of disgust and walked away a few paces and crossed her arms. She stood staring out into the distance as Beatrix watched her.

Gwinni cleared her throat. "Err, ser?"

Buck was staring sadly at his buttle of Bucky. He burped and looked up. "Eh? Me?"

"Ser". The pirate with the moustache chuckled with his friend, another young pirate with a mustache. His friend's moustache was blond and a bit sparser than his, like he couldn't quite grow it properly yet.

"Shut it, Tiger". Buck glared blearily at the pirate with the black mustache. "Plenty called me ser before".

"In your dreams maybe!" Tiger whacked his mate happily on the back.

"And what are you laughin at Wolf? Go twiddle yer lip". Buck hawked and spat.

Wolf self-consciously twirled his half-grown mustache between his long, thin fingers.

"Ignore him Wolf". Tiger shook his head at Buck. "And to think, I used to look up to you".

Buck continued to glare at his crewmates.

"Buck". Beatrix walked forward and extended her hand, introducing herself. "Beatrix".

Buck looked down at her hand a moment, then took it. He straightened himself and puffed his chest out, fixing Beatrix with a fearsome stare. "Captain Buck. Captain of the Buckswift. Leader of Captain Buck's Brazen Baws. And the fiercest pirate this side of the Milky Dipper!" Buck roared this last and pumped his arm into the sky, showering the group with drops of the vicious red liquid.

"AGHHH!" Violet cursed darkly as she rubbed herself down. Drops of the red stuff had sprayed her face and hair.

Beatrix couldn't help but laugh.

Even Tiger and Wolf sniggered.

Tiger was looking at Buck half bemused, half amused. Beatrix sensed there was something of a love hate relationship between Buck and his crew.

"Milky Dipper?" Beatrix looked bemused.

"Ignore him", Tiger said, stepping forward. "Tiger". He extended his hand to Beatrix.

"I know", Beatrix said cooly. "We met".

"Oh, I remember. But we haven't been formally introduced yet", Tiger said silkily, still holding Beatrix's hand.

Cincesse cleared her throat. She was giving Tiger an icy look.

Tiger licked his lips and let go of Beatrix's hand. "Yeah, well. Nice to meet you".

"Is your name really Tiger?" Lucrecia looked fascinated. She cocked her head and looked Tiger up and down.

Tiger nodded.

Lucrecia frowned. "But where are your stripes".

Buck guffawed and choked on a mouthful of his drink.

Tiger smiled in good spirits. He stepped forward and raised Lucrecia's hand to his chest. "Right here".

Lucrecia smiled in understanding.

"Very cute", Beatrix said wrily.

Tiger flashed her a winning smile, that quickly disappeared at another glare from Cincesse.

Edni sniffed. "Got any food?"

Tiger turned his smile on Edni. "Course. What do you think?"

Edni shrugged. "I don't know. What do pirates even eat? Don't you just drink and steal things?"

"HEY NOW!" Violet stormed forward; fists bunched at her side.

"Woah, girl!" Tiger threw out an arm to hold her back. "Easy".

Edni arched her eyebrows. "I was only joking, jeez".

"Yeah, well. Violet don't take pirate jokes so good, you see. And what you said, it ain't good. We get a bad rap, pirates. We don't get no respect y'know?"

"That was rather rude, Edni", Gwinni admonished her friend. "You should apologise".

Edni rolled her eyes. "**Sorry**". She crossed her arms and huffed.

"Sorry about her", Gwinni said quietly. "She's just hungry, I think".

"You know how my blood sugar gets! And what do you expect? After the night we've had!" Edni exclaimed.

"Yes, yes, alright", Gwinni said. Her stomach growled and she blushed. "Come to think of it, I am rather hungry too, actually".

Buck hawked and spat.

Violet gave him a look of disgust.

"Worry not!" Buck yelled. "I'll feed ya".

"Beatrix?" Gwinni looked thoughtful.

"Yeah?" Beatrix said.

"How did you know..." Gwinni paused and looked at Buck, as if considering how to address him. "Buck..." She paused again as Buck gave her a handsome smile, that was a little bit lopsided, and ruined by his luminescent red teeth. "And his...crew...would be here?"

Beatrix grinned cunningly and tapped her nose.

"Oh, come on, do tell", Gwinni wailed.

"Fine", Beatrix said. "It was Gregor that give me the idea".

"How so?" Gwinni asked.

Beatrix shook her head. "Gregor mentioned allies. I knew he didn't mean anyone in the castle, and I knew he had links to the moon pirates".

Cincesse clapped her hand to her head. "The waterfall!"

Tiger grinned at Wolf.

Beatrix nodded. "That's right. And who else would you turn to, to break someone out of a dungeon?"

Gwinni smiled. "That's very clever, Beatrix".

Beatrix sketched a little courtly bow. "Why thank you". She seemed in high spirits now she was rescuing her parents, and not just sitting doing nothing.

Buck guffawed loudly. "You'd make a good pirate, you know", he said, sizing Beatrix up. He made to slap her on the back, but Beatrix raised a finger in warning.

Buck snorted. "A great one, maybe".

Tiger nodded, as he stared thoughtfully at Beatrix.

Violet was poker faced, but she was also watching Beatrix.

"If you've all finished appraising me", Beatrix said, rather adultly. "I could do with a drink. And while we're at it, you can tell me how we're gonna rescue my ma and pa".

There was silence for a moment. Buck looked at Beatrix like he'd just discovered his long last daughter, then burst into hearty laughter. He was too quick for Beatrix and thumped her on the back before she could stop him. Beatrix scowled. She looked up and caught a smirk flash across Violet's face, then it was gone.

"Come on!" Buck this thew his meaty arm around Beatrix's shoulder and steered her toward the village in the distance.

Cincesse looked most aggrieved, but hitched up the bottom of her pinafore, even though it was nowhere near touching the ground, and followed gingerly after them.

Gwinni, Edni and Lucrecia followed a few paces behind, talking with the pirates about this and that.

Above them, the stars sparkled prettily, and a comet raced across the sky, leaving a lazy trail of white dust in its wake.

Back To Brightcastle

"You want to do what!" Buck looked aggrieved at Beatrix's suggestion that they go to Brightcastle. He cast his eyes conspiratorially around the packed tavern then shook his head and carried on eating. He'd led the group to the tavern Beatrix and Cincesse had spied on their first trip to the moon.

The woman Buck had been accosting, Maeve, was behind the bar serving drinks. She looked rather tired.

The tavern was packed to the brims with moonlings. Pirates, and villagers of all sorts and persuasions, rubbed shoulders at the little circular wooden tables.

Lucrecia looked like she'd died and gone to heaven. She stopped everyone that passed and asked them who they were, or what they did.

Edni was happily munching away, wolfing down large spoonful's of what looked like goulash, helping it down with mouthfuls of crusty moon bread. It was much the same as human bread, but milky white, and it had tiny, little, crunchy 'moon rocks' in it. Tiger had assured them they weren't **actual** rocks, but they were in fact seeds.

Beatrix ate sparingly. After a bowl of goulash, she'd pushed away her bowl and sat quietly sipping her drink. The barmaid, Maeve, had steered her away from the large barrels of 'Bucky', and had instead poured her a small, squat glass of sherry. When Beatrix had asked how she'd got sherry, the barmaid had smiled knowingly and tapped her nose. It seemed Gregor had his finger in more than one pie up here.

Her enthusiasm was starting to wane, now the novelty of the situation had worn off, and she was thinking more critically. Was she doing the right thing? Should she have just bolted off like this, dragging her friends into danger? Would Gregor have rescued her parents fine without her? She shook her head. She couldn't doubt herself now. Onwards. She'd come too far to back out now.

Buck seemed to have sobered up now, after several large bowls of goulash. Pirate slop, he called it. Beatrix didn't think it was very sloppy. It was pretty tasty, actually. But the moonlings looked down upon it. It was a 'pirate dish' apparently. The other moonlings in the tavern looked at is distastefully, and many of them gave Buck and his crew a wide berth.

Beatrix had learned that even though the pirates brought money to the village, spending it in the taverns and the shops, they were viewed much the same as human pirates. Rogues. Vagabonds. Scoundrels. It was a dangerous life. And a volatile one. Pirates could die young or be captured. Or disappear without a trace. Beatrix secretly thought it sounded rather glamorous, and a little romantic.

She'd caught herself looking at the girl, Violet, more than once. She was exquisite. She had short, spiky, violet hair, which had the same weightless quality as the waterfall Beatrix had visited with Cincesse. It seemed to float ever so slightly. Her eyes were shockingly white with black pupils, and seemed to flash and shine from time to time, like shooting stars. And her skin wasn't the same milky white as the other moonlings. It was more...human.

"Beautiful, isn't she?" Tiger leaned in close to Beatrix.

"I don't know what you mean". Beatrix blushed. Cincesse was laughing loudly at a joke from Wolf and thankfully didn't hear the exchange.

Tiger winked. "Just like her mother. But don't get on the wrong side of her", he warned.

Beatrix said nothing, and Tiger continued eating his dinner.

A moonling started playing a harp in front of the fireplace, and the villagers started clapping and bouncing their feet in time to the music.

Cincesse smiled at Beatrix and took her hand. Beatrix smiled automatically and watched the harpist. Her thoughts were elsewhere.

The harpist called for a volunteer from the crowd to inspire his next song.

Edni, who had consumed a large glass of sherry at Beatrix's recommendation, grabbed Cincesse's other hand and stuck it high into the sky.

"Edni!" Cincesse hissed.

"Ah, what a beautiful lady", the harpist purred. This seemed to mollify Cincesse somewhat.

"Well..." Cincesse rubbed her hand under chin.

"Come on, my love". The harpist beckoned Cincesse into the centre of the tavern.

Edni cackled and forced Cincesse to her feet. She gave Cincesse a not too gentle push, and Cincesse stumbled out from their table into the centre of the tavern.

Cincesse glared angrily back at Edni, who was still cackling away.

"That wasn't very nice", Gwinni said, but her eyes were laughing.

"Hehehe". Edni clapped her hands together. "This should be good".

"Right here, that's it". The harpist plunked down a wooden stool in front of where he was standing. "Where we can all see ya".

Cincesse allowed herself to be led to the stool and sunk down on it reluctantly. She petted her face hesitantly and pulled her hair into place. She looked around uncertainly, as if expecting to see her shadows, Eli and Clio. She licked her lips nervously.

"**Beautiful**". The harpist measured Cincesse on the chair like she was a work of art. "Isn't she beautiful?" He turned to the crowd for confirmation.

"Aye!" Buck yelled. "A fine lassie!"

"Oh, yes", a woman yelled from the crowd. "So beautiful". She clasped her hands over her chest as if she were swooning a little.

Cincesse blushed. She was starting to enjoy the attention. "Thank you", she murmured.

"Now". The harpist addressed the crowd. "What'll it be?"

"Belle My Beau!" A voice called.

"Am I For Thee!" Another called.

The harpist frowned, like these songs were not quite right.

"A Princess Fair!" A voice called from the back of the tavern.

The harpist raised his hand and started nodding enthusiastically. "That's it, perfect".

The tavern roared in agreement.

"A Princess Fair?" Cincesse mouthed silently at Beatrix across the room.

Beatrix shrugged and grinned happily. Her eyes were still distant, but she was glad Cincesse was enjoying herself. She wasn't sure if Cincesse would have been as good natured it had been her on the stool. She frowned.

The harpist struck a note on his harp, and the crowd went silent.

The woman who had swooned earlier closed her eyes and back to sway silently from side to side, as the harpist strummed more notes on his harp.

To Beatrix's surprise, Buck had also closed his eyes. She hadn't taken him for a romantic.

Tiger snorted and elbowed Wolf to look at Buck. They both sniggered silently, and Violet shook her head as if she found them immature.

Beatrix cocked her head as she watched Violet.

"Her hair was **spun**, as if from **gold**". The harpist's dulcet tones drifted out into the packed tavern.

"Her skin was **soft**, as down and **dae**".

The song had a whimsical, theatrical cadence to it. The harpist would speak softly, and then emphasise the words at the end of each sentence.

"Dae?" Beatrix murmured to Tiger.

Tiger just smiled at her.

The cadence of the song changed now, becoming more romantic.

Many in the crowd had closed their eyes as they listened to the song.

"Never a day, she'd turn me away". The harpist covered his heart with his hand.

"A princess fair, a princess fair".

The villager who had first closed her eyes had tears running down on her face now.

Beatrix looked bemused. It was only a song. Why were they crying?

Tiger looked serious now. Stoic, in his own way, but Beatrix sensed he was feeling something deeply. She looked at Cincesse, who had her hand over her mouth. It seemed Cincesse was wrapped up in the magic of the song too.

Violet was pokerfaced as always, but her eyes were shimmering a little.

Even Edni and Gwinni were quiet.

Beatrix resolved to listen more intently to the song. Perhaps she was missing something.

"From lands unseen, from ken unknown, a princess fair, a princess fair".

Many of the women had taken the hands of their husbands, or lovers.

"From fae and free, to love for thee, a princess fair, a princess fair".

"Her heart was pure as foals first fur, a princess fair, a princess fair".

"But not all's as pure as a princess's heart. A dark was done, a dark was done".

"And the trap was sprung, and the dae was done. A princess fair, a princess fair". The harpist looked terribly sad now and was staring down at his harp as he strummed, instead of into the eyes of the crowd.

"The blood was red, the dawn lay dead".

"Back to the fae, back to the fae". He began speaking softer and softer.

"Not this day, not this day". He was almost whispering now. He looked up suddenly and struck a harsh note on his harp.

"But the dawn was nae done". His tone had become dramatic.

"And none were so fae as they".

The mood in the tavern changed and whispers broke out.

Beatrix frowned as she tried to make out they were saying. She didn't have to wait long, as the harpist continued speaking.

"The olden ones. The olden ones".

Several of the women in the tavern gripped necklaces around their necks and raised them to their lips.

A man at the table next to them closed his eyes and bowed his head. At the same time, he bunched his fists and raised them to form an 'x' in front of his head.

Beatrix thought this was rather bizarre. But she daren't interrupt the song to ask. Everyone was taking it so seriously.

"They took the fae, and they took the dark, and they made their mark...they made their mark".

The enthusiastic woman who'd been swaying side to side shook her head sadly as if this was a great loss.

"The princess was saved, but her dawn was done. Her night was nigh, her night was nigh".

"A princess fair, a princess fair".

"And she took my hand, as she took my heart, and she spoke those words, those dreaded words".

"No", the enthusiastic woman wailed, as she extended her hand toward the harpist, and Cincesse on the stool. "No..."

"Back to the fae, back to fae".

"No!" Another woman wailed. "Princess..."

Beatrix felt sad, though she didn't know why. The harpists song had touched her. She felt invested in the story and wanted to know what happened to the princess. It was rather wordy and obscure. She wasn't sure she understood all of it.

The harpist stood suddenly and strummed to a crescendo. "A princess fair, a princess fair".

The mood shifted and became a little more upbeat.

The harpist sung the chorus a few more times and then waited.

Thunderous applause erupted from the tavern. Men and woman got to their feet and clapped loudly above their heads. Maeve wiped a tear from her eye behind the bar.

Buck sniffed emotionally and wiped the back of his hand across his eyes. "Was good", he mumbled. "Was good". He got up suddenly and stumbled over to the harpist. He stuck something in the harpists pocket and tenderly slapped his cheek, then ambled back to the table, like an ungainly bear.

"What was it about?" Beatrix asked Buck.

Buck sniffed again. "Love, girl. Love".

Beatrix sensed this would have to suffice for now.

Cincesse came back over to the table, red faced and flushed. She immediately pulled Beatrix into a tight embrace. She pulled back and gripped Beatrix's face and kissed her fiercely on the mouth.

"What was that for?" Beatrix asked.

"Nothing". Cincesse smiled sheepishly. "I just wanted to kiss you".

"Thanks". Beatrix grinned.

Violet was looking anywhere but Beatrix.

Tiger and Wolf rolled their eyes.

The evening was starting to wind down now, and the harpist was strumming absentmindedly on his harp without singing. People were leaving in dribs and drabs.

"So", Beatrix said quietly to Buck. "How are we going to get into this castle?"

"Whisht". Buck reached in his jacket for his pipe. He pulled it out and filled it. "How do you even know they're in there, girl?"

"Where else would they be? You know they're in there, don't give me that", Beatrix said quietly.

Cincesse was talking enthusiastically to Wolf.

Buck shook his head. "Don't know that". He began smoking his pipe.

Beatrix gripped his arm. "Don't lie to me. I know you spoke to Gregor. I know Gregor told you. That's why you were there waiting. You were waiting on him, weren't you?"

Buck shook her hand off. "Rubbish".

Beatrix shook her head. "I don't think so".

Buck looked away, pretending to listen to the harpist.

"The one thing I don't understand is, why didn't you just walk away?" Beatrix asked.

"What do you mean?" Buck asked.

"When you saw it was us, and not Gregor", Beatrix said.

Buck ran his tongue across his teeth. "Maybe Gregor told me you'd be coming".

"Did he?" Beatrix asked.

"You'll never know", Buck said mysteriously.

Beatrix stared intently at Buck.

"Maybe he told me to expect you. Maybe he told me, you're just like your mother, and once you're set on doin somethin, there's no stopping you", Buck said.

"My mother?" Beatrix frowned. "You know my mother?"

"Oh yes". Buck nodded sombrely. "Much as I wish I didn't".

"Hey, that's my ma you're talkin about", Beatrix warned.

Buck nodded, as if accepting he had overstepped the mark.

"But why'd you come, if you're scared of the castle? Why didn't you just hide here in this pub", Beatrix asked.

"I don't hide anywhere, girl", Buck replied testily.

"But you're scared of the castle, aren't you?" Beatrix asked.

"Girl, you'd have to be stupid **to not be scared** of the castle", Buck said.

"Why's that?" Beatrix asked challengingly.

Buck shook his head. "Now who's playin games?"

Beatrix stared haughtily back at Buck but didn't say anything.

"You know as well as I what's in the castle girl. Aside from the knights, and the guards, and The Sacred Sisters..." Buck trailed off.

"What?" Beatrix asked.

Buck shook his head. "You don't wanna know". He shuddered.

Beatrix wasn't sure if she did or not. She was already a little frightened. But her stubbornness got the better of her. "Yes, I do".

Buck sniffed and put his pipe down. "Well, you might find out sooner than you might like".

Beatrix swallowed. "So, you're gonna help me?"

Buck shook his head, as if thinking he was crazy for considering it.

Beatrix smiled. "Thanks, Buck".

"Don't thank me", Buck warned. "There'll be a price".

Beatrix's face hardened. "Of course".

Buck stared into Beatrix's eyes. "I'm a pirate, girl. I don't do nothin in this life for free. And neither should you".

"What about loyalty? Friendship? Honour?" Beatrix asked.

Buck snorted as if he thought this pigswill. "Girl I'm a pirate! Didn't I just tell you that?"

"But even pirates have...codes of honour", Beatrix said.

"That's right". Buck nodded. "But that's to my crew". He nodded at his crew. "You ain't crew. Why should I help you? Why should I endanger my crew for you and yours?"

Beatrix went quiet. She didn't have an answer.

Buck nodded. "So, there's a price".

"What is it?" Beatrix asked.

"I don't know yet", Buck said.

Beatrix grimaced. "I don't doubt it will be a hefty one".

Buck snorted. "Girl, you better believe it".

"Beatrix, look at this!" Cincesse grabbed Beatrix's arm excitedly. "Wolf, do it again, do it again".

Wolf stared straight faced at Beatrix, then began inflating his cheeks with copious amounts of air. He kept going and going and going. Beatrix thought his cheeks might burst. After a moment, he began floating a few inches off of his seat. Beatrix couldn't help but laugh, it was rather impressive, and rather amusing.

POP!

Tiger leaned across and popped Wolf's cheeks, and the air in them exploded out of his mouth with a massive **whoosh**.

Cincesse giggled girlishly and pushed Wolf playfully on the arm.

Wolf grinned as if he was most impressed with himelf.

Beatrix felt Violet's eyes on her and looked across at her.

Violet stared back appraisingly then looked away.

"So, what'll it be?" Buck asked.

Beatrix nodded. "Whatever it is. I'll pay it", she said grimly.

Buck hawked and spat on his hand then held it out for Beatrix to shake.

Beatrix grimaced, then spat on her hand.

She took Buck's hand in a pirate's handshake.

Gwinni watched the exchange with a rather worried look on her face.

"Once everyone's asleep", Buck said, nodding at the last remaining villagers in the tavern.

"A pirate's life for me", Beatrix said quietly to herself, once Buck had turned away.

The Buckswift

"Beauty, aint she?" Buck said proudly, as his ship rose out of the water.

They were gathered in front of the waterfall, the witches and the pirates. An odd bunch they made. The girls were shivering and had wrapped themselves in their arms.

The pirates had given them heavy coats made of what looked like wool. But it was still cold. It was hard to tell on the moon, because the sky was always dark. But it was night. Deep night. And there was a chill in the air.

The pirates didn't seem to mind. But then, they hadn't stopped sucking down the red stuff that Buck seemed to love so much. They weren't drunk though. It looked like they drank it sparingly to stay warm. And maybe the nerves.

Buck leaned across and grabbed a bottle from Tiger. He took a deep swill. Violet snatched the bottle from him mid gulp. "Enough!"

Buck scowled at her and wiped his mouth. "Was only a mouthful".

"It's never only a mouthful with you", Violet said.

Buck turned and spat on the ground. His ship continued rising out of the waterfall pool. He smiled as the bow emerged fully. "A beaut!"

Tiger and Wolf watched respectfully with arms crossed behind their back.

Violet looked like she could take it or leave it.

"Wow", Lucrecia said softly. "A real pirate ship".

"Do you like it, Luce?" Beatrix asked.

"Oh, yes". Lucrecia nodded fervently.

"It's beautiful", Cincesse said, as the ship emerged fully from the water. The water rolled off its sides as if from a duck's back.

Buck nodded. "She is indeed".

Edni frowned. "Why are we getting in a ship?"

"Why do you think?" Gwinni looked exasperated.

"But..." Edni looked thoughtful. "There's no...how are we gonna get to Brightcastle in **that**". She pointed at the ship.

Buck grinned. "She'll surprise you, girl. You wait". He bounded quickly into the water over to the ship. He whacked the hull affectionately on the side. "Best ship in the sky".

"In the **sky?**" Edni's mouth was open. "You don't mean-"

Buck interrupted her. "That's right girl. Don't need a cat to fly, me". He looked rather smug at this fact. "Just this ol girl". He whacked the hull again with a **thunk**.

Beatrix was surprised and impressed. She had only learned to fly recently, and that was only with Felix's help. A flying ship was...wonderful.

Felix rubbed his face on the back of her legs.

She smiled down at him and gave his head a little scratch.

The cats had particularly enjoyed the tavern and had snuggled up together in front of the fire, joining them later when everything quietened down.

A gangplank fell suddenly from the top of the ship onto the ground at the edge of the pool. A massive **boom** rang out that scared Cincesse and Gwinni, who almost jumped out of their skin.

"Oh, my goodness!" Cincesse cried, grabbing onto to Gwinni.

"Oh, oh, oh!" Gwinni was also holding on to Cincesse.

Edni cackled. "Wusses".

"Shut it", Gwinni warned.

"Can I go up?" Lucrecia asked Buck.

"Of course! Up you get girl!" Buck gave Lucrecia a gentle push up the gangplank.

She pranced daintily up the gangplank and disappeared for a moment. Then her face appeared over the edge of the ship, grinning excitedly. "Beatrix, come up!"

"Coming", Beatrix called.

"After you, m'lady", Buck said, sketching a bow.

Beatrix rolled her eyes and walked up the gangplank.

"Be careful!" Cincesse called.

"I won't", Beatrix mumbled.

"Come on". Gwinni took Cincesse's hand and pulled her up.

"And you", Gwinni said, turning back to Edni.

Edni smiled. "Sure".

"Ooh! Look!" Lucrecia called from atop the ship.

Beatrix paused at the top of the gangplank to look. Tiger and Wolf were climbing up the hull like monkeys, nimbly pulling their way up. It only took them a few seconds until they both disappeared over the side.

"What you waitin for?" Tiger appeared, beaming over the side. Then he swung out over the side of the ship like a gymnast, hanging on with one hand.

"Oh, Tiger, be careful!" Cincesse cried.

"What about me?" Wolf did a handstand on the edge of the ship and started walking upside down on his hands.

Cincesse giggled. "Wolf, be careful! Don't you fall!"

"I won't", Wolf promised.

"Enough!" Buck boomed.

Beatrix jumped and almost fell from the gangplank. A strong hand gripped her arm and pulled her up onto the ship proper. Violet.

"Thanks", Beatrix breathed.

"You should be more careful", Violet said gruffly.

"I know", Beatrix admitted.

Violet looked like she didn't know what to say, so she walked off and started pulling at some ropes. Beatrix didn't know what she was doing, but it looked very professional.

"ALL ABOARD!" Buck boomed.

Cincesse and Gwinni squealed and hightailed it up the gangplank.

Buck came stomping up behind them, four cats and Edni at his tail.

He whacked the hull twice and the gangplank started juddering. It rose from the ground so that it was pointing straight into the sky, then started to fall downwards toward them.

"AHHH!" Cincesse and Gwinni both screamed. It looked like the gangplank was going to fall on their heads.

Beatrix frowned.

It wasn't falling on them. A hole had appeared in the floor of the ship and the gangplank was falling into the hole, getting shorter and shorter as it went. Finally, it disappeared and the hole in the floor closed with a snap, like a trapdoor.

Buck knelt to examine the trapdoor. Once satisfied, he got to his feet and whistled.

Tiger and Wolf began climbing the mast.

The girls clapped excitedly at their display of athleticism.

A flag whipped loose and began billowing in the twilight wind. On it was a jug crossed by two cutlasses.

Beatrix shook her head.

"You don't like my flag?" Buck appeared behind her and leaned in close.

"It's wonderful", Beatrix said drily. "However, did you come up with the inspiration?"

Buck smiled and showed her some rather discoloured teeth. "Magic!" His eyes popped madly in his head.

Beatrix arched an eyebrow and snorted. "Fool".

Buck smacked his lips. "Full speed ahead!" He ran to the bow and flung his hand out with a debonair flourish.

"Aye, aye, captain!" Tiger called from the mast. He grinned down at Beatrix, then slid down the mast, landing on the floor with a **thump** that startled Gwinni. Her hand flew to her chest.

"Sorry". Tiger grinned.

Gwinni tried to whack him, but he nimbly sidestepped her hand and ambled off to the bow.

"What an adventure!" Cincesse gushed, lacing her arm through Beatrix's.

"You're glad you came now, huh?" Beatrix asked.

"Oh, don't be silly. I would never have left you to do this alone", Cincesse said.

"I know", Beatrix admitted.

"But it is exciting, isn't it?" Cincesse asked.

"Oh, yes", Beatrix said. Her eyes were faraway. Cincesse didn't notice, excited as she was.

"Hey, Cin. Watch this", Wolf called from the mast.

Cincesse looked up expectantly.

Wolf climbed out along the mast on a wooden beam, stepping softly with his hands stretched out to either side.

"Oh, careful!" Cincesse clapped her hand to her mouth.

Wolf paused at the end of the beam, then swung out to the side as if he would fall.

"OH NO!" Cincesse cried.

At the last moment, Wolf turned in midair and caught the beam with his hands, using his momentum to swing himself back onto the beam.

"Oh, bravo!" Cincesse cried. "Did you see? Did you see?"

"I saw", Beatrix said tiredly. Truth be told she found it rather cute how excited Cincesse was. But her mind was on other things. She kept thinking back to the image of her ma and pa in the dungeon. Her father standing protectively in front of her mother. The tired, scared look in her mother's eyes. She hoped they were ok. She hoped they'd be alright until she got there.

Cincesse frowned at the look on Beatrix's face and gripped her shoulders. "They'll be ok. I promise".

Beatrix nodded and smiled. "Thanks".

Cincesse pulled her into a little hug.

"Hey, Cin!" Wolf called.

Cincesse broke off the hug, distracted. "What?"

Beatrix turned away, and looked over the edge of the ship as it started to judder and rise into the sky.

Felix rubbed himself against her leg and purred.

"Thanks", Beatrix muttered. "Love you too".

"Who said anything about love?" Felix thought.

"You just did. I felt it", Beatrix thought.

"Did not", Felix thought haughtily, turning away from her and raising his tail high.

Beatrix grinned. "Did too".

Felix didn't reply but waved his tail affectionately at her and padded off to the mast where Katy was licking her paw. He sunk down beside her and Katy began cleaning him.

Beatrix smiled and turned back to her gazing. She peered over the edge. The ground seemed so far away now. The moon was getting smaller and smaller.

A hand pulled her back.

"I don't want to be rescuing you again, thank you". It was Violet.

"Who says you'll have to?" Beatrix replied.

Violet's mouth twitched. "I do".

"Maybe you want to rescue me", Beatrix volunteered.

Violet's eyebrows arched. "What makes you think that?"

Beatrix shrugged.

Violet smiled mysteriously and walked away.

The exchange left Beatrix feeling a little stupid and wrongfooted. She didn't know why she'd said that. It wasn't like her. She shook her head. Time to worry about that later.

"BRIGHTCASTLE! I'M A COMIN!" Buck yelled from the bow, pumping his hand into the sky.

*

Travel by ship took longer than travel by cat, as the girls quickly found out.

Buck informed them the trip should take about an hour.

They were still flying rather fast.

But it was significantly slower than by cat.

A fact that Beatrix wasn't sure if she was grateful for or not. Her stomach hadn't settled since they'd left the moon.

The stars were whizzing past like little silver bullets, as they soared through a midnight sky.

Beatrix was at the bow now, staring at the blue and green sphere in the distance.

Buck had gone below deck to "get things ready". Violet had quickly followed him.

Tiger approached her, a stone jug in his hands. "Drink?"

"What is it?" Beatrix said apprehensively.

"Bucky", Tiger said.

Beatrix frowned. "Isn't that the name of the ship?"

"Not quite", Tiger said awkwardly.

"And isn't Buck's name...Buck?" Beatrix looked bemused.

"Don't ask", Tiger said.

Beatrix took the jug and pulled the cork plug out of the top with a **pop.** She looked dubiously into the jug. The roiling red liquid rolled softly side to side, much the same as the ship.

"It'll help", Tiger said. "I promise".

Beatrix wasn't so sure. She sniffed the bottle. It smelled pungent. Like strong wine gone slightly off. She took a swig on the bottle and wiped the back of her mouth. "Eugh". She handed the bottle back to Tiger who was smiling.

"What?" Beatrix asked. "Oh". She felt a warmth rush through her, starting in her belly, then reaching her head and her hands. "Oh!"

Tiger laughed.

Her eyes felt like they were on fire for a second and started to shine red. It wasn't entirely unpleasant, and there was no pain, but it was very strange. Suddenly the sensation was gone.

"Bucky", Tiger said, taking the jug and swigging it,

"What is it?" Beatrix asked.

"Bucky", Tiger said unhelpfully.

Beatrix shook her head. "Helpful".

Tiger chuckled and walked away, bucky in hand.

She did feel a little better after the bucky. It had certainly warmed her up a bit.

At the stern, Cincesse was giggling with Wolf, who was showing her how to tie knots with rope.

Beatrix frowned. Should she feel jealous? She felt like she should. She just couldn't muster it right now. Perhaps she was just tired. Perhaps she was distracted. She was worried about her parents, after all.

Buck ambled up onto the deck from below. He didn't look very happy and was grumbling about something or other. Violet followed him up dutifully, like a child that had just scolded its irresponsible parent. She shook her head at Tiger and then disappeared back below deck.

Buck joined Beatrix at the bow and sniffed loudly. He eyeballed her suspiciously then sniffed at the air, as if he could taste something on it. "Been at my bucky, have yeh?"

Before she could respond, he aggressively patted his pockets and pulled his pipe out. He seemed tense.

"Don't know what you mean", Beatrix replied.

"Ah, rubbish", Buck said. He packed his pipe tightly and lit it with his finger. He pulled deeply on it and seemed to relax a little as the smoke hit his lungs.

He turned and looked at her speculatively. "Got any left?" He looked behind her and around her.

"No", Beatrix said bluntly.

Buck cursed. "Bet she has". He looked grumpily over his shoulder toward the lower deck.

"Who?" Beatrix asked.

"**Her**", Buck grumbled.

Beatrix turned to see Violet emerge from below deck. She cast her eyes around the deck like a hawk. Spotting Buck looking at her, she hesitated.

Buck scowled and narrowed his eyes threateningly.

Violet muttered something under her breath, then moved away to speak to Tiger, as if deciding she would chance leaving Buck alone for a few moments.

Beatrix frowned. "Is this a usual occurrence?"

"What?" Buck belched.

Beatrix grimaced as the smell hit her and waved it away from her nose. "This. You two". She nodded at Violet.

"Ah". Buck waved his meaty hand dismissively. "Never you mind about that".

"But I do mind", Beatrix said.

Buck sniffed. "And why's that then". He was leaning over the bow smoking his pipe.

"Because my parents are in your hands", Beatrix said. "I can't have you asleep at the wheel".

"Asleep at the-" Buck straightened himself and looked down at Beatrix, affronted. "I'll have you-"

"Save it", Beatrix said coldly. "I know you're drunk...or were drunk. I don't care what you do on your own time, but pay attention tonight. My parent's lives depend on it".

Buck's jaw worked furiously. He looked mad as hell that he'd been told off by a girl. And not even a pirate girl to boot. He breathed deeply through his nose and slouched down over the bow again, resting on his forearms. He shook his head. "You think you know me, little witch. But yeh don't...yeh don't".

"I know you well enough", Beatrix said astutely.

She walked away before Buck could respond, and he watched her over his shoulder as she approached the other girls.

He shook his head again, sadly this time, then sighed. "Maybe you're right". He turned his eyes to the stars above. "Maybe I shoulda gone with you...Bev".

Here We Come

An hour went faster than any of them expected, and before long, they were dropping lower, and lower, and lower.

It was cold, and the clouds were passing through them like icy fluff.

"Brrr". Gwinni shivered and wrapped her arms around her.

Beatrix smiled absentmindedly.

"Are you nervous?" Gwinni asked.

Beatrix nodded. "Of course".

"I would be", Gwinni admitted.

Cincesse giggled at the stern with Wolf.

Beatrix glanced over her shoulder at the sound.

Gwinni frowned. "Everything alright?"

"Mmm?" Beatrix replied, still watching Cincesse and Wolf.

"You and Cin", Gwinni said pointedly.

"Oh, yeah, fine", Beatrix said.

"Really?" Gwinni pressed.

Beatrix sighed. "I guess".

"Tell me", Gwinni pressed.

"I don't know", Beatrix admitted. "At first it was great, but I think we rushed into it. We don't even know each other".

Gwinni nodded. "Perhaps".

Beatrix turned to face her. "Perhaps?"

"Well..." Gwinni looked thoughtful.

"Out with it", Beatrix said.

"Maybe a **little** rushed", Gwinni admitted.

Beatrix nodded. "I know".

"But I do love her", Gwinni hastened. "Cincesse, that is. She's wonderful".

"I know", Beatrix said. "But I've felt a...distance...between us".

"Oh?" Gwinni asked.

"Yeah...since after the...pub", Beatrix said.

Gwinni licked her lips. "It was a tense situation".

"That's one way of putting it", Beatrix said.

"We're only young, you know", Gwinni said insightfully. "I don't think it's abnormal for us to...experiment". She blushed.

"Experiment?" Beatrix grinned wolfishly.

"Try new things...rush into things. We're young", Gwinni repeated. "We're not supposed to know what we're doing. We follow our hearts, act on...impulse".

Beatrix's eyebrows arched in surprise. She knew Gwinni was smart, but this was a different kind of smarts. A kind of smarts she hadn't expected from her.

"I suppose as we get older, we think about things more". Gwinni looked thoughtfully at Edni and Lucrecia. She shook her head as if making up her mind about something. "But where's the fun in that! We're young! Let's make mistakes! Let's do what we want!" She was rather flushed in the face and gripped the side of the ship tightly, gazing excitedly over the edge into the unknown.

Beatrix's eyebrows were dancing with merriment. She was enjoying this new side of her friend. Perhaps the pirates were rubbing off on her. "Can't argue with that", she said quietly.

"Land ho!" Buck bellowed from the front of the ship, where he was steering a large wooden wheel.

Wolf, Tiger and Violet all ran toward Buck and began conferring quietly with him.

Beatrix swallowed. "It's time".

"I guess so", Gwinni said tightly. "Come on". She led Beatrix over to Edni and Lucrecia. Cincesse joined them at the same time.

"Hello", Cincesse said airily to Beatrix. It sounded a little forced, and perhaps a little guilty.

"Hello", Beatrix replied, smiling weakly.

"Are we landing?" Cincesse asked quickly, looking around the group to avoid eye contact with Beatrix.

"It would seem so", Lucrecia said sagely.

"Brace yerselves!" Buck yelled. "It's gonna be a bumpy landin".

Tiger and Wolf shimmied up the mast and stood staring into the distance, eyes shielded from the wind by their hands. They both wrapped bandanas around most of their faces to protect against the cold wind.

"Violet!" Buck yelled.

"I'm right here", Violet said tiredly from a few feet away.

"Ah, right". Buck looked taken aback. "C'mere!"

Violet approached Buck. He beckoned that she should lean in close. She looked a bit creeped out but obliged. Buck whispered something to her. She shook her head. He whispered again and looked over at Beatrix.

Beatrix frowned. "What are they talking about?"

"I don't know". Cincesse folded her arms.

"Are they talking about you?" Gwinni asked.

Beatrix shrugged.

"Oh, look, how pretty!" Lucrecia ran to the bow and leaned right over the edge.

"Woah, easy there little one". Tiger appeared behind her and pulled her back.

"Sorry". Lucrecia blushed. She peered shamefaced over the bow, careful not to touch it. "Beatrix!" She gestured hurriedly for Beatrix to join her at the bow.

Beatrix smiled and joined her.

"Isn't it beautiful?" Lucrecia asked.

Beatrix nodded in agreement.

Below them, the walls of Brightcastle were glowing softly, illuminated by the golden lights of dozens of lanterns.

"The Torchbearers", Beatrix said quietly.

Lucrecia watched her, uncertain.

As they drew closer, the lights began to move quickly from side to side, like fireflies.

Beatrix frowned. "Are they..."

"EVASIVE MANOUEVRES!" Buck bellowed at the top of his voice suddenly.

"Jeez!" Beatrix almost jumped out of her skin. She turned angrily to Buck at the wheel.

"DON'T SHOUT LIKE THAT!"

"DON'T SHOUT LIKE THAT!"

There was silence as everyone tried to figure out what had happened.

Gwinni gaped as she figured it out.

Both Beatrix and Violet had shouted at Buck at the same time. It seemed they'd both now figured that out too, and were staring at each other a little uncertainly.

Beatrix snorted, then Violet joined her. Then they both started laughing.

Lucrecia raised her eyebrows, the way a schoolteacher might when watching a kindling classroom romance.

Edni sighed and approached Buck where he was standing flabbergasted, mouth hanging open like a drawbridge. She thumped him on the back. "You really can't take her anywhere". She shook her head sadly at Beatrix.

Gwinni looked at Edni as if she was crazy. "You're one to talk!" She yelled.

Edni looked wounded. "I don't know what you're talking about".

Buck guffawed and slapped Edni on the back. He was rather weightier than Edni, and she stumbled a little and looked a little scared. "Bahahaha. I like you, girl. Like me, you are".

Edni seemed pleased at this and puffed her chest out. "Always fancied myself a pirate", she said uncertainly.

Buck roared. "Then a pirate you shall be!" He whacked her on the back again, but she was ready this time and absorbed it. She grinned up at him proudly, then stuck her tongue out at Gwinni over her shoulder.

Gwinni shook her head and watched her fondly.

"Quite the group of friends you have", Wolf said silkily from her shoulder.

"Oh, goodness!" Gwinni's hand flew to her chest. "Don't sneak up on me like that, you pest!" She whacked Wolf on the arm.

"Ow". He rubbed his arm dramatically. "Most uncourteous".

Gwinni looked aghast. "**Me? Uncorteous!**"

"Enough flirting!" Buck bellowed. "We've a castle to crash!"

Gwinni looked away quickly, embarrassed.

Wolf cleared his throat and hurried away to busy himself with important looking ship duties.

The sound of a chest popping open distracted Gwinni from her self-imposed shame. Her mouth fell open. "What is...is that?"

"Catch!" Wolf yelled, as he chucked a Violet a delicate looking dirk.

Violet caught it and belted it to her waist.

"Tiger!" Wolf threw Tiger a cutlass.

Tiger caught it high in the air and twirled it flashily before belting it to his waist.

"Oh, my", Gwinni said. She looked rather scared now. The swords made it real. These were **pirates**, and they were aboard a **pirate ship**. She looked rather feint.

Edni saw and walked over to her. "Relax". She polished what looked like an apple and held it in front of Gwinni's mouth.

"Is that an...apple?" Gwinni looked flabbergasted. "Where did you get an apple?"

Edni shrugged. "Buck gave it to me". She pointed at Buck, then waved happily at him.

Buck grinned a wolfish, gap tooth smile.

"He did?" Gwinni still seemed disoriented.

"Mhm. Eat". Edni guided the apple into Gwinni's mouth.

She took a bite and began to chew quietly. After a few swallows, her colour seemed to improve. "Hang on, where did Buck get an apple from?"

Edni shrugged. "He's a pirate", she said, as if this answered everything.

"Can't argue with that", Gwinni mumbled, in a manner reminiscent of Beatrix.

Edni cackled. "A pirate's life for me!" She pulled another apple out of nowhere and used the side of her mouth to take a huge chomp out of it. She looked down at the teeth marks, then rubbed the apple against her leg. "Good apple, Bucky!"

"Bucky". Buck chuckled merrily to himself as he gazed out at Brightcastle.

Gwinni swallowed.

They weren't very high in the sky now, and the castle and the town were visible.

The Torchbearers on the wall were gesturing frantically at them and running back and forth, trying to get into some sort of position that would advantage them against a giant flying pirate ship. Gwinni giggled as she contemplated the hilarity of the situation.

"What are you laughing at?" Edni asked.

"I don't know", Gwinni wailed, switching back to worried.

Edni smirked. "It is rather funny, isn't it?"

"Yes!" Gwinni cried.

They both started giggling into their hands.

*

Below on the wall, the Torchbearers were panicking.

"Captain Helmet, Captain Helmet!" A mousy haired young boy cried.

A brusque looking man in full plate armour jostled over to the boy, clanking loudly as he went. "What is it, Conny?"

"What do we do? What do we do?" Conny looked petrified. Sweat was dripping from his face, and he looked like he was close fleeing the wall.

Helmet leant forward and slapped Conny firmly across the face.

Conny swallowed and stared at Helmet. "Thanks, capn".

Helmet nodded and put his hand on Conny's shoulder. "I believe in you, Torchbearer. Hold fast. Be the light".

"Be the light". Conny nodded and breathed out deeply. He looked up, resolved, at the pirate ship.

"Captain". Another Torchbearer arrived, breathing heavily.

Helmet nodded curtly. "Report".

The new Torchbearer looked uncertainly at Conny, as if uncertain whether he should speak.

"Report, Lieutenant", Helmet repeated.

"From the markings on the ship it's the..." Lieutenant paused again.

"Out with it", Helmet said.

"It's the Buckswift", Lieutenant said gravely.

Conny frowned. "The Buckswift?"

"Thank you, Lieutenant", Helmet said, ignoring Conny.

"Captain-" Conny started. But Helmet had already strode away to the other end of the wall and was barking orders at another group of Torchbearers.

Conny swallowed and looked up at the stars. "I miss me ma".

*

The ship had started to vibrate heavily.

"Is this thing safe?" Beatrix cried to Lucrecia from the bow.

"I hope so", Lucrecia admitted.

"WooHOO!" Buck yelled and pumped his fist into the air. "I'm comin for you, BRIGHTCASTLE!" He boomed.

Violet shook her head and took the wheel.

Buck ran to the bow of the ship. "You hear me! I'M COMIN!"

"You're crazy", Beatrix said in disbelief.

"You better believe it!" Buck said, grinning madly at her, eyes popping crazily in his head. He pulled a small flask out of his jerkin and unstopped it before anyone could say or do anything. "AHHH!" He sucked down a large mouthful of bucky. "The nectar of the gods!"

"BUCK!" Beatrix yelled. "Now is not the time!"

"Now's the ONLY TIME, GIRL!" Buck yelled back.

He ran back to the wheel and unceremoniously barged Violet out of the way. She stumbled and almost fell. She reached angrily for the dirk at her waist, but Tiger appeared and gripped her hand. He must be strong, because she looked like she was trying her hardest to free the dirk, and he didn't look like he was struggling to restrain her. After a moment, she shrugged him off and brushed herself off.

"Now's the only time", Buck mumbled fiercely, eyes on the castle.

"Woah!" Beatrix yelled, as they soared over the wall, and the heads of the Torchbearers below.

"I'm scared Beatrix!" Lucrecia cried.

Beatrix pulled Lucrecia close, cradling her head into her chest. "Me too", she mumbled. "Me too..."

Beatrix's eyes narrowed as she realised Buck's plan. "Get down!" she yelled suddenly at the girls. She dragged Lucrecia to the floor and covered her with her body. She looked up and cried once more. "Down!"

Wolf pulled Cincesse below deck along with Gwinni, Edni and Violet.

Gwinni looked fearfully at Beatrix lying by the bow. Her terrified eyes were the last thing Beatrix saw before an almighty judder exploded through the ship and everything went black.

The Castle

"Ughh".

Beatrix awoke to the sound of moaning. She swallowed, and immediately started coughing harshly. She rolled onto her knees and hawked up a load of dust and dirt.

"Beatrix". A voice moaned weakly from her side.

"Luce". Beatrix turned Lucrecia gently to her side. "Are you alright?"

"Mmm", Luce said, eyes still closed. "Where are we?" She slowly opened her eyes. "Why is it so dark?" A note of fear crept into her voice.

"We're in the dungeons", Beatrix said grimly, getting to her feet. "Well, sort of".

The bow of the ship had punctured a huge hole in the side of the castle. Rock and debris were everywhere.

"Bloody castle". An angry grumble came from the middle of the ship. Buck. He was getting slowly to his feet. He'd been on his knees, hands clasped to the wheel. It seemed he'd faired a little better than Beatrix and Lucrecia, but then, she reasoned this might not be the first time he'd crashed a flying ship into a castle. Something in his satisfied smirk affirmed this theory.

"HAH!" He stood up straight and shook his fist in the darkness. "Take that, yeh pompous curs!" He coughed suddenly and a cloud of dust exploded from his mouth. He licked his lips

and looked around for his flask of bucky. He bent and snatched
it up quicker than lightning. "Mmm". He smacked his lips as he
swallowed down another gulp.

"Enough!" Violet appeared behind him and yanked the flask
out of his hands.

His fingers closed on dead air, and he scowled, then smirked.
"Plenty in the castle".

"I doubt it", Violet said. "They don't drink pirate swill down
here".

Buck scowled again. "Will you shut it?"

Violet scowled back.

"Come on", Tiger interjected. "Now's not the time".

Buck pulled his pants up around his belly. "Let's go", he said
authoritatively. "Get the others", he ordered Tiger.

"Oi!" A dirty faced man called from the darkness below the
ship. "Let us out!"

"Shut it", Buck barked into the darkness.

Violet frowned, then leapt nimbly from the bow of the ship
into the darkness. They heard her run off to try and free the
man. "Where's the..." she mumbled, as she arrived at the man's
cell.

"Over there!" The man leant through the bars and pointed
at a silver key, hanging from a big hook at the entrance to the
dungeon.

Beatrix approached Buck. "They should be here", she said
quietly.

Buck nodded.

He grabbed a long stretch of rope and tied it to the mast in an elaborate sailor's knot. "Follow me". He climbed over the edge of the ship and began lowering himself into the dungeon.

Beatrix followed him. She landed lightly on her feet, picked up a torch from the wall and immediately began checking the cells. Most of the prisoners looked terrified and shied back against the walls. A few of them looked curious, or hopeful. But all were in bad condition and emaciated.

Beatrix looked disgusted. "They're not feeding them".

"Not much", Buck said gruffly. "Enough to keep em alive".

"Alive for what?" Beatrix asked.

Buck shrugged. "Beats me what goes on in the mind of a king".

Beatrix shook her head. "This is disgusting. It's...wrong".

Buck looked like he agreed. "Cruel world".

"Crueller people", Beatrix said.

A key turned in a lock and a cell door swung open. "Thank you, thank you!" The dirty faced man ran out and threw his skeletal arms around Violet's neck. "Kind ser!"

"Ser?" Violet threw the man's arms off. "I look like a ser to you?"

"Oh, kind madame! Kind madame!" The dirty faced man started waving his hands up and down like he was worshipping her.

"Knock that off", Violet ordered.

"Yes, madame", the dirty faced man agreed.

"What's your name?" Violet asked.

"Cletus", the dirty faced man responded.

"Cletus. Get these other cells open". She handed Cletus the key.

"You sure?" Cletus asked.

"Why wouldn't I be?" Violet asked sharply. "I freed you, didn't I? Why shouldn't they get their chance?"

"No, it's just..." Cletus looked sad. "Some of em don't wanna leave. They ain't got nowhere else".

Violet looked taken aback. "I don't care, just get those cells open".

"Yes madame", Cletus said obediently. He scampered away and started opening the cells.

"Why aren't they here?" Beatrix said quietly.

The prisoners filed out of their cells after much cajoling and encouragement and reassuring from Cletus. Some of them could hardly stand and were supported by others.

Beatrix was pacing up and down between the cells. "Hang on". She frowned. "Who was in this cell?" She'd stopped at a cell in the middle of the dungeon. She looked around for an answer from the prisoners. "Who was in this cell?" she repeated.

The prisoners looked away shiftily, or down at their feet.

"Please madame", Cletus replied.

Beatrix swung to face him.

"Was a man and a woman", Cletus informed her.

Beatrix gripped his shirt. "Where are they?" she hissed.

Cletus raised his hands in front of his face, as if begging her not to hurt him. "Please. They were taken".

"Taken? By who?" Beatrix hissed, shaking Cletus fiercely.

Violet's hand appeared on her arm.

Beatrix looked down at it and her face fell. She let Cletus go immediately. "I'm sorry".

"S'alright", Cletus said, straightening his shirt, which was very moth eaten and had many holes in it.

"Where were they taken?" Beatrix asked. "Please", she added as an afterthought.

"Don't know madame", Cletus said sadly.

Beatrix looked devastated.

"But..." Cletus started.

"What is it?" Beatrix asked.

"Chances are...they're in The Sanctum", Cletus volunteered.

"The Sanctum?" Beatrix frowned. "You mean...The Sacred Sisters?"

Cletus nodded enthusiastically. "That's right, Madame".

Beatrix considered this. "Stop calling me madame", she said absentmindedly. "I'm not a noble. Can't you tell?"

"Assuredly, madame", Cletus responded automatically.

Beatrix shook her head. "Thank you, Cletus". She extended her hand.

Cletus took it and grinned.

Violet smiled, unseen in the darkness behind them.

"Hello", Lucrecia said brightly.

Beatrix jumped. "Oh, I didn't see you there".

"It is rather dark", Lucrecia agreed.

"You can say that again", Edni said, arriving quietly behind them. She looked around apprehensively. "Don't like the dark".

"Me neither", Gwinni said, crossing her arms.

Cincesse arrived and said nothing.

Beatrix smiled at her. "Are you alright?"

"Yes...thankfully. You?" Cincesse asked.

Beatrix nodded.

"Right", Buck said gruffly. "We're all here. Time to go. Best not hang around".

He grabbed a torch from beside the key hook and took a step up the spiral stone staircase. "Stay close", he said, turning back to face them for a moment.

Violet went next, then Tiger, then Wolf. Then finally, the girls.

"Go on", Beatrix said to Cincesse who was next to last. "I'll watch your back".

Cincesse smiled nervously and began ascending the staircase.

When they emerged from the dungeons, the light was blinding.

A servant, carrying a pile of bedding, saw them, squealed, then ran away.

Buck chuckled.

"Can we get to The Sanctum from here?" Beatrix whispered.

"No need for subtlety girl. They know we're here", Buck replied. "And yes, if we're quick about it".

"Come on", Violet said gruffly, pushing past Buck. "Follow me". She hurried off down a corridor to the right, that looked like it led to the kitchens. They were on the lower level of the castle proper, where the king lived.

Cincesse looked very nervous.

"What is it?" Beatrix asked.

"Nothing. Let's go", Cincesse said. She ran off after Violet.

They hurried through the kitchens, which were full of hundreds of pots and pans, knives, chopping boards, hanging meat, onions and a few bleary-eyed cooks who didn't quite register their presence until they were already almost through.

"Now where?" Gwinni asked as they paused.

"Now where indeed?" Buck folded his arms and glared at Violet.

Violet growled. "This way". She took a left and they emerged into a stone tunnel. She peered ahead then nodded.

Buck didn't look happy. It seemed she'd picked the right path.

"C'mon!" Violet called over her shoulder.

Behind them, raised voices could be heard in the castle.

They quickened their pace.

After a few minutes, the tunnel started getting lighter.

"Through here!" Violet pointed at a low, curved wooden door at the end of the tunnel.

She pushed the door open slowly. It creaked loudly and she stopped, cursing.

"Just do it", Buck said gruffly.

She glared darkly at him and turned back to the door. She pushed it open further and peeked into The Sanctum.

"It's empty", she said. "Come on". She held the door open for them to walk through.

Beatrix was the last through. She paused opposite Violet. There wasn't much space, and she had to lower her head due to the low ceiling of the tunnel by the door. "Thanks", she said awkwardly, as she shuffled past.

Violet smiled and nodded.

Then they were through. She closed the door behind them.

"Wow", Lucrecia said. "So, this is The Sanctum. I've always wondered what it looked like".

The Sanctum looked like a very dark cathedral, with an incredibly high ceiling.

There were elaborate paintings on the glass windows, which spanned the walls and most of the roof. It must have been beautiful in the summer with the light shining through.

"Now where?" Beatrix asked. She was eager to find her parents.

"Must be a dungeon or a cellar or something in here", Buck mumbled.

"You mean you don't know?" Beatrix said.

Buck mumbled something inaudibly.

"What was that?" Beatrix asked sharply.

"Never been in The Sanctum before", Buck mumbled a little louder.

"Oh my..." Beatrix put her head in the hands. She looked up. "You mean to tell me; you've dragged me and my friends on this harebrained scheme of yours and you don't even-"

"BEATRIX! RUN!"

Beatrix spun at the sound of her mother's panicked voice.

"Ma!" Beatrix yelled.

At the far end of the cathedral, Cath and another woman were standing by a pulpit. The other woman had her arm around Cath's neck.

"Oh, do be quiet", the woman's bored voice drawled.

"Oh..." Cath breathed a surprised sigh and fell forward out of the woman's grip. She hit the floor with a thud.

Beatrix ran forward.

"Ah, ah, ah", the woman said cheerily, waggling her finger. She wasn't shouting, but her voice echoed loudly for them all to hear, due to the acoustics of The Sanctum.

Beatrix stopped mid-run, one foot extended, one hand in front of her. She looked rather silly. She grunted and turned red in the face.

"You", Beatrix ground through clenched teeth, as she got a closer look at the woman.

"Me", the woman replied amiably.

It was the woman from the pub who had fought with Madame. The same woman that had attacked them from the Scrying circle.

Behind, Buck nodded at Tiger and Wolf. They walked forward past the pews into the open space before the pulpit.

They moved apart, left and right of the woman.

"Oh, how quaint. You've brought me something to play with", the woman said to Beatrix.

Beatrix's face twitched furiously. She was still stuck, rooted to the spot by whatever the woman had done to her.

Buck walked forward slowly, Violet in tow, until they were level with Beatrix.

"We've got it from here, girl", Buck muttered.

The woman giggled. "Is that so?" She put her hands on her hips in a way that Beatrix found very unnerving.

Tiger and Wolf looked at each other, then they both nodded.

Tiger growled and leapt forward like a cat.

Beatrix's eyes widened.

As he leapt, his body changed. It lengthened and grew, and stripes sprung up all over it, as his clothes disintegrated.

When he landed, he looked like a cross between a tiger and a man. A tiger-man.

"Of course", Beatrix thought to herself wrily. "Why wouldn't he be able to turn into a tiger? He's a pirate from the freakin moon. And his name is Tiger".

Wolf leapt forward and turned into some kind of wolf-man.

Beatrix would have shaken her head if she could.

"Wow, cool!" Edni exclaimed.

"Edni!" Gwinni hissed, pulling Edni back into the shadows.

Tiger and Wolf prowled forward until they were in striking distance of the woman.

She arched her brows and crossed her arms. She looked rather bored. She held her hand out and began examining her nails. "Well?" she said, without raising her eyes.

Tiger growled and leapt forward.

The woman's hand shot out and caught him by the throat. Her wrist whipped out to the side and Tiger hit the hard stone wall hard. He slumped down weakly.

Wolf leapt as she was distracted.

She lashed out with her other hand like a claw, and bright red weals appeared on Wolf's face.

Wolf whimpered and fell to the floor.

The woman took one forward and casually kicked Wolf off the pulpit platform. He went sliding into the rows of pews, some of which clattered over on top him.

Buck and Violet looked at each other.

Buck nodded, and cocked his head and shoulders back, puffing his chest out. He started to sweat, then he roared, and a giant cannon popped out of his chest.

"Oh my", Lucrecia said quietly.

Violet hunched forward a moment, then threw her shoulders back. Two long, whispery wings popped out of her back and started flapping. They were semi-translucent and a clear, see through colour. Kind of like insect wings, kind of like fairy wings.

"NOW!" Buck roared.

Violet flew forward and started dodging left and right, her wings whipping through the air like paper thin razorblades.

The woman watched her lazily from the pulpit.

Violet surged forward close to the woman and made a sound like Buck spitting.

A blob of green liquid flew from her mouth toward the woman. It looked a bit like poison, or acid.

The woman's eyes widened.

At the last moment, her pupils dilated, and the poison exploded with a great **hiss**, like it had hit some kind of imaginary wall.

It dripped from the imaginary wall to the floor, where it sizzled and burned through the stone.

The woman stepped forward and looked down at the stone. The poison was continuing to burn through the floor.

Five feet, ten feet, twenty feet.

It finally stopped.

"Goodness", the woman said, with mock worry. "And to think, that could have **ruined** my coat".

The woman pulled the collar of her fur coat up around her cheeks and shivered, as if she were cold, or frightened.

Violet moved back quickly from the woman and paused, unsure how to proceed. She looked back at Buck.

Buck took a deep breath and leant right back, so his head was only a few feet above the ground.

"Goodness, I didn't know he was so flexible!" Gwinni hissed.

"Shut up!" Edni replied.

There was a rumble and Buck started to shake, like he was gathering momentum.

"Aghhh", Buck moaned.

"Oh, no", the woman said. "The sweaty pirate is rumbling". She turned her nails over and examined each cuticle in turn.

"NOW!" Buck roared.

He straightened and a giant, flaming cannon ball exploded from his chest. It soared across the room right at the woman.

At the same time, Violet darted forward and spat some more poison at the woman.

Both poison and cannon ball fell limply to the floor.

The invisible 'wall' in front of the woman shimmered and rippled for a moment, then flexed, like it was hardening itself.

"Is that it then?" The woman looked up from her nails. "Yes? Ok? Alright then". Her pupils dilated and her hands flew toward Violet and Buck. There was a horrible 'crack' and they both fell to the floor unconscious.

The woman dusted her hands, as if she'd just taken care of a particularly tiresome, but necessary, job. "Right, what's next then?" Her eyes fell on Beatrix. "Ah yes, you".

At that moment, there was a lot of clattering and the pounding of many feet from tunnel.

A group of Torchbearers ran into the room, followed by Gladius, shining as always in his golden armour.

Beatrix's breath exploded out of her chest in a massive gasp. She found she could move again.

The woman looked distracted and was glaring at Gladius and his Torchbearers. "What are you doing here?" she asked coldly.

"Madame Inquisitress". Gladius stepped forward and bowed his head respectfully, crossing his fist against his chest.

"Yes, yes", The Inquisitress snapped. "On with it".

"Madame. We responded to the...incursion...and a servant tipped us off that the...intruders...may be here in The Sanctum", Gladius said.

"Well as you can see, they are", The Inquisitress said coldly. "But as you can **also see**, I am taking care of it".

Gladius looked uncomfortable. "Madame...Mistress Madele would be-"

"I don't give a horses fart what **Mistress Madele** would be, or wouldn't be", The Inquisitress said viciously, stepping forward suddenly.

The Torchbearers gasped and stumbled backward, their plate armour clinking and clanking as they jostled into one another like children.

Gladius paled but stood his ground. "That may be the case, but-"

"Gladius", The Inquisitress said sweetly, switching from ice to honey.

"Inquisitress?" Gladius looked wary. His hand was slowly moving closer to his sword.

Beatrix, who had been inching further and further away from the woman, paused as the woman closed her eyes.

When she opened them, they were chillingly beautiful. "The Mistress isn't here, is she?"

"No, Inquisitress, but..."

"But, but, but". The Inquisitress waggled a finger and smiled happily at Gladius. "Always the but's with you, Gladius". During their exchange, she had been walking slowly toward him. The closer she came; the more nervous Gladius became. Sweat was coursing down his face. His hand was resting on his sword now.

The Inquisitress was inches away from him now. She raised a finger and pressed it slowly to his lips. "But".

Gladius swallowed. "I suppose...an exception could be made".

The Inquisitress was cocking her head side to side, looking at him as if he were a meal.

His Torchbearers had slunk back into the darkness. One of them had even edged back into the tunnel behind.

The Inquisitress smiled, but her eyes were still frosty. "I'm so glad we reached an understanding".

She spun rapidly, and her hand shot out at Beatrix. "You", she growled.

Gladius breathed a sigh of relief and took his gauntlets off to wipe his head.

Beatrix screamed as black energy enveloped her.

"Beatrix!" Gwinni screamed.

She made to run forward but Edni stopped her. "You can't", Edni wailed.

"Get off!" Gwinni shook off her hand.

"Ugh". Beatrix was floating now, like a puppet on strings. She'd gone limp and her head had lolled forward onto her chest.

Gwinni took a deep breath and closed her eyes. "Find The Place", she whispered to herself.

The Inquisitress, intent as she was on Beatrix, didn't seem to notice. Or perhaps she just didn't care.

Gwinni began to channel. A soft glow enveloped her. "Ah!" She clapped both hands together in front of her, and a vicious wind whipped out from them.

It hit The Inquisitress and spun her from her feet.

Beatrix collapsed to the floor.

The Inquisitress looked up from the floor, seemingly aghast that one of these inconsequential little things had found the audacity to attack her. She spotted Gwinni and narrowed her eyes. "You".

Gwinni paled and stepped back. "Stay away from her!" she warned.

The Inquisitress pushed herself to her feet. But not with her hands. With some kind of black energy. She rose like a reanimated corpse floating slowly to its feet. It was eerie. "And why would I do that, you stupid child?"

Gwinni screamed. Her back arched back, and her hands flew out to the sides. It looked like she was in terrible pain.

The Inquisitress smiled evilly.

On the floor, Beatrix was groggy. She was drifting in and out of consciousness. She couldn't tell what was real and what wasn't.

A memory floated to the front of her mind.

The same memory that had been plaguing her for weeks.

But this time, she saw a part of it she hadn't seen before.

The beautiful young woman was pacing aggressively in front of her. "No, no, no. How many times do I have to tell you?"

"Tell me what", young Beatrix moaned from the cold stone floor.

The woman leant down and gripped Beatrix by the hair, wrenching her head back painfully.

Beatrix cried out and a tear slid down her face.

The woman leant close so that her lips brushed Beatrix's cheek. "That **pathetic** witch's nonsense **does not work on us**". The woman spat every syllable sibilantly, as if she despised the words she was speaking.

"I don't understand", Beatrix wailed, screwing her eyes shut.

The woman slapped her viciously across the face. "Then I will make you".

Something about the slap awoke something in Beatrix. She snarled and her eyes flew open, dilating rapidly. They went from brown, to black, to white, then black again. "I hate you!" she screamed.

As she screamed, her voice distorted and became harsh and grating. A torrent of wind exploded from her mouth. But it wasn't like that summoned by Madame Tempest. It was virulent and filled with thorns and sharp edges.

"Agh!" The woman staggered and beat at the wind with her hands. After a moment she snarled too, and crossed her hands in front of her chest, then threw them outward. The wind disappeared. Her face was cut and bleeding in several places. Beatrix watched as the cuts slowly healed. After a few moments, they were gone.

The woman nodded. "Good". She walked away without another word.

On the floor, Beatrix watched her go, full of hate and loathing, panting heavily.

In The Sanctum, Beatrix's eyes snapped open as Gwinni's scream tore through her.

"Get off her!" Edni ran forward from the wall where she'd been hiding. "Don't you touch her!"

The Inquisitress hissed and raised her hands. Edni and Gwinni began floating and pirouetting in the air. She cackled. A horrible, throaty, dark sound.

Beatrix jumped to her feet and threw herself at The Inquisitress, tackling her to the floor. As she fell, so too did Edni and Gwinni, throwing their hands out frantically to stop their fall.

The Inquisitress landed with an 'oof'; the wind knocked out of her.

Beatrix tried to get up, but The Inquisitress's hand shot out, pulling her back to the floor.

They lay together a moment, staring into the other's eyes. It was surreal.

Beatrix suddenly felt sick. The Inquisitress's eyes were devoid of emotion. Cruel and cunning and chill as the cold stone floor on which they lay. But worse than that. Beatrix realised she knew those eyes. Her stomach lurched and the world stood still.

The Inquisitress smiled and ran a hand tenderly across Beatrix's face. "Hello...Daughter", she whispered.

Thank you Mina Anguelova for creating a beautiful book cover that encapsulates the essence of my book.

Most of all, thank you mon coeur, for continuing to believe in me.